'Where are my clothes?'

'I've burned them for you. They were unwearable anyway.'

The fingers that were free clenched into a fist. Caro wondered what it would take to provoke him into dropping the tiny towel.

'Right, then,' Leander said, his voice very soft. Padding wetly, he crossed the floor to the door.

'Where are you going?' she demanded breathlessly.

'Back onto the streets, where I belong.'

'But…but you'll freeze out there!'

'I'll be arrested for indecent exposure long before I freeze to death, Mrs Gray.'

Caro dragged her gaze away from the disconcerting curve of his buttocks to manage a careless shrug and toss of the head. 'Well, suit yourself, then. If you want to go ahead and make an…an…absolute spectacle of yourself, it has nothing to do with me…'

'Apart from the fact that you're my wife, Mrs Gray, you'...

Victoria Aldridge lives in Wellington, New Zealand, in what she is assured is a haunted Victorian cottage. She shares it with her husband, whichever of her adult children find themselves otherwise homeless, and two bossy cats. She is a fifth generation New Zealander, and finds her country's history—especially that of women—absolutely intriguing.

A previous novel by the same author:

BEN MORGAN'S MISTAKE

A CONVENIENT GENTLEMAN

Victoria Aldridge

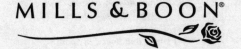

MILLS & BOON®

First published in Great Britain 2004
Harlequin Mills & Boon Limited,
Eton House, 18-24 Paradise Road, Richmond, Surrey TW9 1SR

© Victoria Aldridge 2004

ISBN 0 263 83961 3

Set in Times Roman 10½ on 12 pt.
04-0504-77324

Printed and bound in Spain
by Litografía Rosés S.A., Barcelona

To Sidney—for everything

Prologue

The Hawkesbury, New South Wales, Australia, 1863

For the third night in a row, war raged in the Morgan house.

The skirmishes took place at a number of sites in the huge house—the sitting room, the dining table, and in the kitchen—but all encounters were protracted and very, very loud.

Every farmhand in the cottages behind the main house followed the proceedings with great interest, and a number of wagers were laid on who the eventual winner was going to be. Most of the money was on Morgan. Young Caroline had always been a bit of a tearaway, but her father had always prevailed in the past, hadn't he? And he was not the man to cross, was Ben Morgan. His eldest daughter would come to heel eventually.

Other, perhaps more knowledgeable, money was on Caroline Morgan. For all that she had her father's lungs, she was her mother's daughter, wasn't she? And who was it who really ruled inside the big Morgan house? The older farmhands nodded and winked to each other. Wait and see, they said.

On the third evening, the two protagonists faced each other across the kitchen table, a pot of cold tea marking the battle line between them. The bread-scented air was virtually crackling with animosity. Emma Morgan, sitting quietly in a chair beside the stove, put down the tiny nightgown she was stitching and looked at her husband and daughter in exasperation.

'I have had just about enough of you two! When, may I ask, are we going to return to civil conversation in this house?'

Ben Morgan shoved himself back on his chair and glowered at his wife. 'When your daughter learns some manners and some common sense. But I'd advise you not to hold your breath for either!'

'Really?' Caroline tossed her head pertly. 'You will note, Mother, that you have been my sole parent for the past three days? Which means, Father, that if you didn't sire me, you've no right to order me around like one of your chattels!'

'Caro!' her parents chorused in shocked tones, just as they had almost daily since the time Caroline could talk. Emma looked at her daughter with the oddly mingled feelings of love and dismay that she always felt for her eldest child. She was so much her father's child, with the same fair colouring and striking good looks, and the same volatile personality. Only her green eyes were her mother's, but surely, Emma thought in despair, her own eyes had never glittered with such ferocity? Sometimes she truly feared for Caro. She possessed a hard, determined core just like her father's and, while that quality might be considered desirable by some in a man, in a woman it was simply not… feminine.

'All your father is asking you to do, Caro, is consider Mr Benton's offer of marriage—'

'And I've told him! How many times do I have to tell him? The answer is *no*!'

Emma transferred her steady gaze to her husband. 'She doesn't want to marry him, Ben.'

'Then she's a bloody fool! Benton is his father's sole heir. When he inherits, he'll own one of the best farms in the Hawkesbury, and when it's adjoined to this place—'

'So you're selling me off, are you?' demanded Caro.

'No, I'm not! I'm just pointing out a few salient facts! There's nothing wrong with young Benton—'

'He's an idiot and his ears stick out.'

'Caro, they don't,' her mother remonstrated gently. 'Well, not all that much. And he just adores you! And you've known him all your life.'

'Exactly, Mother! Father wants me to marry a boy he can order around, and you want me to marry a boy I think of as a brother! Although if I'd had a brother, Father wouldn't be in such a hurry to marry us all off!'

Her father looked at her through narrowed eyes. 'A son would have taken over the farm when I'm gone, would have looked after you girls so that there would be no need to find you good husbands.'

'Then leave the farm to me!' Caro said wearily, for the umpteenth time. 'I can run it better than any jug-eared boy you can pick out for me! You know that!'

'Try to show a little common sense, Caroline,' her father snapped. 'A woman can't run a farm, or any other sort of business for that matter. That's not what they were made for.'

Caro looked in appeal at her mother. Usually Ben's daughters fell about laughing at their father's pronouncements on the female ideal, and took not one whit of notice of them. But for once his firmly held beliefs were holding Caro back from what she wanted more than anything in the world. She loved the huge, fertile lands that had been in the family for three generations. There had been a brief period in her grandfather's day when the farm had been in the mortgagor's hands, but under Ben's sober guidance the Morgan family had grown to be one of Australia's wealthiest, with extensive interests in both farming and shipping. But Ben was now ancient—why, he'd had his fiftieth birthday the previous month! He was in his dotage, whereas Caro was young and clever and full of innovative ideas. She could easily see herself in charge of everything. Very easily.

'I suppose you want me to be like Olivia,' she said truculently. 'All sweetness and light, and marrying who you tell her to.'

Emma picked up the small nightgown she had been sewing for her first grandchild and held it closer to the light, frowning as she noticed the irregular stitches she had made in her agitation. 'Your sister always wanted to marry William, Caro. He was her choice, and we're both delighted that she is so happy. Now she's settled down, with a baby on the way—'

'How perfect!' Caro said sarcastically. 'Not, of course, that either of you have ever made any comment on the fact that Olivia's baby is due in January, just seven months after her wedding!'

'Caro, that is enough!' Emma rose to her feet and Caro realised that for once she had gone too far, even for her eternally patient mother. 'That was a spiteful and completely unnecessary thing to say. Go to your room!'

'Mother—'

'I said, go to your room! And don't bother coming out until you have decided to conduct yourself with some degree of civility!'

Caro thought about staying to argue, but her mother was perilously close to tears. And if she made her mother cry, her father's rage would be truly terrifying. He had never once, that she could recall at least, raised a hand to her or any of her sisters, but there was always a first time for everything. With her head held high, she made a dignified exit, although she could not resist banging the kitchen door so hard behind her that the sound reverberated through the house and woke her sleeping younger sisters.

In the kitchen, her parents looked at each other.

'Mercenary little baggage,' Ben said savagely. 'I swear I'll throttle that girl one day. A husband is what she needs, to keep the reins on her. Although I'm not sure that Frank Benton would be able to do that for more than five minutes.'

Emma folded her sewing slowly as she carefully edited what she was about to say. She had to be tactful— the faults that her husband and her daughter shared were the ones they found hardest to tolerate in each other.

'I'm not so sure,' she said slowly, 'that marriage is the answer for Caro. Not yet. She needs to see the world a little, to realise that she doesn't know everything and that she can't always have her way. I think we should let her go. To England, perhaps. Meg Parkins is visiting Home in a month or two, and taking her daughters with her. I could ask her if Caro could accompany them. I'm sure Meg wouldn't mind in the least…'

Ben groaned. 'Not England, Emma! It's so far away! We wouldn't see her for years, and you don't know what could happen to her on the other side of the world.'

She smiled up at him. 'You always were too soft on them, Ben. That's why Caro is the way she is. Let her go—you'll have to some time, you know.'

'I suppose so.' He bent over and kissed the top of her head. 'We should have had sons. They wouldn't have been this much trouble.'

It was just before dawn when Ben heard the faint clink of the dogs' chains from the yards in the valley below the house. The dogs weren't barking, so whoever was moving past them was someone they knew. Damn her, he thought. Stupid little bitch. He carefully removed his arm from around the waist of his sleeping wife and left her warmth to pad out into the chilly hallway.

He was standing on the front porch, moodily buttoning his trousers and staring down the valley to the darkness that was the Hawkesbury River when Mr Matthews loomed silently out of the darkness.

'She's gone.'

'Yeah.' Ben rubbed his chin thoughtfully with the back of his hand.

'She ain't coming back.'

Ben tried to make out his expression in the gloomy light. Mr Matthews had been with him since the days when Ben's father had lost the farm to the mortgagors. A transported convict who had long since earned his ticket, he was an indispensable and much-treasured family member. Mr Matthews's only fault, to Ben's mind, was that Caroline had always been his favourite child and he'd never been able to deny her anything. If she had confided in anyone, it would have been him.

'She told you that?'

'Nah. But she wants to run this place real bad. You should have let her.'

'Don't be ridiculous,' Ben snapped. 'Anyway, she'll be back soon enough, when she realises what a pampered life she's had here. She won't last an hour out there.'

'Unless something happens to her, of course,' Mr Matthews said after a while. 'Like she gets abducted, or raped, or robbed, or sold to the bars down by the Sydney docks or—'

Ben slammed his hands down hard on the veranda railing. 'Dammit! All right, then, go after her and make sure she's all right. And you'd better take some money with you. She won't have much on her.'

'She took Summer.'

Ben swore, remembering just in time to drop his voice. 'That horse is worth a bloody fortune! She won't sell him...'

'She will to spite you. And that'll give her a heap of money. Enough to leave the country with, I reckon.'

Ben thought for a moment and then nodded slowly. 'You're probably right. I... Oh, hell, we can't bring her back in chains. She'll just run off again. I wish I could bring myself to take to her with a horsewhip.' He glared at Mr Matthews's sudden snort. 'What's funny?'

'Nothing. You want me to follow her, then?'

'Yeah. Only I don't want to have to pay an arm and a leg to buy the goddamned horse back.' He turned to go back into the house, but stopped as a horrible thought struck him. 'Oh. Just one thing, Mr Matthews.'

'Yeah?'

'Whatever you do, don't let her go to Dunedin.'

Chapter One

Dunedin, New Zealand, 1863

Dunedin was covered with a light layer of snow, the first Caroline had ever seen. Entranced by the picture-book prettiness of the white-speckled hills, she stood at the dock gates, heedless of the crowd buffeting her. She had seen pictures of snow before of course, in books about Home. But this was much more exciting than England could ever have been. This was a real adventure!

The fact that she had nothing but a single change of clothes in her bag, and twenty-five pounds to her name, simply added an edge to the excitement. Being on board ship for three weeks had been much more boring than she had anticipated: three meals a day, a narrow little bunk to sleep in, nowhere to walk but to the limits of the cabin passengers' deck. It had been a lot like boarding school, really. But now, for the first time in her life, she was on her own, and she had never been happier.

She felt in the pocket of her coat for the envelope,

turning it over in her gloved fingers, not needing to take it out and read it to remember the return address.

Mrs Jonas Wilks, Castledene Hotel, Castle Street, Dunedin.

Dunedin was not as large as she had thought it would be—certainly nowhere as large as Sydney. Built along the shores of a natural harbour inlet, cradled among steep hills, the town that was the hub of the Otago goldrush was still in its infancy. But whereas Sydney had a quiet, settled feel to it after eighty years of colonisation, Dunedin seemed to be teeming with energy.

Fed by the Otago goldfields, the richest since Ballarat and California, Dunedin's prosperity was obvious. Spanning out from a small central park, called The Octagon, were streets of substantial buildings with ornate façades, between which were empty spaces and busy building sites. Over the lower reaches of the hills spread a canvas town of tents, hundreds of them, which Caro guessed belonged to either transient miners or people unable to find or afford accommodation. There was a vibrancy to the town, almost a sense of anticipation, which thrilled Caro to the bone.

A gust of icy wind blew along the quay, billowing the dresses of the women and loosening a few hats. The half-dozen ships tied up at the docks creaked as the gathering gale plucked at their furled sails and hummed along the ropes. Caro realised that she was growing cold. In fact, she could never recall being so cold in her life. Another new experience to savour!

Pulling the fur trim of her jacket collar up around her chin, she strode along the quay and up the road that lay straight ahead, quite unaware, as always, that she was turning heads as she passed. She had always been hard to overlook, being well above average height for a woman. What was more unusual was the way she bore herself, with a loose-limbed, graceful walk that in a man would have verged on being a swagger. Combined with classically blond beauty and a pair of sparkling eyes, Miss Morgan's looks had always drawn admiring comment. Most remarkable, however, was that she had always remained blithely oblivious to the fact that her appearance was anything out of the ordinary.

She might as well get her bearings first, she thought, stepping up on to the narrow wooden footpath that ran below the shop awnings. There was only room for three people walking abreast, so she kept politely to the left, holding her bag close to her side so as not to bump into other walkers. Despite the foul weather the streets were busy, and she noted with interest the preponderance of Scottish accents she heard. She passed no fewer than two Churches of Scotland within five minutes' walk and half the shop names began with 'Mac'. It was true, then, the description she had heard on the ship of Dunedin being the Edinburgh of the South.

'Excuse me, sir,' she said to a man obstructing the footpath as he loaded up his dray. He looked rough, a miner perhaps, and he had a scowl on his face.

'Get lost,' he snarled, not looking up. She waited patiently. Her parents had always insisted on the utmost courtesy to everyone, no matter what their station in life, and she was not going to break that ingrained habit now. She could, of course, step down into the road and walk around the horse and dray, but the snow had turned to sleet, and the icy mud looked most uninviting.

'Will you be long, sir?' she enquired after a moment.

'Long as I need to be.' He slammed down a box

with unnecessary force and turned to hoist up the next one. There were still two high piles of crates to load.

'I see.' Caro put down her bag. 'What if I help you load? That will speed you up, won't it?'

He turned around then with a curse, which died unspoken on his lips as he saw her wide green eyes, utterly devoid of malice or sarcasm. A slow flush rose over his face as he shuffled ponderously to one side to allow her to pass. He was staring at her in the way lots of men did whenever her parents had taken her into Sydney or Parramatta. She really wished they didn't—one usually couldn't get any sense out of them when they looked like that. However, this was New Zealand. Perhaps men were a little more sensible here. She gave him a smile and pulled out the envelope from her pocket.

'Thank you, sir. I wonder if you could tell me where I would find Castle Street? Is it close by?'

He ignored the envelope—too late Caro realised he might not be able to read and that she might have inadvertently given offence—and waved his arm in the direction she had been heading.

'Down there. Second on yer left.'

'Thank you so much.' She picked up her bag and went to move past him, but he had recovered by now enough to move to block her way.

'Heavy bag for a young miss,' he said ingratiatingly. 'Like a hand with it?'

'How kind. But you couldn't leave all these boxes here.' She looked down at him—he was at least two inches shorter—and added with a touch of asperity, 'And your poor horses. They must be cold. You'll want to get them moving, won't you?'

She flashed him a smile and moved smartly away

down the sidewalk before he could detain her any further. Already she could see the signpost for Castle Street, and her heart began to beat a little faster. She wasn't sure what she would find, or what sort of reception she would get at the Castledene Hotel. Indeed, would Mrs Wilks still live there?

Charlotte Wilks. Aunt Charlotte. Her mother's sister. Caro had never seen her, knew nothing of her except that there was some sort of scandal surrounding her aunt, and not of the common or garden danced-twice-in-a-row-with-the-same-man sort of scandal that would have had female tongues astir on the Hawkesbury. No, Aunt Charlotte's sins were too dreadful to name, if her parents' tense reactions to her occasional letters were anything to go by. Caro didn't know if her mother had ever written back, but she did know that her father would have sternly disapproved. He always went rather...*rigid*, she thought, when one of Aunt Charlotte's letters had arrived, or when Caro had mentioned her name, which she had made a point of often doing. Whatever Aunt Charlotte had done, Ben had never forgiven her, and he never would. He loathed her more than anyone else alive. Caro couldn't wait to meet her.

She turned the corner into Castle Street and caught her breath in relief. Standing proudly at the end of a cul-de-sac, the Castledene Hotel was a magnificent, double-storeyed building, the finest Caro had seen so far in Dunedin. Her fears that she would find Aunt Charlotte starving in a cobwebby attic somewhere began to evaporate. The last letter from here to Caro's mother had been posted only three months before, and if Aunt Charlotte could afford to board here, she must be reasonably in funds.

Caro gave a wide berth to the entrance to the public

bar—although it was only mid-morning, there sounded as if there were already a number of noisy patrons inside—and pushed open one of the big front doors.

Very nice. She put her bag on the ground and looked around in approval. The entry was most imposing, if very cold, being paved and colonnaded in pale grey marble. Carved kauri staircases swept discreetly up on either side, almost obscured by rich velvet drapes. Immediately in front of her, panelled doors stood ajar, giving a glimpse of tables set with heavy damask and sparkling silver. It was as impressive as any of Sydney's grand hotels, with only the underlying smell of recently sawn wood betraying its newness.

'Can I help you, miss?'

Caro turned to the thin, neat-looking man behind the reception desk with a smile. 'I hope so, sir. I'm looking for Mrs Wilks. Mrs Jonas Wilks. I understand she was a guest here some months ago. Is she still here?'

The man cleared his throat. 'Indeed, miss.' She was subjected to a politely swift scrutiny. 'May I tell her who is calling?'

Caro hesitated. She had thought long and hard about this situation, and had decided that a little vagueness might initially be desirable. After all, what if Aunt Charlotte felt the same about Caro's family as Caro's father did about Aunt Charlotte?

'I'm a relative,' she said warmly. Then, as the clerk hesitated, she smiled encouragingly. 'I know she'll want to see me.'

He disappeared up one of the great staircases, his shoes noiseless on the thick carpet, and she sat down to wait on one of the elegant chairs placed between the aspidistras around the foyer. Despite her care, her walking shoes were covered with a light layer of wet mud, and she glared at them in irritation. They and a pair of boots were the only footwear she had now. At home, in her closet, stood rows of boots and shoes and slippers. And as for her dresses—she thought with regret of the wardrobe she had been forced to leave behind her. While it had seemed a good idea at the time to run away from home virtually empty-handed, to show her father that she didn't need anything from him to stand on her own two feet, it was now proving to be very tiresome managing with a single change of clothes. She sincerely hoped that her aunt wouldn't mind her shabby appearance. Caro always liked to make a good impression.

She started as she realised that the clerk was standing beside her. Waves of disapproval were almost tangibly emanating from him, and she wondered what she could possibly have done to have earned his censure.

'This way, miss,' he said abruptly. 'You can leave your bag behind the reception desk.'

She followed him up the staircase and along a wide hallway. Her mittened hands were trembling slightly and she clasped them together tightly in front of her waist. The clerk rapped quietly on a door and stood back to admit her.

The hotel room was large, with long windows that let in what winter light there was. A fire burned brightly in the hearth, illuminating a clutter of silver-topped bottles and jars on the dressing table. The air was scented with an odd, but not unpleasant, mix of rosewater and tobacco. Clothes and shoes were flung carelessly over the big bed and on the floor, as if someone had simply stepped out of them and left them lying there. Caro bent and picked up a dress that had impeded the opening of the door. The gentle scent of roses escaped from its folds of soft lace as she smoothed it out and looked around the room for the owner. The room, for all its mess, was charming and utterly feminine.

'Mrs Wilks?'

There was reluctant movement under the pile of clothing and linen on the bed.

'Who is it?' a woman's voice asked croakily. She sounded cross, too, and it only then occurred to Caro that there would be only one reason why someone would still be in bed in the middle of the day.

'I'm sorry if you're not well, Mrs Wilks.' Caro backed towards the door. 'I'll call later.'

The bedclothes were pushed back and a scowling face appeared. Caro's mouth dropped open. For a few seconds it looked exactly as if her mother were lying there, blinking sleepily at her, except that her mother's hair was red, not yellow, and her mother's nightgowns were considerably more modest than her aunt's. Then Mrs Wilks propped herself up on one elbow and Caro swiftly averted her eyes. Her aunt's nightgown was not immodest, it was non-existent.

'You,' her aunt said flatly after a moment, 'have to be one of Ben's children.'

'I'm Caroline,' Caro said carefully. 'The eldest.'

'Mmm.' Her aunt eyed her balefully. 'So what are you doing here? I suppose it's too much to hope that your father has at last decided to act like a human being and apologise for everything he's done to me?'

This was much, much worse than Caro had dared dread. She took a deep breath and said somewhat shakily, 'I don't know, Mrs Wilks. He…he doesn't know I'm here…'

'Really?' Her aunt sat bolt upright and again Caro

had to avert her eyes. 'You mean you've run away from home?'

'Yes...'

'May I ask why?'

'Because...because my father is unreasonable and unfair and...and...' Her voice gave out through a combination of nerves and sudden, unexpected homesickness. There was a rustle of silk as her aunt mercifully pulled on a pink gown and then enveloped her in a soft, rose-scented hug.

'You poor darling. He's a brute of a man, I know. An unfeeling, callous bastard! Oh, what you and my poor sister must have had to put up with all these years...'

This was not strictly fair, but as Caro carefully extracted herself to say so, her aunt smiled at her with all the charm that had seen her through forty-four years and hundreds of men, and Caro felt herself melt into an adoring puddle. With her long, tousled hair tumbling over her pale-blue silk dressing-gown, and her eyes glowing with warm sympathy, her aunt looked like just like an exotic version of her beloved mother. Only the lines of experience and worldliness around Charlotte's eyes and mouth were different, giving her a wistful, rather vulnerable look.

Charlotte watched the awestruck look on her niece's face with satisfaction.

'It's lovely to meet you at last, Caroline.'

'Thank you, Mrs Wilks...'

'Aunt Charlotte, please, darling!' She glanced swiftly over her shoulder at what looked to be a dressing-room door, and added, 'Now, why don't you go and tell Oliver downstairs that you want something hot to drink—your poor face is frozen!—and I'll get dressed. Just give me half an hour, hmmm?'

Out in the hallway again, Caro hesitated. Who was Oliver? She raised her hand to knock on the door, but the sound of murmuring voices from inside her aunt's bedroom made her pause. Perhaps her aunt was given to talking to herself. Caro shrugged her shoulders and went back downstairs.

The man who had first greeted her looked up from the papers on the registration desk. 'Yes, miss?'

She had not imagined it before—his tone was distinctly chilly. 'Are you Oliver?'

'Yes, miss.'

Caro bit her bottom lip. 'My aunt, Mrs Wilks—'

'Your *aunt*, miss?'

There was a wealth of frosty disapproval in the question. Caro drew herself up to her full and impressive height and looked down at the top of his head.

'Mrs Wilks, who is a guest of this hotel—'

'Oh, no, miss—she's not a guest.' Oliver looked up at her searchingly, seemed to come to a conclusion and suddenly there was a glimmer of a smile in his eyes. Whether it was malicious or not, Caro couldn't tell. 'She's the owner, miss.'

'The owner,' Caro repeated blankly.

'Yes, miss. Since Mr Wilks died six months ago and left the hotel to his widow.' He shut the registry book carefully. 'What can I do for you, miss?'

'Ah…Mrs Wilks suggested perhaps a hot drink while I wait…'

'Certainly, miss. Please come with me.'

She followed his stiff, black-clad back as he led her through the doors into the dining room. Her first impression of opulence was tempered a little when she saw the dining tables at close quarters. The tablecloths were stained, and the silver looked to be in dire need of a good polish. A general air of neglect lay over the room, from the crumbs lying unswept on the floor to the spiders in the chandelier above. Automatically Caro righted a spilled glass as she passed.

The kitchen was no improvement on the dining room: dirty pots and pans covered the benches and food scraps filled buckets by the door. The huge ovens were lit and had their doors open. The heat was welcome, but not the smell of rotting food wafting on the warm currents of air.

The two women sitting toasting their feet by the ovens looked up as Oliver banged the door shut.

'Who's this, then?' demanded the older of the women. She was a tall, hatchet-faced woman with heat-reddened cheeks. Her rolled-up sleeves and voluminous apron marked her as a cook. The other, who was little more than a girl, smiled shyly at Caro and wiped her nose on a sooty shirtsleeve.

Oliver motioned Caro politely enough towards a chair by the table and moved to rub his hands together before the fire.

'This, ladies, is Mrs Wilks's niece. Miss…?'

'Miss Morgan. Caroline Morgan.' She waited for him to introduce the other women, but when no introduction came, she sat down in the indicated chair. It looked as if she was not going to be offered a cup of tea, either, but there was a teapot and pile of cups sitting on the table. The teapot was still warm and so Caro helped herself, discarding several cups until she found one that bore no obvious marks of recent use.

The silence dragged on, but Caro was determined that it was not going to be she who broke it.

'You're one of the rich relations, aren't you?' said the Cook at last, her voice fairly dripping with sarcasm. 'Come to bail Madam out, I hope.'

'I beg your pardon?' Caro said politely.

The Cook's chin came up pugnaciously, and the girl with the sooty dress gave a nervous giggle.

'You're one of them Australian relations Madam tells us about. The ones that kicked her out of her home in Sydney when she were first widowed and left her penniless on the streets.'

Caro frowned. 'I don't think that was us. I can't imagine my mother ever doing that to anyone, let alone her own sister.'

The Cook nodded slowly. 'Well, she did. Leastways, according to your aunt, your father did.'

'Oh.' Caro put her cup down carefully. 'My father. Yes, I suppose he could have done. He's very unfair like that.'

She tried to imagine what poor Aunt Charlotte could possibly have done to infuriate her father so. Probably very little. Really, Caro thought, she and Aunt Charlotte had a lot in common—both forced out of their home by Ben's total lack of reason. It was extraordinary that Charlotte had found it in her heart to welcome Caro as she had!

'So,' said the Cook, 'you brought any money with you?'

'No,' Caro said blankly. 'Well, I've got twenty-five pounds…'

As her aunt's three employees all sat back in their chairs with various sounds of disgust and dismay, Caro gained the distinct impression that she was proving a great source of disappointment.

'I suppose,' Oliver said heavily, 'it would have been

too much to hope for, that you might have been the answer to our prayers.'

'I'm sorry,' Caro said sincerely. 'I don't think I've ever been the answer to anyone's prayers.'

From behind the Cook's forbidding exterior came an unexpected chuckle. 'Never mind, dear. Miss Morgan, was it? Not *your* fault if Madam's living beyond her means now, is it? Agnes—' she elbowed the young girl off her chair with a degree of viciousness that Caro took to be habitual '—Agnes here will fetch you a fresh pot of tea. And some of those scones I made yesterday, too.'

Agnes wiped her nose on her sleeve again and scurried around the kitchen, setting out a fresh pot of tea and a plate of rather stale but nicely risen scones.

'Got no butter, Miss Morgan,' the Cook commented as she saw Caro look around her for a butterdish. 'Got nothing very much of anything, come to mention it. No more tea leaves than are in the jar, no meat, no milk, no cheese…'

'No wages,' Oliver chipped in glumly.

'But that's dreadful!' Hungry as she was, Caro forgot all about butter for her scones. 'Is no one paying you? Not my aunt?'

Her aunt's employees looked at each other and then moved their chairs closer to where she sat.

'Mrs Wilks is a most attractive woman…' Oliver began.

'Handsome is as handsome does,' the Cook said darkly. 'She's got not so much as a pinch of business sense!'

'…but she is being poorly served by her business adviser,' Oliver went on doggedly, ignoring the Cook's rude snort of derision. 'When the late Mr Wilks left this hotel to her, it was in fine shape, Miss Morgan. Dunedin's finest hotel, it was called, and rightly so. But since he died…' He shook his head sadly. 'Things are not good, Miss Morgan. Not good at all. We served the last of the meals in the dining room last night, there are creditors at the door day and night, Mrs Wilks can't and won't see them, we haven't had a paying guest under this roof for a week now…'

'There's a non-paying guest I'd like to see the back of,' the Cook snapped. She fixed Caro with a piercing stare. 'Did you see him up there?'

'Who?' Caro was by now thoroughly bewildered.

'Mr Thwaites. Up there. With her.' Caro shook her head and the Cook slumped back in her chair. 'Hmmph. Well, I dare say you'll meet him soon enough if you stay on. You are staying on, are you?'

'If my aunt invites me to,' Caro said earnestly. 'If I can be of any use, that is. I can cook and clean, and I'm sure I could learn to wait, too…' Her voice faltered as she saw the expressions of the faces of the others. 'Is there something wrong?'

'No, Miss Morgan,' Oliver said after a moment. 'It's just that a lady like yourself, coming from a privileged home, could hardly be expected to lift a broom or a duster. It wouldn't be right.'

'Oh, we all had our tasks at home,' she assured him. 'Mother didn't believe in other people doing work we were quite capable of doing ourselves. ''Hard work is good for the soul, the figure and the complexion'', she always used to say, and I'm sure my aunt believes the same.'

The Cook spluttered into her tea and Oliver rose creakily to his feet.

'Well, I'm sure Mrs Wilks will be ready to see you

by now, Miss Morgan. I shall take you to her rooms, if you wish.'

'Oh, please don't trouble yourself! I remember the way very clearly. And thank you for the tea and scones, Mrs…'

The Cook smiled. 'Mrs Webb, dear. Now do make sure you call in after you've seen your aunt, won't you? On your way back to Australia,' she added darkly as the door closed after Caro.

'Ooh, I thought she were nice.' Agnes sniffed dejectedly. 'I hope she don't go.'

'She might be nice, but she came down in the last shower,' Mrs Webb informed her. 'Gawd help her, she's still sopping wet! I give her a day before He tries to put one over her…'

'You mean *across* her, Mrs Webb,' interjected Oliver.

'That, too, Mr Oliver,' the Cook snapped. 'Oh, it's better by far that she leaves here with her virtue than That Man has his way with her. Just look at Madam.'

Oliver leaned forward to prod the embers in the stove. 'You're right, of course, Mrs Webb. It will be in her best interests to leave as soon as possible. She won't be safe here, not with her looks and Madam and That Man…'

They all nodded in sad accord and sat staring at the dying fire, lost in their own thoughts.

Chapter Two

Caro tapped on her aunt's door and, hearing no response, opened it slowly.

Her aunt was standing before the long mirror, smoothing her pale ringlets over her shoulders. She was dressed now, in an elegant gown of dark blue that enhanced her milky skin and slim figure. Deep ruffles of ivory lace covered any victory of gravity around her neck and décolletage, and provided a perfect frame for her heart-shaped face. There was much more than a passing resemblance to Caro's beautiful mother, but Charlotte had an air of fragility and wistfulness that was all her own, and Caro felt a surge of protectiveness towards this glamorous relative she barely knew.

'Come in, darling. Sit down.' Charlotte waved a lethargic hand in the general direction of the bed. Caro carefully moved aside a few of the dresses and assorted slippers lying in disarray over the eiderdown and sat.

'Now, you must tell me all about yourself and what wonderful stroke of fortune has delivered you to my door!' Charlotte perched herself on her dressing-table chair and regarded her niece with tilted head and affectionate smile. 'Do you know, you were only six months old when I last saw you? What a perfectly beautiful girl you've grown into! You obviously favour your father's side of the family. My darling first husband, Edward—who was, of course, also your grandfather! Just fancy that!—had the same chin as you, you know, with that little dimple. Your fair hair, of course, you got from my side of the family… On the other hand, your father is fair, too, isn't he? Or…I imagine he's gone grey by now…'

'Only a little bit,' Caro assured her.

Charlotte turned and began fiddling with the hairbrushes on her dressing table. 'Has he gone bald?'

'No.'

'Has he got fat?'

'No.'

Caro was almost certain her aunt said 'Damn!' under her breath, so hastened to add that her mother and her mother's younger sisters were all happy and in good health. Her aunt, though, didn't seem to be listening with any great attention. She showed a little more animation when Caro went on to describe her own family, and got her niece to repeat several times the information that Caro had seven sisters and no brothers. For some reason she seemed to find it most amusing.

'Poor Ben,' she said, and laughed. 'I'll wager he's not happy about *that*!'

'He isn't,' Caro agreed. 'He says he has to take great care about who we marry as a result. That's what I'm doing here.'

'You didn't like his choice, hmm?' Her aunt watched Caro's reflection in the mirror pull a face. 'Ben never did like being thwarted.' She sighed prettily. 'I'm living testament to that, my dear.'

'My parents never spoke of you, Aunt Charlotte,'

Caro said hesitantly. 'Was there…ah…I mean, I don't know what happened between you…?'

Charlotte gave a light, brittle laugh and waved her hands dismissively. 'Darling, it was all a long time ago, and all really rather silly. Your father never did forgive me for marrying his father, you see, and when Edward died on our honeymoon to England, and I had to come back to Sydney, he cut me off without a penny. If it hadn't been for some very kind friends I would have…well, I would have *starved* on the *streets*, darling.' She gave a little sniff as her eyes filled with bright tears, and she went on bravely, 'But I survived and married again—to the sweetest man imaginable!—and when he died my heart was broken all over again, and so I came here and married again, and—well—I've done all right, haven't I?'

Immeasurably moved by her aunt's stoicism, Caro leapt to her feet and embraced her warmly.

'Of course you have, Aunt Charlotte! Oh, you poor, poor thing! But why would Father have done such a thing to you? I can't believe that he could have been so cruel!'

Charlotte dabbed at her eyes with a scrap of lace. 'I couldn't say. Well, I *shouldn't* say this, darling, but…' she managed a tight, courageous little smile and said in a rush '…oh, I rejected him in favour of his father, and I don't believe he's ever forgiven me! Isn't that silly, to hold such a grudge over so many years?'

'But Mother and Father have always been so happy,' Caro said in bewilderment, remembering the easy affection she had always witnessed between her parents, the way her mother's face lit up whenever her father came into a room, the way their eyes would meet over the heads of their children in amused camaraderie.

Lovely as Aunt Charlotte probably used to be, Caro simply couldn't imagine her father ever looking at any woman other than her mother. Charlotte, correctly reading the expressions on her niece's face, leaned forward to tap her gently on the wrist.

'It was years ago, darling, before you were born. Why, I've almost forgotten about it myself. Except that…well, things would have been very different if your father had been one to let bygones be bygones. But, here I am and here you are and…oh, isn't this just lovely?'

She clasped Caro's hands in hers and smiled warmly. She was being so kind that Caro, remembering what the hotel staff had told her about her aunt's straitened circumstances, felt a twinge of guilt.

'Aunt Charlotte, I haven't any money with me,' she said in a rush. 'I can't pay very much for accommodation, but I can work hard at anything that needs doing…'

'Oh, darling!' her aunt chided her fondly. 'Don't you even think about such a thing! How could I put my own niece to work? The very idea!'

'But I know that the hotel isn't doing very well,' Caro said bluntly. 'If I can help in any way at all, then that's what I want to do.'

'How terribly sweet of you.' There was a slightly speculative tone in her voice as she put her head on one side and looked assessingly at Caro. 'You are a *very* pretty girl, aren't you? I'm sure we could find you something to do, if you *really* want to help. In fact, a friend of mine will know what's best…'

'Mr Thwaites?' Caro asked, and was taken aback by the sudden snap of suspicion in her aunt's eyes.

'Who's been talking to you about him? No, don't

tell me—the kitchen staff!' At Caro's nod she heaved a dramatic sigh. 'Harold's doing all he can to turn this business around. He runs the public bar and bottle shop downstairs, and if it wasn't for the profits from that we'd be in even more of a pickle. You'd think the staff would show some appreciation for all his hard work, wouldn't you?'

'I think they want to be paid...' Caro ventured.

'Oh, the silly things! They'll be paid, of course, as soon as the business gets back on its feet—and it will, in a few weeks! In the meantime, they've got a roof over their heads, and food to eat. I don't know what they're complaining about.' She got fluidly to her feet. 'Anyway, darling, I'm being a dreadful hostess, aren't I? I'll show you to your room—you have a choice, you know. Isn't it fun?'

Chatting all the time, her hands fluttering like animated, delicate little birds, her aunt took Caro down to the far end of the hall, and flung a door open dramatically.

'Here you are, darling! Now make yourself at home. We'll be dining downstairs around six, I imagine.'

She floated off back down the hallway, leaving Caro staring into a darkened room. The drapes had been pulled, presumably against the cold, and after some groping in the dark Caro drew them back to reveal a surprisingly luxurious little bedroom. Plush rugs lay over the polished floorboards, and the large bedstead and matching washstand were of carved mahogany. Yet every surface had a layer of dust, and the sheets on the bed might have been of the finest quality cotton, but they were unmistakably damp.

The room overlooked the avenue, giving an interesting view of the traffic below. It had stopped snowing and so Caro opened the big, double-hung window as wide as possible. Finding it a positive pleasure to have something to do, she went in search of clean linen and cleaning materials and found both in a cupboard in the hallway. It took almost an hour until every surface was dusted and polished to her satisfaction; by the time she had finished, the pale winter light filtering between the lace curtains had all but gone. Closing the window against the encroaching dark, she lit a small fire in the grate and was soon able to put a warming pan filled with hot coals between the clean sheets to dry them out.

Hands on hips, she surveyed her handiwork with satisfaction. The room looked cosy and welcoming now, and smelt warmly of beeswax polish, just like home. She thought of all the other rooms in the hotel, no doubt waiting to be cleaned, and found herself viewing the prospect with pleasure.

In the hallway she found her bag, sitting forlornly where someone—she suspected Oliver—had left it. It did not appear that the staff here were inclined to be in the least bit helpful. While she unpacked her single change of clothes, Caro thought about that.

The staff had told her that her aunt had no business sense and, as utterly charming as Aunt Charlotte was, Caro could see how that could be true. It would take both business acumen and hard work to keep an hotel this size running, but why the hotel should have run out of funds was a complete mystery to her. There had obviously been a fortune spent on establishing the place, with no cost spared in the furnishings or decor. In a town as thriving as Dunedin, with an all-too-evident accommodation shortage, the hotel should have been fully booked every night. So why was there no food in the kitchen and no guests in the rooms?

Caro had always taken an active interest in the book-keeping side of her father's businesses and Ben had been too intrigued by her persistence to really discourage her. She now possessed a sound grasp of the principles of good business, and she had never been afraid of hard work. What better way to repay Aunt Charlotte's hospitality than by restoring her business to its full health?

The clock in the civic building down the street chimed six o'clock, but for Caro the few unbuttered scones in the hotel kitchen were far too many hours ago, and her stomach rumbled hungrily. Her aunt had said that they would be dining—presumably in the hotel dining room—but the staff had told her that there was no food left. She decided that now was as good a time as any to discover the truth of the situation.

She changed into her second dress, of serviceable green wool, and pulled a shawl around her shoulders against the chill; she had allowed the fire to burn down and the air was now so cold that she could see the mist of her breath.

The foyer of the hotel was deserted, and when she looked through into the dining room it looked as if nothing had been cleaned or moved since the morning. The great chandeliers hung unlit and palely gleaming in the crack of light showing from beneath the kitchen door, but the place was eerily quiet. A single lamp shone forlornly on the registration desk. Caro revised downwards her chances of a gracious meal in the dining room that night.

There was a muffled roar of laughter from somewhere beyond the hotel walls and she remembered the public bar that she had passed earlier in the day, the one that Aunt Charlotte had told her that Mr Thwaites ran. Well, that at least sounded like a thriving business. They would probably have a fire going there. Maybe even something to eat! It was snowing again and she stood for a captivated moment on the veranda, watching the fluffy flakes twirling delicately in the air. Light from the long windows of the bar streamed out over the ground, illuminating the white layer of snow, giving a fairytale appearance to the otherwise mundane street.

She knew she had made a mistake the moment she set foot over the doorstep. The bar was much bigger than she had thought, and filled with men. Dozens of them. One by one they stopped laughing and shouting and put their drinks down to stare at her. The heat and smell of alcohol hit her face like a blow.

However, it was too late now to back down.

She wove her way between the tables, ignoring outstretched hands that would have detained her, to the bar, where a scruffy-looking individual in shirtsleeves was wiping out glasses.

'Sorry, lass, can't serve you,' he said shortly before she even reached the bar.

'Aw, go on with you, Bill,' someone very drunk bellowed behind her. 'She looks like she needs a little servicin'!'

The coarse male laughter gripped Caro's insides with terror, but not for the world would she have shown it. She rested the tips of her fingers lightly on the bar to stop their trembling.

'I'd like to see Mr Thwaites if he's here, please,' she said quietly enough, but as for the anticipatory hush in the room she may as well have shouted the words.

The bartender's eyes travelled down assessingly and up insultingly. ''Fraid you can't, lass.'

'Is he here?' she persisted, dreading the thought of having to brave the male barrage alone on her way out.

'Maybe.' He lifted his lips in something between a smirk and a sneer.

'Then I'd like to see him, please.'

''Ere, me darlin'.' A red-faced little man nudged her elbow as he fumbled with his trousers. 'Why don't you see me instead, eh?'

'I beg your pardon?' she began blankly, wondering what conceivable interest the little man thought she would have in his belt. A second before his trousers dropped to his knees a tall body interposed itself between them.

'I think, madam, you should leave.'

She looked up to an unshaven, weary face of indeterminate age.

'I'm here to see Mr Thwaites,' she said tersely, resenting the light pressure being exerted on her upper arm. She was not used to being manhandled.

'Then I suggest another time, madam. In the morning, perhaps.' He turned her around to face the door, raising his elbow as he did so and accidentally jabbing the throat of a man who was about to lunge at her. 'I'm so sorry,' he said politely as his victim staggered back with a yelp. 'Very careless of me.'

There was a grumbled chorus of disappointment as she was marched to the door, but no one impeded their progress. Within seconds she was back out on the veranda, rigid with rage and the cold.

'I'm not going to thank you, you know!' she snapped.

'I wouldn't dream of presuming that you would, madam.'

'I only went in there to see someone,' she went on, cross with herself that she had to somehow justify what was now apparent as recklessness.

'I think you were about to see quite a lot for a young lady,' he said evenly. Despite her humiliation and anger his voice intrigued her, with its clipped perfect enunciation that she had only ever heard before in the Governor-General's residence in New South Wales. Her mother would have been most impressed.

But not if she had seen him. His clothes were old and worn, his hair was unkempt and—Caro could not help but wrinkle her nose—he *smelt*, mostly of drink. I should feel sorry for him, she reminded herself, but that was impossible. Someone who looked like a tramp had no right to the irritating mannerism of sounding apologetic when he plainly was not. She met his gaze squarely and then rather wished she hadn't. There was a deadness in his brown eyes that chilled her. She found herself wondering if he was really even seeing her.

'Well, I suppose I *should* thank you,' she began indifferently, but already he had turned on his heel and returned to the bar with only the most cursory of nods. Incensed by his rudeness, she thought for a moment about following him back in and telling him what she thought, before common sense prevailed. Drawing her shawl tightly against the cold, she turned back into the hotel.

The foyer was still dimly lit, but no longer deserted. Charlotte was there, talking in rapid, hushed tones to a tall, well-dressed man in his thirties who was leaning nonchalantly against the desk, apparently listening to her with only half his attention. His pale eyes swept over Caro with the appreciation of a connoisseur as she made her entrance in a flurry of snowflakes.

'Well, well, well. Now, you must be the niece,' he said softly as he straightened up. 'There's no mistaking the resemblance.'

'Oh, Caroline, there you are!' Her aunt seemed flustered, her fingers working nervously at the fine silk shawl clutched around her shoulders. 'Come and meet Harold, darling.'

'Miss Morgan,' he murmured, extending his hand. 'What an unexpected pleasure. Although I'd never expect Charlotte to have a niece who *wasn't* utterly lovely.' Caro was well used to flattery, and this man was obviously a close friend of her aunt's, but still she hesitated before offering her hand to him. When he brought it to his lips she had to make a real effort not to flinch away. She wasn't sure why she should react to him so—perhaps it was his boldness or air of absolute confidence. He seemed to mistake her unease for shyness and he held her hand for much too long, amusement lighting the etched lines of his face. The word 'dissolute' flashed into Caro's mind.

'Where have you been?' Charlotte said to the man beside her with just a trace of reproach in her voice. 'I couldn't find you in your room when that dreadful Oliver was threatening me...'

'Come now, Charlotte,' Harold said in tolerant amusement. 'He merely told you he was leaving your employment.'

'But it was the *manner* in which he told me! He was so *rude*, Harold—you've no idea!' She pouted prettily.

'You should try paying your staff, my dear—then I can guarantee they won't be rude to you.'

'Oh, don't preach so. You know I hate it.' She looked up at him appealingly. 'Now what shall I do? There's only the cook and that silly chit of a girl left now—and goodness knows how long they'll stay. I'll have to shut the hotel down soon!'

He shrugged as if Charlotte's problems were entirely trivial. 'Let's talk about it over dinner, shall we?'

'I'm sure I could find something in the kitchen,' Caro began uncertainly, but Harold and her aunt turned to her with looks of genuine surprise.

'We'll eat elsewhere, tonight,' Harold said firmly. 'We can't have you cooking, Miss Morgan. That would never do.' He held out an arm to each of them. 'Come along, ladies.'

Charlotte snuggled into his side with alacrity, but Caro held back. That they should dine out elsewhere when her aunt owned this huge hotel and could not afford to even pay the staff seemed completely nonsensical. However, Harold remained where he was, arm outstretched, his smile not faltering, and it seemed churlish to refuse him.

'I'll just get my coat,' she said hurriedly and ran upstairs so that she would not have to take his arm. In her room she stood for a moment, struggling to regain her composure. Encountering Mr Thwaites so soon after the unpleasant episode in the bar had left her head whirling. She didn't like him, and she didn't understand the relationship between him and her aunt. She thought for a moment about excusing herself from dinner, but a low growl from her stomach reminded her that her last meal had been well over twelve hours ago. At least if she went she would be fed. She changed into her stout boots, buttoned her coat up to the neck and went downstairs.

The snow was still falling thickly when they stepped outside and a bitter wind had sprung up, making visibility past a few yards impossible and piling the snow in drifts along the side of the road. The Castledene bar was doing a roaring trade judging from the raucous sounds coming from within. Despite herself, Caro edged a little closer to Harold as they passed.

Along an almost-deserted Princes Street he led them to another hotel, nowhere as near as grand as the Castledene, but where they were welcomed into a very pleasant dining room by a neatly uniformed maid.

'Somewhere close to the fire, please,' said Charlotte with a shiver in her voice. It was then that Caro realised that her aunt had not put on a coat, but was still wearing only the silk shawl over her evening dress. As they took their seats at a table close to the fireplace, Charlotte removed the by-now sodden shawl and Caro's jaw dropped. Her aunt's pale-blue satin gown was beautifully cut and obviously very expensive, but the sleeves were almost non-existent and Caro was sure that with one deep breath her aunt would reveal far more than could ever be deemed socially decent. The waiter, on his way over to them with the menu, collided into another diner's chair in his stunned state.

'Aunt Charlotte,' she whispered urgently.

'Yes, darling?'

'Aren't you *cold*?'

'Frozen rigid, darling. I need a drink!'

Harold chuckled and summoned the red-faced waiter with a flick of his wrist. 'Your aunt always drinks champagne with dinner. What's your preference, Miss Morgan? Or may I call you Caroline?'

'I don't drink, thank you,' Caro said a little too tersely. She was aware that he was looking at her oddly, but she was still too shocked by her aunt's appearance to care if he thought her over-prim. Mind you, she thought twenty minutes later, *anyone* would appear prim next to Aunt Charlotte. The first bottle of champagne was swiftly dispatched and the second took only a little longer as Aunt Charlotte, it seemed, had mastered the art of elegant gulping. By the time the soup dishes had been cleared and plates of steaming-hot ham and potatoes set before them, the third bottle of champagne had been opened. A pang of unease went through Caro as she realised that Harold drank only a little himself, and appeared to be quite happy to encourage Aunt Charlotte's excesses.

She sipped the glass of water she had ordered for herself and looked around the dining room with critical eyes. It was comfortable, certainly, and warm. The service had been attentive enough—overly attentive, in fact, as the waiter had missed few opportunities to ogle down the front of her aunt's dress—and the food was adequate. But if this was one of Dunedin's best restaurants, then the Castledene, cleaned and polished, with the chandeliers dusted and lit, would be in a class of its own. When she had pestered her father to take her on one of his business trips to Sydney—which she frequently had—he had always treated her to lunch in one of the substantial hotels of the town. It was here that she had leaned to appreciate fine dining, surroundings and service. Why shouldn't Dunedin have the same? After all, it was said that there were fortunes made daily in this town and the Castledene had plainly been built to take advantage of those fortunes.

It was just a matter of restoring the Castledene to its earlier glory. As she watched Aunt Charlotte push her untouched plate away and reach for her glass again,

Caro began to understand why the hotel had fallen on hard times in the first place.

As if reading her thoughts, Aunt Charlotte looked archly over the top of her glass.

'Not drinking, darling?' Her voice, soft and musical as ever, was distinctly slurred.

'I don't like alcohol, Aunt Charlotte,' Caro said carefully.

'Hmph! Like your mother, are you? Emma didn't like drinking. Not like your father. Ben used to like a drink.' She gave a laugh and slumped back in her seat. One pink nipple popped up out of her dress and she gave no sign of noticing as Harold considerately tucked it back into her bodice. 'Oh, yes,' she went on, 'your father could put it away, all right. Oh, the things I could tell you about your father—'

'But you're not going to, my dear, are you?' Harold cut in smoothly, much to Caro's relief. 'Let me fill up your glass.' He turned the full charm of his smile on to Caro. 'Now, Miss Morgan. What do you think of Dunedin?'

Caro laid her knife and fork down precisely on her plate. 'Apart from the cold, which is quite a novelty, I like what I've seen so far, Mr Thwaites.'

'Good, good.' He topped up Charlotte's glass and looked askance at Caro. 'Sure you wouldn't like just a drop, Miss Morgan?'

'Thank you, no,' Caro said firmly. 'But what I would like is to talk to you about the Castledene.'

He sighed dramatically. 'What a dreary subject for a chill night, Miss Morgan. Surely we can find a more convivial subject on which to converse?'

'It seems to me that it's a subject we must discuss,

and urgently, too.' She looked pointedly at her aunt. 'Don't you agree, Aunt Charlotte?'

'About what, darling?' Her aunt smiled fuzzily at her and Harold leant over to speak in a stage-whisper in her ear.

'Your niece wants to talk about business, Charlotte.'

'Oh, do you? How tiresome,' Charlotte pouted. 'I don't.' She giggled and Harold propped her up carefully as she began to slide to one side.

Caro took a deep breath and began patiently, 'Aunt Charlotte, the hotel has been forced to close down...'

'No it hasn't, silly,' her aunt murmured into her glass.

'Yes, it has,' Caro corrected her. 'You've lost staff, you can't afford to pay the staff you have, there's no money to stock the kitchen and feed the guests. You're trading insolvently, Aunt Charlotte!'

Her aunt blinked at her. 'I have no idea what you're talking about, darling.'

She plainly hadn't. Caro turned her attention to Harold who, despite his languid pose, had in fact been watching her sharply. 'Mr Thwaites, the bar seems to be doing very well. How much rent do you pay my aunt for it?'

'That, my dear, is between your aunt and myself,' he said courteously enough.

'Well, whatever it is, it's obviously not enough!' Caro retorted. 'That bar was full of men this evening, all buying considerable amounts of alcohol—'

'Which is an expensive commodity in this country,' he broke in. 'Besides which, may I ask how you know how well the bar is patronised, Miss Morgan? You would never cross the threshold of such a place, surely?' As she hesitated, she saw the gleam of amusement in his eyes. 'That was not wise, Miss Morgan. Anything could happen to you in a public bar. I'd advise you not to do anything so foolhardy in the future.'

He was probably right. For one disconcerting second she remembered the cold, dead eyes of the stranger in the bar. But far too much was at stake for her to be deterred by Harold's veiled threats and she plunged on regardless.

'Tomorrow I'd like to see the books for the hotel and I intend doing a thorough inventory.' He shrugged, so she added provocatively, 'And that includes the bar, too.'

His expression grew decidedly chilly. 'The bar is run as a separate business, Miss Morgan. You're not to set foot in it.'

'Oh, stop it, stop it,' Charlotte waved her hands at them helplessly. 'Don't argue. You know I hate people arguing…'

'You're quite right.' Harold said soothingly, even while sending Caro a look of pure malice. 'We don't want to upset you, do we, Miss Morgan?'

Caro looked at her aunt and was instantly contrite. Under her makeup Charlotte was very pale, and the champagne glass was shaking in her hand. Caro helped her aunt to her feet and, when the waiter brought their coats, insisted on Charlotte wearing her own warm coat back to the Castledene. Charlotte protested briefly about how unbecoming the garment was to her, but was either too drunk or too unwell to complain for long. Caro felt her aunt's feverish, bird-like frame as she buttoned up the coat for her and felt an overwhelming sense of protectiveness. Poor Aunt Charlotte, in appearance so much like Caro's mother, but with none of the quiet contentedness that was part of Emma's personality. And while Caro was firmly of the opinion that a woman should be able to look after her own interests, it was all too clear that Charlotte was relying far too much on the highly dubious goodwill of Mr Thwaites.

Resolving to tackle Harold again first thing in the morning, Caro followed his and her aunt's unsteady progress back through the streets of Dunedin. It had stopped snowing, but the sidewalks were slippery with snowdrifts. On the corner of Castle Street Charlotte collapsed and Harold had to carry her the rest of the way. Caro followed him upstairs and into her aunt's room, where she hurriedly lit the lamps while he deposited her aunt on the bed.

'I'll take care of her now,' she said pointedly as he removed her aunt's slippers, silly, frippery little things that they were. He stepped back with a sardonic smile.

'As you wish. I'll be in the bar if you need me. I take it you remember where that is, Miss Morgan?'

As he left Charlotte struggled to sit up, protesting that she was perfectly capable of seeing to herself. Calmly ignoring her, Caro set and lit the fire, and soon had the room in order and Charlotte tucked up warmly in bed with a bedpan.

'Shall I see if there's any milk in the kitchen?' Caro asked, perching herself on the edge of the bed. Propped up against the pillows, her aunt wrinkled her nose in disgust.

'Ugh! Yes, I remember Emma used to make me hot milk and honey before I went to bed at night to help me sleep.' She held out a fine-boned hand to Caro. 'I miss your mother, Caroline. She's an angel…'

Caro fought back the pang of homesickness. 'I miss her, too,' she confessed.

Charlotte sighed and her eyes drooped. Her hand in Caro's felt far too hot for comfort, despite her complaints of the cold. 'Twenty years apart. Such a long time, and because of such a silly quarrel...'

She was asleep in seconds. Caro waited for a while, but her aunt seemed comfortable enough, so she tiptoed back to her own room. The meagre fire she had lit for herself had long since died out and when she pulled back the curtain the room was flooded with cold moonlight. She undressed swiftly without a lamp and pulled on the old, comfortable nightgown that always reminded her of home. Then, shivering, she slipped between the cold sheets, finding the still-warm bedpan with grateful toes.

She was so tired that she had expected to fall asleep immediately, but instead she lay staring blindly at the ceiling, missing the creaking of ship's timbers beneath the wind and the waves. The silence here unnerved her, and although there was an occasional burst of noise from the bar below the sound was so muffled by the snow on the windowpanes as to be almost imperceptible. It was hours later when she heard the creaking of the stairs and the sound of quiet footsteps coming down the hall. Feeling suddenly very alone she sat up, pulling the blankets around her protectively. Too late she remembered that she hadn't locked the door.

The footsteps stopped outside her room. Scarcely daring to breathe, she silently padded to the door and felt for the key. There wasn't one. She gripped the doorhandle tightly, resisting the pressure as she felt it being turned on the other side.

'Caroline?' Mr Thwaites whispered hoarsely. 'Are you awake?'

'Not at this hour, I wouldn't think, mate,' snarled a familiar voice beside him.

'Mr Matthews?' Caro whispered incredulously.

'Yes.'

She wrenched open the door and looked down at the little, whiskery, beloved face. Harold Thwaites seemed to have vanished silently into the shadows.

'Oh, I'm so pleased to see you!' She flung her arms around Mr Matthews and hugged him tight. He tolerated it for a full five seconds before pushing her away.

'Enough of that!' he said gruffly.

She drew him into the room and stared at him incredulously in the moonlight.

'I can't believe it! Oh, this is wonderful! When did you arrive in Dunedin?'

'This evenin'. I shipped out from Sydney same day as you.' He looked disparagingly around the room. 'You ready to come home now?'

She sank down on the edge of her bed. 'No,' she said mulishly.

'You've made your point, girl. Your ma's beside herself, your pa wants you home safe again—'

'But I can't go home!' she burst out. 'Not now! Aunt Charlotte's not well, and the hotel needs rescuing and Mr Thwaite's cheating her, I just know it and—'

'Hey, hey, hey!' He held up a hand in protest. 'Just slow down and tell me what you're talking about.'

So she did, and he stood listening intently, nodding from time to time in what she hoped was agreement. His silence when she had finished, however, was ominous.

'Well,' she said after a moment. 'You can understand why I can't go home.'

He scratched his head. 'I can understand why you

won't go home, girl. But why you should stay here beats me. You don't owe your aunt nothing!'

'But I do! She's so sweet and helpless…' She ignored Mr Matthew's derisive snort and added, 'I'm not leaving Dunedin until she's out of trouble and that's that. Now, do you have any money?'

'What?'

'Money. Did Father give you any before you left Sydney? I'm sure he would have.'

He looked shifty. 'Can't say that he did…'

'Yes, he did. He would have given you enough to get us both home, if nothing else.' She held out her hand. 'That will at least pay some of the staff wages. It may even be enough to open the dining room again,'

Mr Matthews stepped back, his eyes widening in panic. 'Your pa'd skin me alive if I gave your aunt so much as a penny! I'd never dare set foot in his house again!'

His consternation was so real that Caro uncharacteristically stopped arguing and lowered her hand. 'Oh, this family feud is so ridiculous! Well, I'll just have to think of something else.' Somewhere in Dunedin a clock chimed three o'clock and she struggled to stifle a yawn.

'Tomorrow,' Mr Matthews said. 'We'll think of something tomorrow, girl. Now you get back into bed and keep warm.'

She couldn't stop the next yawn. 'I'll find you a room along the hall…' But he told her in no uncertain terms that he was perfectly capable of finding a room to 'bunk down in' and left her after several more admonitions that she return to bed directly. The bed was cold, and her feet felt like ice, but Caro was so happy she scarcely noticed. Mr Matthews was sleeping across the hallway and everything was right with the world. She fell asleep almost immediately with a smile on her face.

Chapter Three

'Ah, here it is!' Caro hauled the heavy book up from under the registration desk, thumped it down triumphantly and blew the light layer of dust off the leather cover. The motes danced in the pale winter light pouring in through the long front windows of the Castledene Hotel.

Outside had dawned the loveliest imaginable spring day. The previous day's snow still clung to the hilltops, but Caro had gone for an early-morning walk around the outskirts of Dunedin, with Mr Matthews puffing behind all the way, and she had returned with a clutch of bright daffodils. They sat now in a fine crystal vase on the registration desk, lending an air of cheerful welcome to the otherwise formal entry hall.

'Oh, dear.' She looked across to where Mr Matthews sat glowering at his feet. 'Nothing has been entered in these books for over four months.' Mr Matthews, who had a profound suspicion of anything on a page, merely shrugged. 'I wonder who's been keeping record of everything bought or sold since then?' she murmured to the empty air. 'I would have thought that would have been Oliver's job.'

'Or yer aunt's,' Mr Matthews said shortly.

Caro glanced up at her aunt's door at the top of the stairs. She had looked in on her earlier, but Charlotte had been still sleeping restlessly and Caro hadn't liked to disturb her.

'She's not well, Mr Matthews.'

He snorted rudely. 'Never has been, that one. Never been sober, neither.'

'Don't be horrible!' Caro said indignantly. 'I meant, she's not well physically. She's not strong, and only recently widowed, and I don't think she's ever had to run a business before.'

'Neither have you,' he retorted. 'What do you know 'bout books and figures and all that? Never noticed you paying any attention to your 'rithmetic lessons when your ma was trying to learn you.'

'But the figures that relate to running a business make *sense*, don't you see?' Caro jabbed her finger at the offending blank space in the ledger book. 'Without that information, I can't tell how much it costs to run this establishment. And I'd really like to know how much Mr Thwaites is—or isn't—paying for the lease on the bar.'

'None of your bleedin' business, I say.'

Caro closed the ledger book with a slap. 'It is, Mr Matthews, because I'm my aunt's closest relative in this town. Come on.'

'Oh, Gawd help us.' He got creakily to his feet. After weeks of inactivity on the ship from Sydney and a night spent sleeping outside Caro's door, he had found the brisk walk around Dunedin exhausting. 'Where're you going now?'

'To the bar. There's bound to be a ledger kept there.'

His eyes widened in alarm. 'A public bar? Now look here, girl…'

But she wasn't listening as she strode out the front door and along the veranda to the bar. With Mr Matthews audibly following her, she wasn't in the least bit afraid. In fact, the bar was deserted apart from a bartender—a different one from the unpleasant man the previous night—and a couple of comatose bodies slumped on the tables. Although she would not have admitted it even to herself, Caro was relieved that there was no sign of Mr Thwaites. The air was fuggy from tobacco smoke and beer and she left the door open behind her to allow in some fresh air.

'Good morning,' she said firmly to the bartender. He opened his mouth, caught the look on Mr Matthews's face and closed it again.

'Mornin', miss,' he said after a moment.

'I'm Caroline Morgan, Mrs Wilks's niece. My aunt is indisposed, so I will be in charge of the Castledene for a while.' She smiled engagingly at him. 'Could I see your books, please?'

'Books, miss?'

'Yes. Your ledgers. Please.' Her smile did not falter.

'Don't think I'm allowed to do that, miss…'

'I'm sure you are,' Caro said with steely charm.

The bartender looked from her to Mr Matthews, whose whiskers were literally bristling with belligerence. The little man had to be one of the ugliest people the bartender had ever seen, in contrast to the stunning beauty of the tall and very pushy blonde facing him across the bar. Completely unnerved, he stepped back.

'I don't think…well, I couldn't let them leave the premises…'

'That's quite all right.' Again there was that quick,

enchanting smile before the girl took the ledgers firmly from his grasp and bore them off. In the middle of the bar room she stopped and frowned at the slumped figures at the two tables.

'I think these people should go home, Mr Matthews. The place looks so…so *cluttered*, don't you think?'

Mr Matthews grumbled something, seized the legs of the closest man and hauled him out the door. While he was gone, Caro moved closer and peered at the remaining unconscious customer. Arms splayed out on the table, his face turned to one side, he was still recognisable as the man who had come to her rescue the previous night. She shook him, gently at first, and then harder until his impossibly long lashes fluttered open.

'Sir? The bar is closed now, sir.'

It took a visible effort for him to raise his head off the table, and it was only by using his arms as leverage that he was able to sit upright. The cold, dead eyes that had looked at her so clearly the previous night were half-closed and he looked to be in some kind of private agony.

'Come on, mate! On yer way!' Mr Matthews said testily behind Caro and she held up her hand to stall him.

'Are you all right?' she asked, keeping her voice devoid of sympathy.

After a moment the man nodded, very carefully. 'Yes, madam. I believe that I am.'

Again, the perfect vowels struck her as strangely exotic and behind her she heard Mr Matthews's expelled breath of surprise. Slowly, with great precision, the man lifted his hand and felt inside his jacket. Then his face crumpled and his eyes screwed tight.

'No…!'

'Been fleeced, have yer, mate?' Caro was surprised by Mr Matthews's completely out-of-character sympathy. The man took a steadying breath and nodded. 'Stay off the booze next time,' Mr Matthews advised. 'Then you can keep a hold on yer wallet.'

'Thank you for the advice.' There was not a trace of sarcasm in the man's voice. He manoeuvred himself to his feet and stayed there, propped up against the wall as the room was obviously swimming around him. He didn't look at all well.

'Have you got somewhere to go?' Caro was surprised to hear herself ask.

'Yes, thank you, madam.'

She didn't believe him.

'Mr Matthews, please give me a pound note,' she said, not taking her eyes off the man for a second. He was so pale she thought he was going to faint. With only an insignificant mutter of discontent, Mr Matthews did as he was told.

'Here.' She tucked the note briskly into the man's jacket pocket. 'Please get yourself a meal and somewhere to sleep tonight.'

For a moment he met her eyes and the anger she saw there shocked her to the core. Then he looked away, a faint flush rising to his cheeks.

'Thank you,' he said emotionlessly.

She watched him walk stiffly to the door and out into the sunshine.

'You'll have us both in the poorhouse if you keep giving money to drunkards,' Mr Matthews grumbled as Caro propped the ledger open on the vacated table. She ignored him, as she was certainly not about to tell him what had transpired in the bar the previous night. It pleased her that she had paid her debt to the man, but she still felt unsettled by the expression she had seen in his eyes. He hadn't even had the grace to be grateful.

Ten minutes of perusing the accounts confirmed Caro's worst suspicions. Mr Thwaites was making very healthy profits, indeed, from the bar, but if he was paying any rent to the Castledene Hotel, it was not shown in the books. She sighed and sat back to study the gleaming rows of bottles lined up on the wall above the bar.

'This is dreadful, Mr Matthews. My aunt is facing destitution, the hotel has had to shut down, yet the bar is taking in hundreds of pounds every night! I've got to find out why none of the profits are going to keep the hotel and why the hotel got into financial trouble in the first place. It appears to have been profitable until my aunt's husband died.'

'Well, I'd 'ave thought that was bleedin' obvious.' Mr Matthews rubbed his bristles thoughtfully. 'Yer aunt's spent the lot on men and fripperies and booze. Always has, always will. When yer grandfather—yer aunt's first husband—died, yer pa gave her enough to keep most women for years. She was back with her hand out in a fortnight and cut up rough when he wouldn't give her another penny.'

'But she's my mother's eldest sister—and she was his widowed stepmother! Surely he had an obligation to care for her, Mr Matthews?'

He looked uncomfortable. 'There was more to it than that, girl. Things you don't need to know nothin' about.'

'You mean about Aunt Charlotte choosing my grandfather instead of my father?' Caro said tartly. 'I know all about that, Mr Matthews, my aunt told me.

While I'm pleased that she *did* turn him down, of course, because he married Mother instead, I think Father was petty and mean to send her away without a penny. The least I can do is try to help her out now.' There was an ominous silence. 'Well?' she prompted after a moment. 'Don't you agree?'

Mr Matthews shook his head slowly. 'Darned if I don't know whether to weep or to put you over my knee and paddle yer behind. All I can say, girl, is don't believe a word yer aunt tells you. From what you tell me, she ain't changed one bit in the last twenty years.'

'Then what did happen?' Caro demanded.

'Not for me to tell you.'

'Then kindly mind your own business.' She shut the ledger and returned it to the cringing bartender with a brilliant smile. 'Now, I must go and see if Aunt Charlotte has improved.'

But Aunt Charlotte hadn't improved at all. She lay shivering and as pale as the satin pillows of her bed, giving anguished little cries as Caro tried to open the curtains.

'Oh, the light, Caroline! Oh, I can't bear it! Please, go away, darling. I just want to die!'

'I've brought you a jug of water, Aunt Charlotte— Mother always makes us drink lots of water when we're feverish.' Caro sat down on the bed and, despite her aunt's protestation that it had been *years* since she had drunk plain water, she persisted until Charlotte had completely emptied a glass. She then dampened a cloth for her aunt's forehead and tiptoed silently around the room, tidying and straightening, until Charlotte was asleep again. After leaving a window open to let in some of the crisply fresh air, Caro left, closing the door carefully behind her. There was so much she wanted to ask her aunt, but this was clearly not the time.

There had been no staff in the kitchen in the early morning and there were none there now. Mr Matthews stood alone at the kitchen table, preparing one of the delicious soups he always seemed able to produce from nothing at all, grumbling away to himself all the while. Caro sat and watched him, her chin propped on her fists, her forehead furrowed with thought.

'You'll get wrinkles,' he advised her after a while.

'Mmm. Mr Matthews, I'm going to have to go to the bank.' He sucked in his breath with horror, but she plunged on. 'Aunt Charlotte's in no condition to do so and Mr Thwaites won't lift a finger to help and there's no other way to get the money we need to start up the hotel again.'

'How much're we talking about here?' he asked in alarm. 'I've got a little bit on me, not much, mind, and yer pa'd kill me if he knew...'

'By the time I've paid the staff wages, provisioned the kitchen, bought firewood, had the chimneys cleaned... I'd say five hundred pounds at the very least.'

'I ain't got that much.' He slumped into a heap of misery. 'But you don't want to go off to a bank. Nasty, thievin' places, banks. Have the shirt off yer back in two seconds, they will.'

'My father always dealt with them satisfactorily.' Caro recalled visiting the bank with her father on occasion. She remembered the dark panelled walls, the heavy-handed pleasantry of the manager as he plied her with compliments and pressed a glass of the best whisky on Ben... Why, it had been rather fun. It couldn't be that bad going on her own account, surely?

'Yer father never borrowed 'cept on what he knew were a good business deal. And he were a *man*. They'll never lend to *you*,' Mr Matthews predicted darkly, realising his mistake only when Caro's chin came up.

'Well, we'll see about that!'

There were banks on every street in Dunedin, but it was the work of a minute to look through the ledgers and find out which one her aunt dealt with. It took somewhat longer before Caro was satisfied with the image she wished to present to the bank manager. The better of her woollen gowns was perfectly presentable, but her coat and bonnet were too plain to give her any confidence. She crept into her aunt's room and managed to extract a particularly fetching bonnet in pale blue, together with a matching short walking cape, without waking Charlotte.

She was pleased when she looked at her reflection in the mirror. While Aunt Charlotte's taste ran to the somewhat flamboyant, the bonnet Caro had chosen was a study in understated elegance once she removed the peacock feathers. Just right, she thought, for impressing bank managers with her innate good taste.

Her sublime confidence lasted all the way down Princes Street, past St Andrew's Church and down Carlyle Street. It began to falter a little during the half-hour she was kept waiting at the counter for the bank manager to see her, and by the time Mr Froggatt spared the time to show her into his office, she was decidedly tense.

Mr Froggatt was a big, squarely built Northerner, and not one to waste time on niceties.

'Come to pay off the overdraft, have you?' he boomed loudly enough for any passing customer to overhear.

'Overdraft?' Caro said blankly.

'Aye, overdraft.' The bank manager viewed her through narrowed little eyes.

Caro swallowed hard and flashed him her most engaging smile. 'I'm afraid I don't know anything about an overdraft, Mr Froggatt. I've come to see you about a business proposition. One I think you'll be very interested in.'

'Oh, aye?' he responded drily, completely unmoved by her loveliness. 'And what that might be? Nothing involving this bank lending further to the Castledene Hotel, I trust?'

She leaned forward to hide her shaking hands. 'There's no value to the bank in foreclosing on a business that should and could do very nicely on a small injection of capital, Mr Froggatt.'

He leaned back in his chair to distance himself, splaying his powerful hands on the desk as he bellowed, 'There'll be no more money lent to the Castledene Hotel, I say. No more, until the five thousand pounds already outstanding has been repaid in full, with interest. Am I understood, Mrs…?'

Five thousand pounds? It took all Caro's resolve not to fly from the office there and then. She took a deep breath. 'My name is Miss Caroline Morgan. I'm Mrs Wilks's niece, from Sydney.'

He was instantly alert. 'Are you, indeed? And would your father be Mr Morgan, of the Morgan Shipping Line?'

The word stuck in her throat. 'Yes…'

'Ah.' Something that Caro hoped might have been a smile flickered far too briefly over the impassive features. 'Yes, Mrs Wilks has spoken of your father several times and I understand he'd be prepared to stand for the losses incurred by your aunt. Are you here on his behalf?'

Thinking that she could cheerfully strangle Aunt Charlotte, Caro shook her head. 'No, Mr Froggatt, I'm here on my aunt's behalf. She's not well, you see, and I'd like to put the hotel back on a sound financial footing.' She spoke rapidly, before he could interrupt, outlining her plans for the resurrection of the hotel, speeding up when it looked as if he was about to raise an objection. To her relief he heard her out. When she finally ran out of words, he sat back, his shrewd eyes summing her up in a most demoralising manner.

'I'm sorry, Miss Morgan. You've put forward some convincing arguments, but the answer has to be no.' He almost sounded apologetic.

'But why?' She tried not to wail the words. 'In a town expanding as fast as Dunedin, it would be impossible to run a failing business, if one were prudent!'

'Mrs Wilks is not prudent,' he pointed out patiently.

'But I am!'

'But you, Miss Morgan, are a young unmarried female.'

'And?'

'And the bank does not lend to young, unmarried females, no matter how…*prudent* they may be. That is the bank's policy, it is a sound policy, and it will not be changed, Miss Morgan. I'm sorry.'

She took a deep breath. 'And if I were married?'

'But you are not married, Miss Morgan.'

'I am engaged,' she said brightly.

'Then I offer my congratulations, Miss Morgan. But you are not married.'

'I will be next week,' she said recklessly, prompted

by the dreadful vision of the Castledene Hotel falling into ruin. 'I shall be a married woman then!'

'Then, given the standing of your father, we might revisit the possibility of extending the period of the loan,' Mr Froggatt said cautiously. 'May I ask the name of your intended?'

'My what?' Caro said blankly, her mind whirling at what she had got herself into.

'Your fiancé. The young man to whom you are affianced.'

'Oh, him!' she said quickly, trying not to panic at the note of suspicion in the banker's voice. 'You wouldn't know him. He's not long arrived from England. He doesn't know anyone here. Well, he knows me, but he doesn't know anyone else…'

'My congratulations, then, Miss Morgan. I shall look forward to meeting him when you've tied the knot.' He stood, terminating the meeting. 'Until then, Miss Morgan.'

Somehow she managed to hold herself together until she returned to the hotel. She ran into the kitchen, took one look at Mr Matthews sitting huddled on the kitchen stool and burst into tears.

'Mr Matthews, I've got to get married!' she wailed.

In a trice he was at her side, pressing her down on to a chair, patting her shoulder in helpless sympathy. 'Oh, girl, girl. These things happen. Don't you fret…'

She wiped her nose on her sleeve, struggling for control. 'But I have to get married *immediately*! Within the week!'

He sat beside her, finding a large handkerchief from a pocket and dabbing ineffectually at her eyes. 'Now, it won't have to be that soon, you know. It kin happen to the best of us. Why, me and my missus—'

'You have a wife?' Caro was so amazed by this information that she almost forgot her own problems for a second.

'Had a wife. Might still have one. Dunno. England…' His voice trailed off and she dared not ask further questions. Mr Matthews had once, a very long time ago, been a convict, and no one in the family ever spoke about his origins, respecting him as deeply as they did. He took back the handkerchief and harrumped loudly into it. 'All I'm saying, girl, is it's not the end of the world. When did it happen?'

'Just now, at the bank.'

'At the *bank*?'

'Yes. Mr Froggatt the banker…'

'The *banker*?'

She nodded miserably and Mr Matthews sat looking positively stricken.

After a while he cleared his throat. 'Didn't realise you wanted the loan this bad, girl.'

'Oh, I do. That's why I have to get married, you see.'

'Yes, but you didn't have to… Oh, blasted bankers!' He slammed his fist down on the table. 'I'll do fer him, I will. And when yer pa finds out…'

Caro gave a final sniff. 'Father doesn't have to find out, Mr Matthews.'

'Well, how're you going to hide a baby, girl? Be sensible!'

'What baby?'

'Ah.' He stared at her puzzled face and after a moment said carefully, 'I think you'd better tell me what happened, girl. Slowly, this time.'

So she told him, stalking up and down the kitchen in indignation as she spoke, oblivious to the look of dawning relief on Mr Matthews's face. He was smiling by the time Caro finished, which cheered her up no end.

'So, you think it's a good idea, Mr Matthews?'

'What?' He sobered up swiftly. 'No. No, it's a real bad idea. You can't do it.'

'But I have to. I have to find a husband in the next day, if I'm to get a special licence. The problem is, how?'

'The problem ain't how to get married quick, girl— the problem is the forty years after! You can't just go and get a man off the streets...'

'Yes, I can!' She stared at him as if he was a genius. 'That's exactly what I can do! I'll marry...oh, someone, I don't care who, but someone who needs the money... That drunk in the bar this morning, for instance! All I have to do is pay him off out of the money the bank will give me, and then later I can get the marriage annulled! I mean, I don't ever want to get married, but I might, one day, and no one need ever know... Oh, it's a wonderful scheme! Thank you for thinking of it!'

Mr Matthews slumped on his stool, clutching his chest. His heart was surging in a way that terrified him. 'You can't...' he said weakly, but she wasn't listening.

'Now, I want you to go and find that man and offer to pay him...well, I'll leave that up to you, but don't make it too much. I'll go to the Town Hall this afternoon and arrange for a special licence and then... Oh, I've got so much to do!'

She spun around at the door and raised a cautionary finger. 'And you *will* check his name, won't you, Mr

Matthews, please. I don't want to be saddled with a name like Ramsbottom, or Piggot or...or Froggatt!' She laughed gaily and the door slammed behind her.

Mr Matthews sat alone in the kitchen and listened to his charge's feet exuberantly pounding up the stairs. Bleedin' heck, he thought. What *am* I going to tell her pa?

Chapter Four

Things were progressing very well, indeed, Caro thought. Obtaining a special licence had been easy enough, as was arranging with the minister at St Andrew's to officiate at a small, private wedding to be held later that week. It hadn't even been necessary to give the name of her affianced—she had simply smiled demurely and ignored the question when it came, and effectively given the impression of a shy but eager bride-to-be. She had even bought herself a wedding ring, although she had baulked at the five pounds something so unnecessary had cost. In a town literally built on the goldfields, she had somehow expected that the price of a plain gold ring would not be exorbitant.

She had detoured by the wharves on her way home and had a little chat with the porters there, promising them a generous tip should any disembarking passengers be directed to the Castledene. The afternoon she spent thoroughly cleaning out the remaining spare bedrooms in the hotel, rewarded for her efforts when a party of four—a group of mining engineers arrived just that day from Wellington—rang the bell at the desk to ask about accommodation. While she could not yet offer them a meal in the dining room, they seemed very satisfied with the luxurious private rooms she showed them to. She was kept very busy for the next couple of hours, flying up and down stairs with her arms full of towels, jugs of hot water and boots to be polished. When her guests had left for dinner, directed to the same hotel Caro had dined at the previous night, she sat down at the bottom of the stairs, her head spinning. She was enjoying herself enormously, but she hadn't looked in on Aunt Charlotte for hours, and she hadn't eaten anything since the early morning.

In the kitchen she found the pot of soup Mr Matthews had made earlier that day, together with a couple of loaves of bread, so she prepared a tray and took it up to her aunt. Charlotte appeared a little better, but flatly refused to eat anything.

'But I am thirsty, darling,' she said croakily, and then pulled a face when Caro produced a fresh jug of water. The cold water made her cough, a deep, unsettling sound, and Caro resolved to call the doctor in if her aunt's health was not improved in the morning.

Mr Matthews was waiting for her in the kitchen.

'Well?' she demanded as she put the untouched tray on the table and pulled up a chair. 'Did you find him?'

'I did,' he said ominously, but she chose to make nothing of his sour expression.

'Good. I asked the minister if he could marry us tomorrow—that's Friday, at one o'clock. That gives me time to see Mr Froggatt before the bank closes late afternoon.' She swallowed a spoonful of the soup Charlotte had rejected and licked her lips appreciatively. Mr Matthews surely had to be the best cook in the world. 'Oh, and did you find out what his name is?'

'Gray,' he said. 'Wiv an "a".' Mr Matthews sat down heavily across the table. 'First name's Leander.'

'Caroline Gray.' She tried the name, rolling it over her tongue, deciding that it was a name of distinction. 'Caroline Gray. Yes, I like that.'

'Cost you a hundred quid,' he snarled and she dropped her spoon in shock.

'A hundred pounds! My word, he must fancy himself dreadfully! Tell me you're joking!' At the shake of his head she picked up her spoon again. 'Well, tell him I'll go to ten pounds and no more. There must be hundreds of men who'd get married for less!'

'Not this one.' Mr Matthews propped his chin on his hands and met her eyes squarely. 'Said if you won't pay he ain't interested. He's a toff, girl. Might only be worth ten quid. Might only be worth half a crown. But he's been raised as quality and that lot've got queer ideas 'bout money. They always act like they don't know nothing 'bout money, even when they ain't got none. You follow me?'

'No. I haven't got a clue what you're talking about.' Caro placed her spoon and emptied dish in the washing basin and smoothed her skirt down. 'But if this Gray fellow thinks he's too good to marry me, I'd like to know why. Where is he?'

Mr Matthews's eyes widened in alarm. 'I'm not saying!'

'By which I take it he's in the Castledene bar.' She glanced at the mantleclock. It was only just after five o'clock. The bar would scarcely be busy at this hour, and her guests would only now be sitting down to eat at the hotel in Princes Street. 'I'm going to talk to him, Mr Matthews. Are you coming or not?'

As if the poor man had any choice. He followed

miserably in Caro's wake as she stormed through the doors of the bar. The barman of the previous night looked up in surprise but, when he saw who was following Caro, he rapidly decided against challenging her. The ugly little man had spent almost half an hour in quiet, intense conversation with the young drunk in the corner, and when the barman had gone up to them to demand that they order another drink to justify staying on the premises, the little man had given him a look that had him shaking in his shoes. The barman bent his head and concentrated on wiping out the beer mugs.

Leander Gray was sitting at a table, slumped against the wall, his attention absorbed by the card he was holding in his hand. From right to left and back again he flicked it between his fingers, over and over, at blurring speed. Then he looked up and saw her. As he got to his feet the card disappeared so swiftly that she wondered if she had been seeing things.

'Miss Morgan, I presume?' he said in that irritating manner, so correct and studiously polite that she could not be sure that he was not privately making fun of her.

She inclined her head a fraction. 'Mr Gray. I believe we should talk.'

'About what, Miss Morgan?'

'About the completely unrealistic cost of your services, sir.'

His dark gaze flicked behind her to Mr Matthews. 'In that case, I don't believe we have anything to discuss, Miss Morgan.'

'On the contrary, Mr Gray.' She folded her hands before her waist and raised her chin. He was just a penniless drunk, after all, with nothing to lose by marrying her except the sharing of a perfectly innocuous name. And yet…

His oddly blank eyes challenged her, making her mouth suddenly dry. Damn him, she thought furiously. How dare he act as if she were nothing and he the master of all? He would marry her, and then she would have the greatest of pleasure in tossing him out and throwing his ten pounds—or twenty, or whatever it took!—out into the snow behind him.

Deciding to change tack, she switched on her warmest smile. That usually served to disarm most men. 'Mr Gray, we have a matter to discuss that could be of benefit to us both. But I don't think that *here*'— she inclined her head towards the barman who had drifted over to ostentatiously remove a speck of dirt on a nearby table—'is the most suitable place to hold such a conversation. Could I suggest that we move to the hotel?' She let her eyes flick over his decidedly lean frame. 'I could offer you a light meal, perhaps a warm room for the night?'

He kept her waiting just a second too long to be polite.

'No, thank you, Miss Morgan.'

She stiffened in rage. 'Mr Gray, I don't believe that you're in a position to have a choice!'

His shoulders lifted in the slightest of shrugs. 'One always has a choice, Miss Morgan.'

Damn it, he *was* laughing at her! Not for the world was she going to let him get away now! She leaned forward, her fingers resting on the edge of the table, her face set in contemptuous lines. 'Does one choose to turn one's back on fifty pounds, Mr Gray?'

'My price, Miss Morgan, is one hundred pounds.'

'Sixty!'

'Ninety.'

'Seventy-five or you can forget it, Mr Gray!'

She heard Mr Matthews choke at the vast sum, but it was too late—she'd made the offer, and with money she didn't have. But at least the obnoxious Mr Gray bent his head in acceptance of her bid. She'd won after all, just as she had known she would. Ignoring Mr Matthews's outraged glare boring holes between her shoulder-blades, she nodded graciously. 'Good. I knew you'd eventually see sense. This way, please.'

Scarcely daring to check that he was following, she walked stiffly out of the bar doors and back into the hotel, through the lobby and the dining room into the kitchen. Once there, because she didn't know what else to do, she put the kettle on the stove. When she had regained sufficient equilibrium to look up, he was there, standing by the kitchen table, calmly watching her. She caught her breath on an exhalation of relief. She had done it! He belonged to her now!

Mr Matthews appeared to have made himself scarce, and that suited her. Across the table she and Mr Gray studied each other in silence, the only sound the gentle steaming of the kettle.

'Would you care for a bowl of soup, Mr Gray?' she said at last.

'Thank you, Miss Morgan.'

She served him and sat down opposite him to watch him eat. If he was hungry—and she suspected that he was—then he didn't show it. His table manners were perfect; he broke his bread and handled his spoon in exactly the way Caro's mother had always insisted her children eat, although she noted the slight tremor of his hand that she thought might be a symptom of his addiction to alcohol. His fingers were long and shapely and, despite his rough appearance, perfectly clean. All, in all, he was something of a mystery. But she really didn't have the time to speculate on how a man of obvious refinement had sunk to living rough on the streets. She had a business to save. She put her elbows on the kitchen table and leaned forward.

'Can I take it that Mr Matthews has told you what I require of you for my…seventy-five pounds?' She found the last words very hard to say—what *had* possessed her to bid so much for his services?

He looked at her levelly. 'You require my presence at the church and my name on a wedding certificate, Miss Morgan.'

'And I hope you understand that that's *all* I require,' she said tartly.

'Indeed, Miss Morgan. Anything more would cost considerably more than seventy-five pounds.'

His words were delivered so politely that she almost missed the impudence of his message. Her mouth fell open, but before she could recover herself sufficiently to speak, he rose to his feet. 'If you will excuse me…'

She stood up, too, aware for the first time that he was considerably taller than she was. 'And where are you going, Mr Gray? Back to the bar?'

'I was not aware that your seventy-five pounds entitled you to more than my presence at the church at the designated time, Miss Morgan,' he said mildly enough.

She busied herself tidying up his soup dish and plate. 'The wedding is tomorrow, at one o'clock. We have some guests staying at the hotel, but there is a room ready for you, and I would suggest that you use it. Just for tonight, mind.'

'How very kind of you.'

She glared at him. His deferential manner was far more aggravating than any open hostility could have been. 'I'm not being kind. I'm merely protecting my investment. It will be no end of bother if you get too drunk tonight to remember anything and I have to find someone else to marry tomorrow afternoon!'

He gave a slight bow. 'Then I commend you on your sound business sense, Miss Morgan. You have my admiration, if not my gratitude.'

Caro lit a lamp with swift, jerky movements, too furious to be careful with the tinderbox and consequently burning a finger in the process. She almost wished that she had taken heed of Mr Matthews's warning now, and chosen someone else to marry. Someone who would be grateful for ten pounds—*ten* pounds, mind!—and didn't act as if he were the one bestowing the favour on her. Who on earth did this man think he was, after all? She slid a quick look from under her lashes at him standing by the warm stove. Scruffy, unkempt individual that he was... She found herself wondering what he would look like after a haircut.

She filled a jug with hot water and handed it to him. Then she led him up to his room in silence, the lamp throwing long shadows on the wall as they mounted the stairs. The room she showed him to was the smallest one they had, although perfectly comfortable and she had aired it only hours earlier. She put the lamp on the dressing table and moved over to draw the curtains. It was snowing lightly again, and she thought momentarily about lighting a fire. But the room was small enough to be snug, and there were two eiderdowns on the bed. Besides, she told herself firmly, he was probably used to being cold.

'Would you like me to light a fire?' she heard herself offer.

'Thank you, no. I'll be very comfortable.' He poured the steaming water into the wash basin. He doesn't have a nightshirt, Caro thought absently, watching him. He'll take off his clothes and wash, and I haven't given him anything to wear in bed…

Good Lord! What was she bothering about that for? She nodded abruptly and moved past him, to the safety of the hallway.

'I'll bid you goodnight, then, Mr Gray.'

'Goodnight, Miss Morgan.'

It was past midnight when her other guests arrived, rather jolly from a little too much ale and the boisterous walk back through the snow. Stifling her yawns, Caro lit them each a lamp and saw them to their rooms. By the time she crawled into her own bed she was exhausted.

As her eyes closed she thought of Leander Gray down the hallway. He might be cold in his bed, but at least she had ensured that he would be sober and marriageable for their wedding later that day. Just for a moment she wondered if she might not be making a major mistake… But it had been a long day and any doubts disappeared as sleep overwhelmed her.

The faint sound of agonised coughing awoke her at dawn. She'd forgotten all about Aunt Charlotte! Pulling her shawl around her shoulders Caro ran down the hallway to her aunt's room, almost tripping over her nightgown in her haste.

Charlotte was huddled in her bed, her hair plastered to her skull with perspiration, her face deathly white in the pale dawn light. Caro drew up short at the sight of specks of blood on the pillows and her aunt's night-gown. Mr Matthews, following in her wake, muttered an expletive under his breath and for once offered not one word of complaint when Caro sent him off to find a doctor.

'Oh, Aunt Charlotte, Aunt Charlotte!' Caro wet a cloth and tenderly wiped her aunt's flushed face and hands. 'I'm so sorry…'

But Charlotte was beyond speech. She grabbed the towel from Caro's hands and coughed violently into it. When she fell back against the soiled pillows, her chest heaving with exertion, the towel was bright with blood.

The doctor came within the half-hour, harried by Mr Matthews. By now quite desperate with anxiety, Caro kept herself busy preparing hot water and clean towels while he made his examination. Doctor Scourie was a tall, pleasant-featured Scot, but when he called Caro outside to the hall his face was set in grim lines.

'It's not good news, lass,' he said without preamble. 'It's an infection of the lungs. She's had the condition for a while, I'd say. She should have sought help a long time ago.'

For a second the hallway spun around her, but Mr Matthews's hand, warm under her elbow, steadied her.

'Will…will she die?' she whispered.

Doctor Scourie hesitated, watching her carefully. 'It's possible, lass. She's not a strong woman—almost malnourished. I take it you know she's a heavy drinker?'

'I…I couldn't say…'

'She drinks like a fish,' Mr Matthews interjected and

gave her arm a little shake. 'So, doc—how long's she got?'

'If she stays here and keeps drinking she'll be dead by spring. On the other hand, send her to a kinder climate, dry her out…'

'We'll do that!' Caro said fervently. 'If it will save her life, we'll do it today!'

Doctor Scourie patted her hand. 'Not today, lass—it remains to be seen if she can recover from this fever, first. But after a fortnight or so, and only if she's strong enough, you could risk a journey to somewhere warmer. Auckland, perhaps, or maybe the Bay of Islands. Oh, and you might like to remove the bottles of liquor under her bed, Miss Morgan. I suspect they've been her sole source of nourishment for a while now.'

Feeling horribly neglectful, Caro extracted the doctor's fee from a very grumpy Mr Matthews and paid him. The doctor had given Charlotte something to dull the pain, and her aunt was drowsy by the time Caro returned. Caro made her as comfortable as possible and extracted the four bottles of gin and three of brandy from under the bed, despite her aunt's weak protestations that 'they're just for emergencies, darling!'.

The comings and goings had woken the other guests and Caro was fully occupied for the next hour, seeing them off and cleaning the rooms. As she bundled up dirty sheets and emptied chamber pots, she thought of the two newly-earned pound notes sitting in the drawer of the registry desk. The hotel could have earned twice that amount if the dining room had been open for business. And what had the Castledene bar earned last night? Probably one hundred times that amount, with no rental to pay…

She wondered where Harold Thwaites had taken himself off to. She hadn't seen him since Mr Matthews's arrival in Dunedin, and now that her aunt was sick it was imperative that he be made to contribute to the running of the hotel.

In the kitchen she piled the used sheets into the sink and stopped to think. Presumably the hotel sent all its laundry off the premises; being built in on three sides, the Castledene possessed no wash house. If she were to wash the linen herself, where would she dry the sheets? Even if she laid them all over the kitchen, there was barely enough wood in the stove to boil a kettle of water, let alone gallons of water to wash the linen and provide heat to dry it. And then there were the soiled tablecloths in the dining room—she had simply put them aside while she swept and cleaned up. It would take her days to wash them all. Yet how could they afford a laundrywoman when she had spent money she didn't have on a husband who she only needed in order to get the hotel further into debt at the bank?

For almost the first time in her life she felt utterly worn out. She slumped into a chair and buried her face in her hands.

Mr Matthews tapped her on the shoulder. 'Pot of tea on the bench and I've bought some bread.'

'Thank you.' She smiled at him gratefully. 'I don't know what I'm going to do without you.'

He froze in the act of pouring out the tea. 'What d'you mean, girl?'

'When you take Aunt Charlotte to Auckland, I'm going to miss you.' She pulled a cup towards her and blew gently on the steaming liquid. 'Oh, by the way, can you give me seventy-five pounds? I need it to pay for my wedding this afternoon.'

Mr Matthews slopped tea all over the table in indignation. 'Now see here, girl…'

'In fact, you might as well give me a hundred pounds. We need firewood, and I've got to find out who does the laundry for the hotel—I haven't got time to do it myself. Will that leave you enough money to take Aunt Charlotte to Auckland? And then there's the question of where you're going to stay while you're there. It could take months before she recovers, and you can't stay in just any old place—'

'I'm not taking yer aunt nowhere!' Mr Mathews exploded. 'That baggage brought more grief to yer ma and pa than anyone alive, and I'll be damned before I so much as lift a finger to help her! Yer off yer head, girl! This talk of rescuing the hotel an' getting married in an hour an'—'

'An hour?' Caro checked the clock on the mantelpiece, gave a little scream of horror and stood up so fast that her chair fell backwards. 'It's after midday already! I wanted to get to the laundry this morning, too! Oh, drat!'

Picking up her skirts, she ran up to her bedroom, banging peremptorily on Mr Gray's door as she passed. It was only as she was hastily dragging a comb through her hair that the thought occurred to her that she hadn't seen her fiancé that morning. It would, she decided, be a fitting finale to an already disastrous morning if her intended had vanished in the night. But when she came out into the hallway, tying the ribbons of her bonnet, he was there, standing quietly at the top of the stairs.

'Miss Morgan.' He gave a small, formal bow. She

pulled the ribbons under her chin tight and glowered at him.

'So, you're still here.'

'Still here, Miss Morgan.'

'Well, come on, then.' She ran down the stairs to where Mr Matthews dithered, his bearded little face screwed up in misery. 'Please keep an eye on my aunt, Mr Matthews. I won't be long.'

Outside the sun was shining weakly but cheerfully, and she set a brisk pace to St Andrew's on Carlyle Street, although Mr Gray with his long legs had no trouble in ambling alongside her. Caro didn't bother talking to him—what, indeed, did one talk about to someone with whom one had nothing whatsoever in common? Instead, her mind was whirling with plans for the two thousand pounds she planned to ask Mr Froggatt for that afternoon. A cook—no, a chef. A proper chef—and a scullery maid, and one housemaid to start with until the Castledene became really busy...

'We're here, Miss Morgan.' Her fiancé touched her elbow and she realised that she had walked right past the church in her haste.

St Andrew's was a charming small church, built from the locally quarried stone and lined with glowing kauri timber felled in the forests of the far north. The sunshine filtering through the stained-glass windows was intensified and coloured softest rose as it fell on the polished floorboards. It was the perfect setting for a small wedding, but Caro scarcely noticed her surroundings. All she wanted was to get the event over and done with.

There was a short delay while two witnesses were persuaded to come in from the street, but otherwise the service went with satisfying speed. Caro was aware of the puzzled frown on the minister's face as he performed the ceremony, obviously wondering about the haste of the marriage and the dishevelled appearance of the groom. In truth, she had just the faintest niggle of unease as she signed her maiden name for the last time, but all it took was a few vows and a flourish of the pen and she was officially Mrs Leander Gray. Her husband spoke his vows quietly and firmly and, as she watched him sign his name in a beautifully executed copperplate, she was pleased that she had had the foresight to keep him sober the previous night.

Outside the church she offered him her hand.

'Thank you, Mr Gray. If you return to the hotel, Mr Matthews will have the fee we agreed upon for your services.'

He took her hand but didn't let it go, holding it firmly when she tried to withdraw it.

'I hope you know what you're doing, Mrs Gray.'

A little quiver went through her at the sound of her new name, but she hid it by looking pointedly at their clasped hands.

'I know exactly what I'm doing, thank you. And now that you've done what was required of you, you may leave. I believe Mr Matthews has your payment ready for you at the hotel, should you wish to collect it today. That aside, there is no reason for us ever to see each other again.'

'Not even when the time comes to annul the marriage?'

She tugged her hand free. 'In a month or two I can apply for an annulment, Mr Gray. Your presence would be *most* unwelcome within that time.'

'I see.' For one dreadful moment she thought he might object further, but then he bowed, with that peculiarly out-of-place courtesy. She watched him walk back down Carlyle Street and heaved a sigh of relief. Now for Mr Froggatt.

She was ten minutes early for her appointment with the banker, but this time she wasn't kept waiting at the counter.

'Well, Miss Morgan, and what can I do for you?' boomed Mr Froggatt as he pulled out a chair for her.

'It is Mrs Gray now, Mr Froggatt.' She had pointedly removed her left glove and the plain gold band glinted on her otherwise unadorned hand. 'You did say that the bank would assist me in reopening the Castledene Hotel after I married...'

'I don't believe I said any such thing, Mrs Gray. As I recall it, I said the bank might reconsider winding up Mrs Wilks's business.' He leaned back in his chair, studying her shrewdly. 'Your husband—is he a man of business?'

'I...I beg your pardon?' she stammered, caught completely off guard.

He made an impatient gesture with his hand. 'Your husband, Mrs Gray. Can he guarantee any loan that the bank makes to you?'

She stared at him blankly. 'But I am the one asking for the loan, Mr Froggatt, on behalf of my aunt...'

'Your aunt, Mrs Gray, is up to her neck in debt! I am not prepared to put this bank into further jeopardy by extending the loan!' He saw the stricken look on her face and added a little more gently, 'It should be your husband here, Mrs Gray. This is not a suitable activity for a woman. Is your husband in business?'

'No,' Caro said with only the briefest of pauses. 'He's a gentleman.'

'Ah.' The banker steepled his fingers ominously. 'So he has a private income?'

'Yes, he does.' Well, it *was* private, she reasoned to herself. *She* certainly didn't know what it was.

There was such a long silence that she began to debate with herself as to whether she should walk out or throw herself on the floor and beg for clemency. Mr Froggatt cleared his throat.

'I'd have to meet your husband, Mrs Gray…'

'Oh, certainly!'

'If you could bring him here, perhaps this afternoon—'

'Tomorrow would be better,' she broke in. She was bound to have thought of something by tomorrow. Then, seeing his raised eyebrow and remembering that tomorrow was Saturday, she plunged on. 'You could come to dinner at the hotel and meet him there. You and Mrs Froggatt!'

He looked surprised, but not displeased. 'Well…'

'Then you can see the hotel for yourself, Mr Froggatt, and I can explain what I—what *we*—plan to do with the Castledene. Shall we say six o'clock?'

He rose to his feet and nodded. 'Thank you, Mrs Gray. Six o'clock it is.'

Caro didn't remember getting back to the hotel. Once in the privacy of her bedroom, she threw herself on her bed and stared at the ceiling. She had never before admitted to being wrong, and she didn't want to do so now. But there was no way to avoid the fact that she had made the biggest mistake of her life.

There was a tap on the door and Mr Matthews looked in. With a groan Caro grabbed her pillow and rolled over to bury her face.

'Go away!'

He padded in on stockinged feet. 'Brought you a cuppa tea, girl.' He placed it carefully on the chair beside the bed. 'Thought you might need it.'

Caro raised a flushed, hot face to him. 'What am I going to do, Mr Matthews?' she wailed. 'Now the bank wants to meet my husband! I've invited Mr Froggatt and his wife to have dinner with us tomorrow night! They're expecting to meet a cultured English gentleman with a private income, and *my* husband is a drunken tramp of no fixed abode! I'll never get the loan and I've just wasted seventy-five pounds on a worthless vagabond. And don't you dare tell me you told me so!' she added furiously.

Mr Matthews picked up the cup of tea and sat down heavily on the chair.

'Well, girl,' he said eventually, 'you're going to have to think of something. You're just getting in deeper and deeper. How's about you tell the banker the truth?'

'Oh, I *couldn't*! He'd never understand and then he'd *never* lend me any money! What if we pretend that *you're* my husband?'

'What? That I'm some toff what you married? And me old enough to be yer grandpa?' Caro had never seen him so outraged.

'Then I'll have to say he's ill. But if I do, Mr Froggatt will still want to meet him later. But…but if I said he was *dead*… Why, yes! That's it! He died immediately after the wedding ceremony. His heart gave out, or a carriage ran over him when he came out of the church, or…or…' She came to a halt as she saw the look on Mr Matthews's face and she dragged the air into her lungs with an agonising shudder. 'Oh, dear,' she said in a small voice. 'I'm going to have to find my husband.'

'Or forget all about this stupid loan,' he snapped. 'Much more sensible idea.'

She shook her head. 'I can't let Aunt Charlotte's business fall apart, not when she's sick and she's already so much in debt. I can make the Castledene a profitable business, I know I can! But I can't do it without the loan. And I can't get the loan without showing that I've got a husband. So I'm going to have to find Mr Gray. At least he speaks properly…'

'Reckon he'd scrub up all right, too,' Mr Matthews said and she looked at him with a frown.

'Did you pay him, Mr Matthews?'

''Course I paid him! He showed me the marriage papers, didn't he? Mind you, I only had twenty-five pounds on me. Told him I'd get the rest for him Monday.'

'He'll be able to get very drunk on twenty-five pounds.' Caro sat up and patted her hair back where it had come loose from her chignon. 'Of course, he's only had an hour's start on us. He probably went straight into the Castledene bar. Let's look for him there.'

But Leander was not in the bar, or in any of the other hotels in Princes Street or Carlyle Street. To make matters worse, Charlotte began coughing up blood again, and Caro had to sit with her while Mr Matthews searched the bars of Dunedin alone. Outside the snow had given way to a cold, heavy fog that obscured the high hills beyond the town. Caro kept the fire burning in her aunt's bedroom but she still shivered whenever she looked out the window at the dark swirling mist. In a life that had previously been filled with sunshine, the situation she now found herself in was unnervingly depressing. If Mr Matthews couldn't find Leander... If she couldn't save the Castledene from the clutches of the bank... If Aunt Charlotte died...

She needed to keep herself busy. Her aunt was almost asleep, so Caro drew the curtains against the gathering dusk and turned her attention to her aunt's extensive wardrobe. Charlotte was obviously not given to needlework, as many garments shoved to the back of the wardrobe needed little more than a few stitches to fix a hem or a seam, or to re-attach a border of lace. While Caro was taller and much bigger than Charlotte, she did uncover several beautiful, loose-fitting gowns that could easily be lengthened to fit her.

Charlotte, watching her drowsily from the pillows, waved a limp hand. 'Help yourself, darling. Anything you want. I'm tired of those gowns anyway. There are more in the chest in the corner.'

'Oh, thank you, Aunt Charlotte!' She held a particularly fetching dress in deep rose with ivory lace against her and admired the effect in the full-length mirror. 'I need something for tomorrow night, you see. The banker is coming to dinner.'

'The banker?' Charlotte croaked in sudden alarm. 'Here?'

'It's all right, Aunt Charlotte, really it is,' Caro assured her. 'He's coming here to approve a loan that will get the hotel out of trouble and give you a profitable business once more!'

'But he's a horrible man,' Charlotte gasped. 'You mustn't... Oh, darling...'

'I can handle Mr Froggatt, Aunt.' Caro smoothed the sheet that her aunt had rumpled in her agitation. 'It's all under control. And there won't be any problems, because I simply won't allow it.'

'Oh, my God,' Charlotte said weakly. 'You're just like your father with breasts…'

Caro decided her aunt was probably a little delirious and gave her a good dose of laudanum before returning her attention to the wardrobe. Yes, there were enough gowns here to give her quite a presentable range. Charlotte was fast asleep by the time Caro looked in the chest. There were a number of men's items of clothing there, including several evening suits, that she could only presume belonged to Aunt Charlotte's late husband. He had been a tall, slim man from the looks of it, and the clothes would almost certainly fit Leander.

If they ever found him.

She fetched the sewing kit from the linen cupboard, built up the fire, and sat stitching beside her sleeping aunt while night fell.

Chapter Five

Caro jerked awake, wincing as she did so at the pain in her neck and spine. She had fallen asleep at some stage during the night and the gown she had been repairing lay pooled at her feet. The fire had gone out hours before and her hands felt painfully cold. She tiptoed to the windows and eased the curtains back a few inches to a grey-lit dawn in an overcast sky. In the reluctant light she could see that Aunt Charlotte was sleeping quite comfortably.

She padded silently down the hall to her own room, where a quick wash in the freezing water left in her jug served to wake her sufficiently to remember what had been worrying her the previous night. When she did remember, she heartily wished she hadn't—the wave of dark despair that flooded through her was enough to make her feel ill. They hadn't found Leander. She wouldn't be able to extend the loan. They would lose the hotel. She would have lost. She didn't think she could bear it.

A cup of Mr Matthews's tea would help, she decided. On her way to the kitchen she stopped in the dining room to tweak straight a freshly laid tablecloth.

It had been a week now since a meal had been served in this room. The silver cutlery lay in a forlorn pile on the servery table, only a fraction of its original quantity—the departing, unpaid servants must have helped themselves liberally to them in lieu of wages. Caro supposed what was left of the silver could be sold to help repay Mr Froggatt and his bank, together with the chandelier and the beautiful glassware still sitting on the kitchen shelves. It wasn't likely to be nearly enough, however.

With a sigh, she pushed open the kitchen door to find her husband stark naked and fast asleep in a hip bath before the stove. Kneeling beside him, Mr Matthews was intently cutting Leander's shoulder-length, freshly washed hair.

'Oy!' He seized a face-cloth and threw it over Leander's midriff. 'Look away, girl!'

'Don't be silly—he's my husband!' she retorted, half-shocked and half-thrilled by the sight of so much naked male flesh on display. Mr Matthews moved around to block her view.

''E's yer husband in name only, miss, so you busy yer eyes elsewhere and don't go lookin' where it ain't decent. Make us a cup a tea, why don't you.'

She went over to the stove to put on the kettle. 'Where did you find him?'

'Down by the docks, drunk as a lord. Had the devil of a time getting him back here. Lucky he didn't pass out on me until I got him in the bath.' He ran a comb through Leander's hair and eyed its length critically. 'Nothing left on him of the twenty-five pounds, neither.'

'Well, at least he consistently disappoints,' Caro said with a rare charity born of relief. She drew up a chair beside the warm stove and sat down, hugging her knees. Mr Matthews tut-tutted and found a fractionally larger tea-towel to drape over Leander's middle parts.

'Not a sight you should be seeing, girl.'

'My mother saw my father naked every day!' she retorted.

'Well, all due respect to yer ma and pa, I never agreed with that! It ain't natural! So just you look elsewhere and take yer tea and leave the room, you hear me?'

She ignored him, and after a while he returned to his barbering, grumbling under his breath the while. Caro ran her eyes assessingly over what she could see of her husband's body that was not blocked by Mr Matthews's attempts at decorum. She had thought Leander to be thin, but in fact he was simply lean, with long muscles visibly cording his legs and arms. Caro and her sisters had occupied a fair amount of time over their summers comparing the torsos of the young farmhands who frequently worked stripped down to their trousers when shearing or fencing in the heat. In fact, Caro considered herself to be something of a connoisseur of the male physique, and Leander was far from being a poor specimen. He was a lot paler than the men she was used to, of course, but she found that rather attractive. Mr Matthews was ruthlessly applying the scissors, revealing a well-shaped head and ears.

'Can you leave him with a fringe? Yes, like that.' She leaned forward with interest. Her husband's hair, drying in the heat from the stove, was much fairer than she had expected. 'I want him shaved, too, please.'

Mr Matthews looked up, his own whiskers bristling indignantly. ''E's got no beard as it is, girl! I'm not touchin' what little he's got!'

'I want him shaved,' she said implacably. 'I doubt he's seen a razor in a week.'

'What if he don't want to be shaved? What if he's tryin' to grow a beard? Man's beard's personal. Likely he'd take it amiss if I took it off while he were sleeping!'

Caro got up to pour the boiling water into the teapot. 'He's my husband, I bought him, and I can do what I like with him.' She raised her chin imperiously. 'Go on, Mr Matthews.'

He shook his head. 'Won't do it, girl.'

'Then I will.' Shouldering him aside, she picked up the soap and made a lather in her hands before carefully spreading it over Leander's chin. She had sheared a few sheep in her time, and had even badgered her father into letting her shave him when she was younger, although Ben had always said that he thought it was only because she liked holding a knife to his throat. Ignoring Mr Matthews's dire mutterings, she flicked open the razor and began scraping.

It was a bit like opening a Christmas present layer by layer. Under her fingers she could feel the clean lines of his jaw before she shaved the hair from it. And his mouth... She held her breath as she carefully brought the blade under his nose. His mouth was beautiful. Almost shaking with impatience, she wiped the last of the lather from his face and sat back on her heels.

He was absolutely the most handsome man she had ever seen in her life. He was the most handsome man she had ever *dreamed* of. Much younger than she had thought him—why, he would only be a couple of years older than *she* was—he was the possessor of completely regular, well-proportioned features, saved from boring perfection by the small, hard lines grooving the sides of his incredibly kissable mouth. Caro was filled with exultation and unease. Exultation that this impossibly beautiful man was hers. Unease that his beauty was not a factor she had taken into consideration.

Mr Matthews noted her gloating, rapt expression and glanced down. 'Told you he'd scrub up well,' he said shortly.

She got to her feet and busied herself pouring out two mugs of tea—anything to stop herself from touching her husband. *Her husband.* She could hardly believe it.

'Oh, God…' Leander groaned quietly, his face screwing up with pain. Neither Caro nor Mr Matthews dared move. After a moment he raised a careful hand and ran his fingers through his hair. Then he froze. His eyes shot open, widening as he saw Caro standing over him, a mug of tea clutched defensively to her breast.

'What are *you* doing here?' He looked beyond her to the kitchen range, the table, the walls filled with hanging utensils. 'What the hell am I doing here?' His outraged stare fell on Mr Matthews, kneeling unhappily beside him, and the little man swallowed hard.

'Found you in a bar down by the docks. They'd thrown you out 'round midnight.'

'I see.' Leander nodded with care. He looked as if it hurt him to move his head overmuch. 'May I ask why I'm not wearing any clothes?'

'Because you're in the bath, silly,' Caro chided him lightly. 'They'd get wet otherwise, wouldn't they? Would you like a mug of tea?'

She held out the mug, but he chose to ignore it. 'And may I ask why I'm in the bath, Mrs Gray?'

'Because you're filthy, Mr Gray. That's why.' Caro

sat down in the kitchen chair, very conscious of the height advantage it gave her. In fact, a man in a bath was in a very vulnerable position altogether, she thought with pleasure. 'And we've given you a hair-cut.'

'What…?'

'And you look much better without all that hair, too, if I may say so. A great improvement.'

He ran a rueful hand over his head. 'I've had long hair since I was eighteen…'

'Then it's high time you had a change, isn't it?' She smiled down at him benevolently, thoroughly enjoying herself.

Leander dropped his hand and lay back against the high side of the tub, his stare steady. The odd deadness in his eyes had gone, she realised with a start, replaced with something like a battle-light. Oh, God, he is gorgeous! she thought and gulped her tea unsteadily.

Leander picked up the towel lying over his midriff and peered under it, as if to ensure that nothing else was missing from his person. 'Hmm. I must admit to being somewhat mystified. Am I to understand that you've brought me here for the express purpose of giving me a bath, cutting my hair and shaving me?'

Caro placed her mug very precisely on the table. 'Mr Gray, tonight the bank manager and his wife are coming to dinner here, at the hotel, and I've got to persuade them that I am a competent woman of business. And for that I need to produce you as my husband, looking clean and tidy.'

He tilted his head slightly to look up at her. 'Your financial credibility is hardly my problem, Mrs Gray. Besides, you still haven't paid me in full for the use of my name.'

From upstairs came a faint, plaintive call, followed by a hacking cough.

'I'll see to her,' Mr Matthews said quickly. 'Won't be but a minute.'

'Be as long as you need to be, Mr Matthews,' Caro said calmly, settling back in her chair. 'My husband and I have some important matters to discuss.'

'We've got nothing to discuss.' Leander closed his eyes wearily. She waited while Mr Matthews closed the door behind him, but Leander seemed to have fallen asleep again. Leaning forward, she carefully gathered up her husband's old clothes and poked the bundle into the stove. The sudden roar of the flames as they engulfed the material made Leander's eyes flicker open.

'What was that?'

'Just the stove.' She stood up with her sweetest smile. 'Are you sure you wouldn't like some tea?'

He regarded her suspiciously. 'What I would like, Mrs Gray, is to leave this place with the rest of my money.'

'We can't get you the rest of your money until the banks open again on Monday. Until then, you might as well stay here and enjoy our hospitality.'

'I'm not staying,' he said quietly.

Caro folded her arms. 'Then you're going to have to think about it, Mr Gray. Because you're not going anywhere.'

She could see the comprehension dawn in his eyes. For a long, deliciously fraught moment she wondered what he would do. Not, of course, that he had any options.

'Would you turn your back, please, Mrs Gray?'

'I certainly will not.' She met his eyes squarely, following them up as he got unsteadily to his feet and stepped out of the tub. Water splashed noisily on to the flagstoned floor. With one hand he held the small square of towelling over his private parts. He ran the other hand through his shortened hair in what she had come to realise was a frequent gesture in times of stress.

'Where are my clothes?'

'I've burned them for you. They were unwearable anyway.'

The fingers that were free clenched into a fist. Caro watched him carefully, scarcely daring to breath. She wasn't in the least afraid of him; besides, Mr Matthews was just a scream away. She wondered what Leander would do next. She wondered what it would take to provoke him into dropping the tiny towel.

'Right, then,' Leander said, his voice very soft. Padding wetly, he crossed the floor to the door.

'Where are you going?' she demanded breathlessly.

'Back on to the streets, where I belong.'

'But…but you'll freeze out there!' He was out of range of the warm stove where he stood, and already the satin-smooth skin on his back was raising in tiny goose-bumps.

'I'll be arrested for indecent exposure long before I freeze to death, Mrs Gray.'

Caro dragged her gaze away from the disconcerting curve of his buttocks to manage a careless shrug and toss of the head. 'Well, suit yourself then. If you want to go ahead and make an…an…absolute *spectacle* of yourself, it has nothing to do with me.'

'Apart from the fact that you're my wife, Mrs Gray, you're quite right.'

She thought that through for all of five seconds. Her husband parading himself on the streets of Dunedin, wearing nothing but a small tea-towel and that odiously superior stare... What if Mr Froggatt were to see him? What chance of a loan then?

'I have clothes upstairs,' she bit out furiously. 'Stay here.'

She took care not to touch him as she pushed the kitchen door open, but to her horror he followed her through into the dining room.

'I said, stay in the kitchen!' she snapped.

'I don't trust you not to lock me in there.'

'There isn't even a lock on the kitchen door!'

'Then you'd barricade me in.'

'I wouldn't!'

'You would.'

The argument was becoming childish. She turned on her heel and walked swiftly through the dining room, praying that no intending guests should choose that moment to enter the hotel. Her shoes rang resoundingly on the marble tiles in the foyer, but all she could hear was the damp slap of Leander's bare feet just inches behind her. By the time she ran up the stairs and stopped outside her aunt's door she was quite breathless.

'Now stay out here in the hallway while I fetch you some clothes!' she instructed between gasps.

'Not likely,' was the rejoinder, and he leaned past her to open the door and nudge her inside with his damp shoulder. To Caro's enormous relief she was not going to have to explain what had happened to Mr Matthews. Aunt Charlotte was the only occupant of the room, a thin, pale shadow against the big white cushions.

'Don't wake her!' Caro whispered, but already Charlotte was moving restlessly.

'Caroline, darling, is that you?' She gave a spluttery cough and feebly attempted to sit up. 'That horrible little man of your father's was in here! I thought I was having a nightmare! I demanded he leave immediately of course, he's…' She stopped, her eyes widening at the sight of a naked man standing at the foot of the bed.

'Aunt Charlotte…' Caro decided that there was nothing for it but to pretend that there was absolutely nothing out of the ordinary going on. 'Aunt Charlotte, this is Mr Gray. Mr Gray, this is my aunt, Mrs Wilks.'

'How do you do, Mrs Wilks.' With some considerable grace, Leander changed the hand over the facecloth and extended his right hand to her. 'I'm sorry that you're not feeling well.'

'Oh.' Charlotte placed her fingers limply in his and gave him a wistful little smile. 'Thank you. But, in fact, I feel much better already.'

'I'm glad to hear it—'

'Aunt Charlotte,' Caro broke in rudely as she poured her aunt a glass of water, 'I wondered if I could lend Mr Gray some of the men's clothes I saw in your chest last night?'

'Of course, darling. Help yourself to anything.' Charlotte lay back on the pillows, wheezing softly. Leander gave her the first real smile Caro had ever seen him bestow upon anyone, a wry, slightly lopsided grin that sent Aunt Charlotte into a visible flutter and a nasty, jealous pang through Caro.

'You're most kind, Mrs Wilks.'

'Not at all…'

'Here.' Caro thrust the bundle of clothes violently at his free arm. 'You can change in the next bedroom.'

'Goodbye, Mrs Wilks.'

'Goodbye, Mr Gray. And thank you for coming to cheer me up.'

Tight-lipped, Caro shut the door and led him across the hallway to the room he had occupied the previous night. 'You can change in here and then you can get out!'

Beneath his new fringe, his eyebrows rose fetchingly. 'What happened to your determination to keep me here at all costs?'

'That was before you started...*flirting* with my aunt!' she hissed. 'She's very ill, if you hadn't noticed. She didn't need you pawing her and upsetting her the way you did.'

His eyebrows drew together. 'I'm sorry you saw it like that. I like your aunt.'

'How can you say that? You've known her for all of thirty seconds!'

He shrugged goose-bumped shoulders. 'Sometimes that's all it takes.'

'I hardly think so,' she said scathingly. It was so cold in the small, unheated room that when they spoke their breath was turning to steam. She saw him shiver and was appalled by her sudden impulse to wrap something warm and her arms around him. 'Now get dressed and get out!'

She threw herself into a frenzy of activity in the kitchen, polishing the silver and glassware until they shone. Leander could show himself off the property. All traces of his bath—even his wet footprints across the flagstones—had been carefully wiped away, and only embers remained of his clothes. She never wanted, never needed, to see him again.

Given the hour, she guessed that Mr Matthews had

taken himself to the markets. One of his innumerable talents was that of cooking and, whatever he chose to serve that night, Caro could be certain that it would be as finely cooked and presented as any dish the Froggatts had ever eaten elsewhere. She would not have invited them to dinner had she thought otherwise. Without a husband to establish her creditworthiness, an outstandingly good dinner was all she was going to be able to produce in her defence that the Castledene should remain open.

An hour later, when Caro had polished all she could and was preparing a small tray for her aunt, Mr Matthews staggered in, clutching a crate full of produce.

'I gotta nice piece o' pork and some fresh cod.' He dumped the crate on the kitchen table and began to haul out leeks and cauliflowers. 'I'll make a stew an' a pie an'—' He stopped and looked at her quizzically. 'Whatsermatter, girl?'

'I've told my...my husband that his services were no longer required.' Caro regarded the burnt bread at the end of the toasting fork through a veil of tears. 'So I don't really know if there's any point in cooking a beautiful dinner to impress Mr Froggatt and his wife tonight, Mr Matthews. Leander is probably at the nearest bar as we speak, drinking himself legless, and undoing all our good work...' She couldn't help the snuffle that escaped her at the thought.

'Can't get legless without money, girl,' Mr Matthews reminded her gruffly. 'Anyway, he ain't at no bar.'

'How do you know that?'

''Cause I set him to work polishing the chandelier,

that's why.' He jerked his head towards the dining room. 'Go and have a look, if you don't believe me.'

She didn't believe him, and so she did have a look. Leander was, indeed, cleaning the chandelier, which had been lowered to the floor. Warmly dressed in the flannel shirt and moleskin trousers she had thrown at him, he sat cross-legged on the dining-room boards, frowning in concentration as he scrubbed the dulled crystal with a small brush and soapy water, and then carefully polished each piece with a soft cloth. Even with the smudge of dust on his nose he still looked irresistible.

Caro let out a long sigh of relief and edged her way back into the kitchen unseen.

'Thank goodness! I never thought I'd see him do something useful! How did you bribe him into staying? You didn't give him the rest of the money you owe him, did you?'

Mr Matthews bristled indignantly. 'I don't owe him nuffink! You're the one what said you'd pay him fer marrying you. And no, I didn't give him any money. Got no money to pay him now anyway—spent the lot on this here food, didn't I?'

'Hmm.' Frowning, Caro rearranged the cutlery on her aunt's luncheon tray. 'So why is he staying, if not for money?'

'Beats me.' He untied the string around the butcher's parcel and lifted out the roast of pork with reverential hands. 'Maybe he ain't got nowhere else to go.'

That answer seemed logical enough, but somehow Caro knew it wasn't the right answer. However, there was far too much to do to spend any time puzzling over Leander's unexpected acquiescence with her plans. It was close on five o'clock and the day was drawing to a wintry close by the time everything that needed to be done had been done. Aunt Charlotte had mercifully needed little attention all day, pulling only the slightest of discontented faces when Caro alone took up her tray.

'Where's that nice young man you brought with you last time?' Charlotte managed to prop herself up while Caro rearranged the pillows, a feat of strength on her aunt's part that heartened Caro immensely. 'Couldn't he bring up my tray?'

'He's busy,' Caro said shortly, opening the napkin with a flick of irritation. Her aunt seemed to be labouring under the delusion that Leander had been brought into the hotel for the sole purpose of cheering her up.

'What a pity.' Charlotte settled herself back on the pillows with a dreamy expression. 'He really is the most charming young man, puts me in mind of one of my husbands…unlike that dreadful little gnome you brought with you. What's his name? Matthews? I do wish you'd keep him away from me, darling. He's your father's *creature*, you know. Utterly devoted to him, and so he *detests* me. So unfair. You know, darling, there's a great deal of activity going on today. What's happening?'

Caro chose not to upset her aunt for a second time by reminding her that the banker was coming, and so said brightly, 'We have more guests, Aunt Charlotte! Two parties arrived this afternoon and—guess what? We're opening the dining room again tonight! Isn't that exciting?'

But Charlotte didn't seem to find it in the least exciting, or at least not as exciting as a naked man in her bedroom had been earlier that morning, and she fell asleep a few minutes later after just sipping at her soup. Caro took her tray downstairs again, struggling to remain optimistic. Charlotte had expressed very little interest in the running of the hotel before her illness, so it was unlikely that she would suddenly show enthusiasm now. But for all the effort that Caro was putting into the enterprise, for all the hard work and risks she was taking—for the loss of her single state, for goodness' sake!—she would have appreciated just a little word of thanks from her aunt.

When the two parties of guests had arrived that afternoon, within half an hour of each other, Caro had taken a deep breath and informed them that the dining room would be open for dinner that evening. After all, she had explained to a scowling Mr Matthews later, it would no doubt impress Mr Froggatt all the more if there were paying guests dining at the Castledene that night.

'I have to water me soup then,' he grumbled. 'And you'll have to peel me some more 'taters if we're to stretch the cod pie.'

Caro pulled on an apron with enthusiasm. 'I was wondering, too, whether I should go next door and demand a couple of bottles of good wine from the bar, in case Mr Froggatt likes a glass with his meal.'

Mr Matthews regarded her steadily. 'Yer husband likes a glass or two.'

She considered that and then sighed. 'You're right. We can't risk it. Besides, Mr Froggatt doesn't look as if anything stronger than vinegar ever crosses his lips.'

'You've still got the brandy from under yer aunt's bed fer the end of the meal,' Mr Matthews reminded her. 'You should be safe with that—long as you keep yer husband away from it.'

* * *

It was a quarter to six by the time Mr Matthews physically ejected Caro from the kitchen, assuring her for the tenth time that all preparations for the meal were well in hand, if only she would leave the dishing up and serving to him. In the dining room she stopped short, tilting her head to stare up at the great chandelier, now a brilliant shimmer of crystal and candles that illuminated the elegant room to perfection. Polished candelabra held lit candles on each of the three tables to be used that night and a brisk fire roared in the grate.

Thrilled with pride, Caro ran her fingers over the silver settings on one of the tables. While the ornate wine glasses would have looked more impressive, the plain, cut-crystal water glasses looked very well on the table. It had been with grave misgivings that she had left the dining-room arrangements to her husband, but she could not fault the order of the cutlery, and even the napkins looked professionally executed. It appeared that Leander was no stranger to the finer points of elegant dining. For just a moment she allowed herself to speculate upon what circumstances had turned a man of obviously respectable birth into a hopeless, penniless drunk… But then she remembered the time and raced up the stairs to change.

She had lengthened her aunt's rose gown by unstitching two rows of lace and adding them to the hem. Now the dress hung gracefully to the floor, successfully covering her decidedly scruffy walking shoes. She turned slowly before the small mirror over the washstand, critically examining her appearance. Where the dress would have hung loosely on her aunt, it clung to Caro in a way she was less than happy with, and the bodice was close to overflowing. She shrugged and turned away from the sight. It was the best she could do, and at least it looked expensive. Besides, she was a married woman now, and was thus surely entitled to be a little more daring in her dress?

Leander came out of his room across the hallway at the same time and for a long moment neither of them spoke as they stared at each other. If he had looked startlingly attractive naked, he was positively devastating in an evening suit, Caro thought uneasily. Suddenly he looked bigger, taller and a lot more assertive. Mr Matthews had done a commendable piece of work on Leander's hair and, brushed back from his face, it gleamed dark blond in the lamplight. It was hard to believe that just the day before it had hung dark and matted to his shoulders. Tonight he looked as well heeled and as well bred as Caro needed him to be.

'You look lovely,' he said quietly. His hard, dark eyes scanned her in approval—as if she needed it! But all the same, his obvious appreciation caused a strange little flutter in her stomach and she swallowed, her mouth suddenly too dry.

'We're late. Mr Froggatt...'

'But you might like to put your hair up,' he continued as if she had not spoken. 'A plait is very fetching, but not, I think, appropriate for a married woman at a dinner party?'

He spoke with the utter certainty of one who knew about such matters, and somehow it did not occur to her to question him. Without a word, she returned to her room, brushed out her hair and pinned it into a neat bun at the nape of her neck. Her hands were shaking so much that the simple actions took much longer than usual. When she finally hurried into the dining room Mr Froggatt was already there, shaking Leander's hand. The banker, she saw in astonishment, was actually smiling.

'Ah, Mrs Gray!' he boomed at her. 'You're here at last. Keeping us waiting, eh? Ah, well, lady's prerogative, I suppose.'

He was obviously making some attempt at humour, but the mere sight of Leander standing next to the banker was enough to send Caro's heart leaping into her mouth. She would never pull this off! She had been crazy to think for one moment that Leander—drunken, spendthrift, helpless Leander—would ever be able to convince Mr Froggatt that he was a man of sufficiently substantial means and background to risk lending a medium-sized fortune to. Why, she hadn't even told Leander what to say, because she had expected to do all the talking tonight. And yet here she was, standing like a dressmaker's dummy with her mouth open and no sound emerging, while her all-too-confident husband regarded her with open amusement thinly disguised as an affectionate smile.

'Well timed, my dear,' he said gently. She gave him a swift *don't-you-dare* look before turning her attention to the short, dumpy, leaden-faced woman standing beside him. 'Mrs Froggatt, this is my wife, Caroline,' Leander added somewhat unnecessarily.

'How do you do,' Caro said warmly.

'Well enough,' Mrs Froggatt said dourly, ignoring Caro's outstretched hand. Her deepset eyes travelled suspiciously up and down Caro's length, dwelling somewhat indignantly on Caro's tight bodice. 'Where is she, then?'

'I…beg your pardon?'

'Her. Your aunt.' The disapproval was literally dripping from the banker's wife's thin lips. So that was the problem, Caro thought in a rush of comprehension. She could well imagine how her aunt's flamboyance would jar with staid, plain-living women like Mrs Froggatt. Caro's sense of panic increased. She had not counted on this. The banker's wife plainly did not want to be on Mrs Wilks's premises, and was covering her discomfiture by rudeness. And if Mrs Froggatt held any sway with her husband, as Caro was sure that she did, then this whole evening was bound to be a disaster. Charlotte's reputation would have seen to that.

She managed a polite smile. 'My aunt is indisposed, I'm afraid…'

'You mean she's drunk again,' Mrs Froggatt snapped.

Caro was losing the struggle for composure when Leander turned around and directed his dazzlingly innocent smile at the banker's wife.

'Would you like to step closer to the fire, Mrs Froggatt?'

'I would. 'Tis like an icehouse in here. Far too big and grand and draughty.' Pointedly pulling her shawl around her ample shoulders, Mrs Froggatt moved away to rub her hands before the fire. Caro was wondering about the possibility of an errant spark setting fire to the banker's wife's sensible brown serge, when Leander's fingers coming to rest around her waist startled her from her pleasant fantasy.

'Patience, my darling,' he murmured. 'Always a virtue.'

'Don't "darling" me,' she whispered back. 'What an obnoxious woman! She's nasty, closed-minded, rude—'

'*And* married to your banker. Do be sensible, Caroline.' He chucked her under the chin condescendingly.

His fingers were warm and light and a thrill of pleasurable awareness spread across her skin, adding to her
sense of outrage. She was rapidly losing control of this
situation, and that was not something she was used to.
Twenty-four hours ago this man had been a pathetic,
dirty wretch living on the streets. Now, reborn in evening suit and a decent haircut, he was disconcertingly
persuasive; the worst of it was, she suspected, that he
knew all too well the effect he was having on her. She
had to put him down at once, belittle him with a sharp
word or two, remind him just who was in charge here.
She had to do that…so why wasn't she? Why was she
simply standing there, *blushing*, for goodness' sake, for
all the world like a new bride? And why was the feel
of his fingers on her skin sending intense little quivers
through her whole body?

The arrival of the hotel's other guests in the dining
room covered the awkward silence. Mr Matthews
emerged from the kitchen to seat the guests and tell
them the bill of fare, and Caro used the diversion to
suggest that they, themselves, be seated.

Mrs Froggatt took in the absence of any wine glasses
on the table and pointedly raised her eyebrows. Did
she approve or disapprove? Dimly, Caro was aware
that Leander was saying something to Mr Froggatt, that
the banker was laughing—*laughing!*—and she resolved
that she must say something immediately to exclude
her husband from the conversation. But Leander, it appeared, was highly accomplished at completely incon-
sequential small talk. He placed the dour Mrs Froggatt
in her seat with quite impeccable manners, and the
sour-faced old prune's lips twisted in what might have
passed for a smile. Even Mr Froggatt seemed charmed.

After Leander had taken his seat Caro cleared her throat. 'Now, Mr Froggatt, about the loan…'

'Caroline, my sweet, I'm sure our guests would prefer to enjoy their dinner first,' her husband chided smoothly as Mr Matthews chose that very moment to place a steaming tureen before Caro. Leander's eyes met the banker's across the table and he gave a complicit smile. 'But of course, Mr Froggatt, you know my lovely wife. And her enthusiasms.'

'Enthusiasms?' Caro repeated dangerously.

Mr Froggatt tucked his napkin under his chin and chuckled at her expression. 'I believe, Mrs Gray, that your husband is referring to…shall we say…a certain impulsiveness in your character?'

Leander nodded thoughtfully. 'Well put, Mr Froggatt. Yes, that is it precisely.'

'Mind you, 'tis a characteristic common to all you ladies,' the banker hastened to add, in case Caro should be offended. He cast a fond look at his wife, who Caro doubted had ever had a rash thought in her life. 'And that is why business is best left to men, Mrs Gray.'

'Quite.' Leander raised his water glass to Mr Froggatt in an unspoken toast. 'Caroline, darling, that soup smells quite delicious.'

She should have told him to serve it himself. Better still, she should have thrown the entire, scalding-hot contents of the tureen over his well-groomed head. The smirk on Mrs Froggatt's face was almost more than she could bear. But when she saw Mr Froggatt's approving nod, she remembered what the whole purpose of this dinner was. On the other hand, nothing was worth this humiliation She went to push back her chair.

Leander's hand came to rest lightly on her wrist. 'I forgot to ask, darling. How is Mrs Wilks this evening?'

She sank back in her seat and fought for composure. Dimly she was aware of Mr Matthews materialising beside her to skilfully spoon out the soup—with her hands shaking the way they were, she would never have managed it herself. As if from a great distance she heard Leander explaining that Mrs Wilks was seriously ill, and the murmurings of condolence from the banker. Mr Froggatt was in complete agreement with the idea of Mrs Wilks leaving for warmer climes. The hotel would be in good hands—sound hands!—in her absence, he was sure. Mrs Froggatt pronounced the soup to be quite agreeable. Leander expressed his great pleasure at the fact.

And so it went on, through the pork stew and the cod-and-potato pie and the apple tart. Even in her stunned state, Caro was somewhat taken aback at the unadorned state of the food; Mr Matthews was a dab hand with a sauce and the use of herbs. But when the Froggatts praised the 'good, plain cooking' before them, she realised that Mr Matthews had read his guests well.

If only Leander had exhibited the same good sense. It was true that he said relatively little, and merely encouraged Mr Froggatt to discourse at length on his particular views of the world. He gave only a modicum of information about himself, when pressed to do so, but what he did tell the banker was so outrageous, so utterly preposterous, that Caro was convinced that at any minute Mr Froggatt would realise the deception being practised upon him.

'So *he*'s your father?' Mrs Froggatt scowled at him from over her apple tart and Stilton. 'That makes you mighty grand to be in Dunedin, running an hotel.' She looked balefully at Caro, who was trying not to choke on her mouthful of food. 'Marrying a long way beneath yourself, aren't you, Mr Gray? Or do you have a title?'

'No title, thank heavens, and, at last count, I had five older brothers, Mrs Froggatt, so there's no chance of me ever inheriting. Besides…' Leander spread his hands deprecatingly '…I came here in order to leave all that behind me. This is a wonderful country, with ample opportunities for a man prepared to work hard.' He had the gall to smile tenderly at Caro. 'And with the right wife at one's side, how can one not succeed?'

Mr Froggatt pushed himself back from the table, dabbed at his mouth with his napkin and gave a sigh of appreciation. 'Quite right, Mr Gray, and the two of you make as fine a looking couple as I can recall seeing. I'm of the opinion that you'll do very well here. Very well, indeed. You're just the sort of man the colony needs. I'd be pleased to meet with you Monday morning, in my office, sir. We can draw up a loan agreement then…'

'The loan agreement will be with me, Mr Froggatt.' Caro thought she would burst with either relief or indignation. 'The hotel is my aunt's, after all.'

The banker looked at her indulgently. 'I would not consider an unsecured loan to your aunt for one second, Mrs Gray. This property is already mortgaged to the hilt. But I would consider advancing a loan to a prudent, experienced man of business such as your husband.' He extended his hand across the table. 'Monday morning, Mr Gray.'

'Excuse me,' Caro said icily, 'but I must see to our other guests.' She ignored Mr Froggatt and her husband as they courteously rose to their feet, and strode out to the kitchen. Mr Matthews was carefully pouring custard into a jug to accompany the apple tart for the hotel guests.

'Why didn't we get any custard?' Caro demanded, wanting an argument.

'Not enough milk in the safe. Besides, yer Mr Froggatt didn't strike me as the kind of man who'd see custard as vital to a meal. Plain eaters, folk like them are.'

That was true, but Caro didn't want to hear it. She began to violently stack dishes ready for washing. Mr Matthews watched her cautiously.

'How's it going?'

'Oh, wonderfully,' she said. 'Leander is telling them a huge pack of lies, the Froggatts are practically eating out of his hand...'

'So you got the loan then?'

'*Leander* has got the loan!' she snarled. 'Being a mere female, I'm not considered capable of handling the hotel finances!'

He shrugged. 'Well, now yer married, anything you own goes to yer husband, don't it? Stands to reason that the bank won't lend to you.'

'But I'm a *married woman*!'

'Wiv a *husband*!' He mimicked her dismayed face and took the custard and tart out to the dining room.

Chapter Six

Caro fell into a fitful sleep shortly before dawn, and so was in a suitably unpleasant mood when she banged on the door of her husband's bedroom at eight o'clock. When there was no answer, what small degree of patience she possessed deserted her entirely.

'Come on, get up!' She opened the door and crossed to the bed in a few quick steps. 'It's late!'

'For God's sake, Caroline!' Leander's voice was muffled under the blankets he was vainly trying to wrest from her. 'It's the middle of the night!'

'It's Sunday morning.'

'So what?' He gave up the battle for the blankets and eyed her balefully.

'So we'll be late for church if you don't hurry up!'

He groaned and pulled the blankets back over his head. 'Just go without me then, will you?'

'I most certainly will not!' Caro took two handfuls of bedding and pulled mightily until her husband landed in a tangle of sheets and pillows on the floor. 'You've got two minutes to get dressed.'

'And what if I don't get dressed?' Leander rolled over lazily and sat up. As the sheet slipped to his waist

Caro realised for the first time that he slept naked. 'Are *you* going to dress me, Mrs Gray?'

'Don't be ridiculous,' she snapped. 'You're perfectly capable of dressing yourself, so why should I do it for you?'

'Why, indeed.' He yawned widely and ran his fingers through his hair. 'When you're so much better at taking my clothes off. Give me two minutes, then.'

In fact it was ten minutes, and he still looked half-asleep when he joined her in the entry hall. Dressed in one of the dark suits from her deceased uncle's trunk, he looked presentable enough, but was in need of a shave and his hair was still ruffled from sleep. Tut-tutting, Caro reached up and ran her fingers through the tangles.

'Where's your hat?'

'I haven't got one.'

'Then we'll have to buy you one. You can't go walking around the streets bareheaded.' She brushed a piece of cotton from his lapel and straightened his collar. Leander yawned again. 'And do try to stay awake, please. I don't want you embarrassing me by falling asleep during the sermon.'

Mr Matthews sidled past with a pile of clean sheets and met Leander's eyes sympathetically.

'Oh, do come on,' Caro said in exasperation. 'We're going to be late.'

It was a beautiful morning, with a hint of real warmth in the sunlight, but Caro allowed Leander no time to enjoy it. She set a brisk pace down Princes Street and her husband had to speed up his amble to stay alongside.

'Morning,' he said politely, raising his hand to doff his non-existent hat as a couple passed them.

'Who was that?' Caro said in surprise.

'That rather nice chap who delivers the firewood to the hotel. And I assume the lady with him would be his wife.' He looked at her and shook his head. 'You don't notice much, do you, Caroline? Do you know anyone here? Have you walked around the town at all? Or do you spend all your time slaving away in the Castledene?'

'Of course I know my way around Dunedin,' she huffed as they reached the church. 'I'll prove it to you after church!'

Caro had chosen St Andrew's merely because of its proximity to the hotel, but in fact she liked its atmosphere and the minister gave a thoroughly sensible sermon, which she always regarded as a bonus. Leander, unfortunately, kept dropping off to sleep and needed to be prodded to stand for the hymns. Caro was all too aware of the sideway looks they were attracting from the other worshippers.

A quiet snore half an hour into the sermon was the last straw for Caro and she kicked her husband so hard that he jerked awake and knocked the prayer book from the hands of the elderly woman sitting next to him.

'What?' said Leander loudly. The minister stopped mid-word and every head in the church swivelled to stare. Caro could have died of embarrassment. He made a great show of retrieving the book and returning it to its owner with a charmingly whispered apology, but the service was held up for one of the longest minutes of Caro's life.

'That was disgraceful!' she hissed as they queued to leave the church. 'I'm never bringing you again!'

Leander arranged his features into an expression of remorse. 'I'm really dreadfully sorry, Caroline.'

She apologised to the minister at the door, but he waved her excuses aside with a kindly smile and a wink. 'Och, Mrs Gray, you've only been married these past few days. 'Tis only to be expected that you'll be a little fatigued, is it not?'

Caro frowned. What a peculiar thing to say. 'Well, *I'm* not tired,' she corrected him, and was sure she heard the woman standing behind them smother a laugh.

'What do you think he meant?' she asked Leander as they set off back down the road. 'Why would he assume that we would be tired?'

'I'm sure I have no idea. Are we going back to the hotel now?'

'No, we're not.' She linked her arm firmly through his to deter him from any thoughts of escaping. 'I'm going to show you how well I know Dunedin.'

In fact, she barely knew her way around, but she had a good sense of direction and managed to remember where they were in relation to the Castledene. She avoided the necessity of small chat and the inherent danger of Leander asking her questions about Dunedin by setting a punishing pace. From a vantage point up on the hills she paused for breath, retying the strings of her bonnet firmly against the pervasive southerly gusting from behind. White capped waves ruffled the surface of the harbour below, breaking into high flurries of foam against the stone breakwaters edging the town.

Nestled into a picturesque harbour, Dunedin was an orderly treat for the eyes, branching out from a central octagon, with ample parks and numerous fine buildings testifying to the wealth pouring into the town from the goldfields some fifty miles inland over the mountains. But much of the town's population was transient, composed of miners returning from the goldfields or about to depart, many of them living in a vast and somewhat squalid suburb of tents on the lower hills.

'I can see the Castledene,' Leander commented.

'Where?' She followed the direction of his gaze and squinted. 'I can't see it.'

'That large red-roofed building over there.' He moved to stand immediately behind her and pointed into the distance. 'That's interesting—it backs directly on to the Gold Office.'

His voice was a soft burr in her ear and to her secret shame she found herself nestling closer to him, to follow the line of his arm. 'Oh, I see it. So that is the Gold Office? That big brick building with the colonnades?'

'That's it. All the gold from all the goldfields in Otago, brought to that one building. There would be millions of pounds' worth there at any given time.' He grinned. 'Just think—five minutes in there and you could tell your Mr Froggatt where to put his miserly thousand pounds!'

She turned and looked up at him, her mouth dropping open in dismay. 'Is that all he agreed to? One thousand pounds? I had hoped for at least twice that!'

'It is an unsecured loan, Caroline,' he reminded her mildly. 'Given the five thousand that your aunt already owes the bank, I think we did rather well. Mind you, it is on condition that we start repaying your aunt's loan as well.'

Illogical as it was, it was oddly comforting to hear him use the word 'we', she thought. For, in truth, the loan would do little but give her a breathing space to re-establish the hotel. She could not see the fortunes of the Castledene turning around until Mr Thwaites could be persuaded to pay a fair market rental for his bar. With a last, wistful look at the Gold Office and its invisible millions, she turned away and continued on their walk.

Down in the streets the miners were easy to spot, with their swags on their backs and heavy workman's clothes. Caro was sure she could guess which of them were about to go out to the goldfields and which of them had already returned, from the air of expectancy or sturdy resignation each man wore like a hat. She caught her breath in horror, however, at the sight of a group of men limping painfully around the town's botanical gardens in feet wrapped with nothing but rags. Despite the sunshine, the ice remained like flawed mirrors over the puddles in the muddy paths and the wind held the promise of more snow to come.

'They've jumped ship,' Leander said, noticing her sympathetic look at the men's agony. 'When the ships dock at Port Chalmers, the ships' captains lock up the sailors' shoes to discourage them from running off to the goldfields. Not that it appears to be an effective deterrent even in the middle of winter. It's a common enough sight in Dunedin.' He grinned. 'If you're familiar with the town.'

'Of course I am. I knew that,' she said, and was about to move on when Leander gently disengaged his arm from hers and seated himself on the nearest park bench. She clicked her tongue in irritation, but he appeared not to hear. 'Leander, we must hurry up. We've wasted enough time as it is.'

He sighed and settled himself more comfortably on

the bench, tilting his head back to catch the sunlight and closing his eyes. With his fair hair and pallid skin he looked in dire need of the warmth. 'Must we? I'm afraid I'm exhausted already.'

Caro thought of all the work waiting to be done at the hotel. 'You don't do any physical exercise, do you?'

'Not if I can possibly avoid it,' he agreed.

'And when was the last time you ever did an honest day's work?'

Leander frowned. 'Now let me think…' He closed his eyes and stretched his long legs out as far as they could reach.

'Well?' she demanded after a moment.

'I'm still thinking.'

Caro became aware that they were attracting some amused attention from passers-by. Exasperated, she sat down on the far side of the bench. Her husband gave every appearance of having gone back to sleep.

'You look very comfortable. I expect you're quite used to sleeping on park benches.'

A murmur that sounded like agreement was all the response she got. She sat fidgeting impatiently for a few moments, although she did have to admit that it was a pleasant spot to sit. The botanical gardens were a somewhat eclectic mix of English and native plants, mostly in their infancy, but surrounded by the dense, damp, evergreen forest that was typical of New Zealand. For a moment she thought wistfully of the flat, sunbaked country that was her home, but just as swiftly she pushed the memories aside. She had spent a few nights sniffling into her pillow thinking of her family, and when she began to remember even her father with nostalgia, she knew things had gone too far. Home-sickness was not a luxury she could afford.

'Leander, I need to talk to you,' she said at last to her husband. When he didn't answer she leaned over and kicked him on the shins.

'I am listening,' he said drowsily without opening his eyes.

'You're not. You're asleep. How can you do that? Sleep all day, I mean?'

'Mmm. Routine, I suppose. For the last year I've stayed up every night and slept every day.'

'Really?' She stared at him in amazement. 'Why?'

He opened one eye and looked at her. 'Why do you want to know?'

'Well...' She hesitated. It would not do to show any concern or interest in Leander's background or nefarious night-time habits but, all the same, she was beginning to feel a small pique of curiosity. 'Well, it's such a peculiar thing to do. And I would think it to be most unhealthy.'

'Most unhealthy,' he agreed and shut his eyes again.

She remembered afresh the events of the previous night. 'Leander, please do me the courtesy of waking up and listening to me. I *have* to speak to you,' she said urgently.

'Mmm?'

'About the money.'

'What money?'

She clicked her tongue in irritation. 'You know very well what money! The bank's money. Mr Froggatt's money. *My* money.'

'Your money?' He opened his eyes and smiled at her lazily.

'Yes, my money! And it *is* my money!'

'Of course it's your money,' he agreed urbanely. 'Lent to me, of course, and less my fee for marrying you…'

'So,' she said uncertainly 'you are going to give it to me to keep the hotel running?' He roused himself to give her a look of such indignation that she went on hurriedly, 'I mean…well, it's not a ridiculous question, Leander! You patently have not a proverbial bean with which to keep yourself…'

'Not one bean,' he agreed.

'And when someone does give you a bean—or beans—then you promptly go out and spend it all on drink. So of course you're going to be interested in keeping the money from the loan!'

'It's true that one could buy a great many beans with one thousand pounds.' He crossed his arms behind his head and closed his eyes, the long dark lashes startling against his pale skin. 'As it happens, I am perfectly content to settle for the outstanding portion of my fee which, as I recall, stands at fifty pounds.'

Relief and amazement warred within Caro's breast, to be replaced with a growing suspicion as to Leander's real motives. 'Why?' she demanded bluntly.

'Why don't I want to take the whole amount?' He shrugged. 'I gave up giving a damn about money quite some time ago, Caroline.'

Such heresy was completely beyond Caro's comprehension. 'But…but *why*? How could you *not* care about money? When it's so *important*!'

'It's not important,' he said flatly.

'Only someone who has never had to worry about money would say such a stupid thing,' she retorted. 'And you…well, you're penniless! How can you say money doesn't matter?'

He gave a short, oddly bitter laugh. 'People matter. Sunshine matters. Fresh air, children, a smile… Those things matter.'

'What twaddle. You have no idea what you're talking about. Have you ever had money? Lots of money, I mean?'

'Yes.'

'And weren't you happy?'

He gave that serious thought before saying slowly, 'No. No, I wasn't. At least, not as happy as I am now.'

Caro frowned. 'So…what happened to the money? Was it stolen? Did you gamble it away? Did it go on drink and riotous living?'

'No. I walked away from it.'

'Then you're insane,' she said flatly. 'No one walks away from money.'

He turned to look at her through lazily narrowed eyes. 'Not even when there are strings attached?'

She wondered how much Mr Matthews had told him about her own family history and decided it might not be wise to pursue the point. It was all too likely that Leander's background bore some strong resemblance to her own.

She sniffed by way of defiant retreat and sat in stiff-backed silence beside him while the clouds rolled back to reveal a flawlessly blue sky. The wind had dropped to a light breeze, bringing with it the sweet scent of English spring flowers. She thought of all the work waiting for her back at the Castledene. The vacated bedrooms waiting to be cleaned. The linen that had been returned by the laundress yesterday and now needed to be put away. The rows of silver and glassware to be cleaned. She was going to face all that and much, much more when Mr Matthews took Aunt Charlotte to Auckland to recuperate. Oh, she would employ help, of course, although she had heard that good domestic servants were hard to come by. It was the prospect of running the hotel day to day that she found most daunting. And if Mr Thwaites ever came back, she would not know what to do.

She took a long, unsteady breath, before becoming aware that Leander was studying her with an expression of concern. He did *seem* to care about her wellbeing, she realised with a pang that was almost physically painful. Although God alone knew why he *should* care when she had given him as little encouragement as she could. She had always thought of him as some kind of aristocratic alley-cat; completely self-contained, interested only in his next meal and somewhere to lounge in the sunshine and yet, inexplicably, he had stayed with her thus far. If only…

'Will you leave now?' The words left her lips before she could stop them.

'Do you want me to leave?'

She looked away, unable to bear it if he should find her answer ridiculous. 'No. I mean… Well, it would be dreadfully inconvenient if you should leave now, what with Aunt Charlotte having to leave with Mr Matthews. I would have to run the hotel by myself with just hired help. So…you might as well stay on, don't you think? It's not as if you have anywhere else to go, is it?'

He threw back his head and laughed. 'Put as graciously as that, how could I possibly refuse, Caroline?'

So he did find her answer silly, but she was so relieved that for once she didn't mind. Besides, when his eyes glimmered with laughter and his mouth took on that certain twist at the corners, she found him almost irresistible.

'Thank you.' She stood and primly pulled her jacket straight. 'And you might as well call me Caro. Everyone else does.'

He rose to stand beside her, so close that his breath was warm on her face and she felt the tiny hairs on her nape prickle in anticipation. 'All the more reason for me not to then, don't you think?'

The constriction in her throat suddenly made breathing rather difficult. 'Stop this!' she said, when she could.

'Stop what?'

'What you're doing! This…this is a business arrangement…'

'I never thought otherwise, Caroline.'

She closed her eyes for a moment, fighting for equilibrium. He was playing games with her again, games at which he was far more experienced than she. Games in which he sought to master her, body and soul. Games in which she rather desperately wanted to join.

He surprised her by dropping a quick kiss on the tip of her nose. 'I'm sure there are a million and one things you have to do at the hotel, Caroline,' he said abruptly, offering her his arm. 'Let's go back, shall we?'

Chapter Seven

Caroline sighed and slowly shut the ledger book. No matter how many times she added up the numbers, and in whatever combinations, the facts remained depressingly and all too obviously the same. The hotel was running at a loss. For over a month now they had had full occupancy every night and the dining room had done a healthy trade. But settling all the outstanding bills, hiring the new staff needed and replenishing the supplies had quickly eaten through the thousand pounds from the bank. The income from the guests who ate and slept in the hotel was barely covering the interest repayments.

As if to taunt her, an outburst of raucous laughter from the Castledene bar penetrated the wall behind her. How many hundreds of pounds changed hands a night in there, while here she slaved away for nothing!

She couldn't talk to Mr Matthews about her worries. He would only give her the I-told-you-so look that she detested and advise her to return home to Sydney. Besides, he and Aunt Charlotte—together with the last one hundred pounds—were booked to leave for Auckland the following day. Doctor Scourie had recommended a small and inexpensive boarding house by the sea in Auckland. There, it was hoped, the temperate climate and careful nursing would soon return her aunt to good health. Charlotte's condition had vastly improved this past month, but she remained as resolutely uninterested in the running of her hotel as ever.

And as for Leander...

He had been affability itself, doing whatever she asked of him without complaint. He was charming at the reception desk and endlessly obliging when called upon to help out in the kitchen. How many times had there been when she had panicked over some domestic drama and he had stepped in to calm her down and help sort out the problem? He had been all she had required him to be and more.

Except for the nights, that was. Most evenings, when his day's duties were done, he would pull on his coat and quietly slip out of the front door. Only occasionally was she roused from sleep when he returned, in the small, dark hours, as he carefully climbed the stairs to his room, across from hers. Once she had heard the hushed rumble of male voices, and the footfalls on the stairs were heavy and unsteady, as Mr Matthews helped Leander to his bed. She had lain awake until dawn, fuming with the thought of the money her husband was spending in the bars. In fact, she was not sure which was the greater sin—drunkenness or wasting money. She was determined to make his life a misery when he woke up the next morning, but he had been perfectly amiable when she shook him awake at dawn. Of course, he always was amiable. She found herself becoming very tired of his amiability.

The hall clock chimed ten. Struggling to keep her

eyes open, she ensured that the front door was locked, and made her way to the kitchen.

The stoves had been banked low for the night. In the frugal light of a single lamp Mr Matthews was bent over the table, intently polishing silver. Leander was stretched out on a chair, scribbling on a sheet of paper. Caro caught herself smiling at the scowl of concentration on his face and the way his bottom lip was caught between his teeth. So great was his absorption in what he was doing that he started when she walked over to the stove.

'Caroline! Would you like a cup of tea?'

'I'll get it.' She stopped to look over his shoulder. He had drawn Mr Matthews, capturing his likeness so perfectly that she caught her breath. 'You…really are very good,' she said, somewhat inadequately. 'Have you ever thought of drawing professionally?'

'Is that what you was doin'?' Mr Matthews folded away the silver cloth and stood up indignantly. 'I'm off, then. I ain't no artist's model.'

'But it's an extraordinary likeness,' Caro commented. 'Look.'

Mr Matthews peered at the sheet of paper she held up. 'Hmm. Not bad, but you've done better than that with some of them pictures you done of yer wife, Mr Gray.'

Leander shrugged. 'You're probably right,' he said to Mr Matthews's departing back. He went to open the stove door, but Caro grabbed the paper before he could throw it into the embers.

'Don't do that, I'd like to keep it. And…is it true that you've sketched me before?'

'I have. But I've thrown them away.' He grinned at her unconscious pout. 'They didn't do you justice.'

'Really?' she said, somewhat mollified. She poured herself a cup of tea and slumped down in the chair beside him. 'You really do have a talent, Leander. Have you ever thought about making money from it?'

'Money?' He looked up from under his fringe, a small smile playing at the corners of his mouth. 'Oh, I don't think so, Caroline. It's just a hobby.'

Too tired to correct him or comment on his wasteful ways, Caro leaned against the hard-backed chair. The stairs up to her bedroom seemed a long way away in her present state of weariness and she found herself beginning to nod off, wrapped in the soft, warm cocoon of the stove and the lamplight. Even the muted racket from the bar next door had all but died away.

'Tell me about it, Caroline,' Leander said quietly.

'About what?' she said drowsily, scarcely able to open her eyes.

'About why you've spent the last three hours poring over the books. About why that little frown between your eyebrows is becoming permanent.'

She absently rubbed the offending wrinkle. 'It's nothing you can help with, Leander. It's just this bank loan, and I really don't think… Oh, I say! What do you think you're doing?' she ended on a gasp as he bent down and grasped her left ankle.

'You were limping when you walked over to the stove. I imagine your feet hurt,' he said calmly. He placed her foot in his lap, slid off her slipper and began to firmly massage her toes. 'So, tell me. What is the problem with the bank loan?'

Caro sat stunned into silence for a long moment, completely taken aback at the casual way her husband was handling her with such intimacy. But his touch was so soothing, and the look on his face was so concerned and she really did need to tell someone about the worries that were twisting her insides so miserably.

She began to tell him about the accounts, and her frustration at not being able to pin down either her aunt or Mr Thwaites as to why the profitable bar next door should not be paying rent to the hotel. About how the employment of servants and the purchase of new silver and linen had all but depleted the borrowed funds from the bank. And how her aunt's desperately needed trip to the warmer north was going to leave them perilously close to not being able to meet the next payment to the bank.

'And when is that due?' he asked, concentrating on smoothing out a sore spot on her right instep.

'Next Friday. Six days away.' She sighed luxuriously, despite herself. 'You really are very good with your hands, Leander.'

He raised one eyebrow. 'Two compliments in one evening. One more and I swear the shock will kill me.'

'I pay compliments where compliments are due,' she said, defensive in the knowledge that she had never, to date, paid him any. 'All I'm saying is that…was very pleasant.' All too aware that she was in an exceedingly compromising position, she tried to extract her feet from his hands, but his light grip on her ankles tightened.

'Leander,' she said warningly.

He ignored her, holding her fast as he studied her ankles with a professional eye. 'You know, you do have remarkably pretty ankles. Well turned, as they say. I must sketch them, some time.'

'I really would rather you did no such thing.' She wrenched her ankles from his grasp but, as he offered no resistance, she almost overturned her chair. To hide her embarrassment, she busied herself by putting her slippers back on.

'So,' she said into the silence, 'in your opinion, what should I do about the hotel?'

He sighed and stretched out, his arms behind his head. 'I think you've only got two choices, Caroline. Stay here and work out the problems, or walk away from a poor business proposition that was not your problem to begin with.'

'I'm not walking away from this hotel!'

'Now, why did I know you'd say that?' he interjected.

'And neither solution would solve the problem of my debt to the bank,' she pressed on. 'Or are you saying that I should just run away and leave my aunt in debt?'

'No, of course I'm not. But is there really any harm, Caroline, in telling Charlotte that the hotel is unprofitable and persuading her to sell it? She shows no interest in it whatsoever and she is too ill to run it even if she did want to. Selling it would leave her in a comfortable position, able to live permanently in a warmer climate…'

He was making altogether too much sense. Caro shook her head firmly. 'Charlotte already has a huge mortgage on this place. Selling it will only give her enough for a very modest pension…'

'At least it will be a pension and not a debt.'

'No!' Unwilling to hear any more, Caro got abruptly to her feet. 'There is no reason why this hotel should not make a good income for my aunt. The bank's money has helped us make it habitable again, and once I can convince Mr Thwaites to pay rental—'

'Pigs will fly before that happens, Caroline.' He unfolded himself and stood up slowly, his face sympathetic despite his blunt words. 'I've never met the man, but it's clear that your aunt and Harold Thwaites have enjoyed a very…intimate relationship in the past. They are, or they have been, lovers for quite some time, and Charlotte won't charge him rental for that reason.'

'But why not?' she wailed in frustration. 'Business is business! *I'd* charge him in that situation!'

'I'm sure you would. But your aunt does not have your keen regard for business. And, with her health as fragile as it is, now is not the time to try and change what is fundamental to her character.'

'She can't change, but Mr Thwaites can! If he has only the slightest regard for Aunt Charlotte, I'm sure he would easily be persuaded to pay his way.' She hesitated, taken aback by the cynical expression on her husband's face. 'You don't agree?'

'Not knowing him at all, I couldn't tell you. But let's say that I would be more inclined to agree with you if Mr Thwaites ever made an appearance at the hotel. In his absence… Well, I wouldn't rely on his generosity, Caro, no matter how sick Charlotte is, or how dire your need.'

For a long moment she stood, staring at the faintly flickering embers, coming to terms with the fact that he was right. *Leander* was right. She had, until now, managed to regard everything he had said as being the irresponsible meanderings of one of the world's most abject failures. To finally have to admit that, in point of fact, the tramp she had married was possessed of an acutely observant brain was not an admission she was happy to make. It made their relationship more equal, and consequently much harder to stay detached from.

She absently swallowed the last of her by-now cold

tea as Leander bent to tend to the fire and shut the oven door. When sober, he moved with a grace and economy of movement that always took her by surprise, and she had long since resigned herself to the fact that she took pleasure from watching him. Outrageously handsome in the broad light of day, in this soft half-light he looked flawless. Which, of course, she would do well to remember he was not.

He turned and caught her looking at him hungrily. Caro covered her embarrassment by putting her cup and saucer in the washing basin, appalled at the noise she made while doing so.

'Caroline, I think it's time for bed,' Leander said gently.

Her shoulders went rigid. 'Oh. I…I don't know…'

'It is late,' he persisted. 'And you look exhausted.'

'Late,' she said blankly. 'Oh. Yes, it is. You're right.'

Feeling somewhat disoriented, she followed him to the foot of the stairs and watched as he lit two candles and turned the night lamp down to a dim flame.

'Leander,' she said impulsively. 'Thank you.'

'Whatever for?'

'For listening to me. For the…' She swallowed and managed to say it. 'For the good advice.'

'Even though you're not going to take it?' he teased, and she laughed, for once not minding that he was making fun of what she considered to be her strength of will. He cared about her—she knew that now and, inexplicably, that knowledge filled her with exultation.

It was by now so late that there was no sound from the bar next door. The candles and lamp did little to light the dark panelled entry hall. Caro was suddenly, achingly aware that she and Leander were completely alone. She moved closer, but not to take the candle from the table. Greatly daring, she raised her fingers to touch the pulse beating swiftly at the base of his throat. His skin was warm under her fingertips, and she heard him catch his breath.

His response to her touch aroused her unbearably. She could never have stopped herself moving forward the few inches into his arms and lifting her mouth to his. He kissed her twice, lightly, as if testing her response. But then she wrapped her arms around his neck and sought his mouth greedily.

Above them, at the top of the stairs, Mr Matthews smiled to himself and padded silently back to his room.

Caro knew that if Leander let her go she would fall. Utterly trusting, she clung to him, responsive to the feel of his hands around her waist, the way his body pressed against hers. She knew his body, had seen it naked, had been fascinated by its contours and masculine mysteries. But this touching, this world of sensations, was even more exciting. She could feel his heart beating hard and fast against her breasts. With a moan of pleasure she opened her mouth under his.

Dimly she registered the sound of an upstairs door being carefully closed and, with a sigh of reluctance, Leander pulled back to study her face.

'You have the sweetest mouth I've ever tasted.'

'Really?' Caro said breathlessly. 'And just how many *have* you tasted?'

'Enough to know that you're the sweetest.' He grinned and chucked her under the chin as if she were a child. 'Come on. Bedtime.'

He picked up the two night candles and she followed him upstairs, scarcely able to breathe for excitement. She knew what was going to happen, of course—her mother had touched on the basics some years before. It all sounded very awkward and undignified, and more than a bit silly, and the thought that her parents had actually done *it* eight times scarcely bore thinking about. But her mother had finished her little talk with, 'And only when you're married and in love, Caro. Otherwise it will never be the truly special time it is meant to be.'

Well, she wasn't in love, but she *was* married. And no matter how ridiculous this lovemaking procedure turned out to be, she knew that it would be special— Leander would make it so. Upstairs, he opened her door and stood back to let her pass. Holding her hands tightly before her, she dropped her eyes, unwilling to show him how anxious she really was. She was amazed at his composure—she was sure he could hear the pounding of her heart.

'Goodnight, Mrs Gray.'

He was holding out her candle. She took it dumbly and watched as he turned to his own door.

Alone in her room she held her hands to her scorching cheeks, telling herself in a harsh whisper how grateful she was that she had not said anything to embarrass herself. What a fool she would have been if she had said what she had thought...what she had expected...what she had hoped...!

The following morning dawned still and unseasonably warm, a welcome respite from the cold brisk gales of the previous days. It was a good omen for Aunt Charlotte's departure, Caro told herself as she pulled back her bedroom curtains. And, indeed, everything went very well, indeed.

Charlotte was pale beneath her powder, but perfectly

cheerful, leaning heavily on Leander's arm as she
climbed the gangplank to the *Lady Clarence*. Mr Matthews and a stream of porters struggled in her wake,
laden with all the hatboxes and trunks that Charlotte
deemed essential luggage. Having a father who owned
one of Australia's premier shipping lines, Caro knew
enough about the rigours of sailing to have paid the
extra three pounds to secure a superior cabin for her
aunt's comfort. Once she had settled her aunt into her
bunk and inspected the cabin's facilities, she decided
it was money well spent.

'After all, the journey will take the best part of a
week.' She carefully stored the last of Charlotte's hatboxes on the high-rimmed shelves. 'With your own
commode and washing facilities, you should be perfectly comfortable.'

'I'm sure I will be, darling.' Charlotte nestled her
narrow shoulders into the plumped pillows and gave a
little sigh of contentment. Ill as Charlotte undoubtedly
was, she seemed to thoroughly enjoy the fuss and pam-
pering that went with being an invalid. 'After all, I shall
be in the best of hands, won't I?'

Caro watched with a mixture of irritation and affection as her aunt reached for her ever-handy mirror and
began to smooth down the locks disturbed by the re-
moval of her bonnet. Poor, poor Charlotte, she thought.
She was a woman who had always relied on her looks
to get her through every conceivable situation in life,
and now that those looks were beginning to disappear,
her vanities and vulnerability were all too readily exposed. Men like Mr Thwaites were, it seemed, given
to walking in and out of her life as the whim took them.
To be so beautiful, and so reliant on that beauty, must

be a curse. Why, even her own father had fallen out with his father over her...

She gave herself a little shake. And it was just as well that he had, she reminded herself. What if Charlotte had chosen to marry the son and not the father! Charming as Charlotte was, Caro could not imagine her as anything other than the most appallingly self-centred mother.

Charlotte finished preening herself and laid down the mirror with a smile.

'How can I ever thank you, Caroline? You've been such an angel, looking after me, and taking on all this tedious business of the hotel after Harold left!'

'Oh, heavens! It's no trouble at all,' Caro lied blithely. She perched beside her aunt on the bed. 'All that you should have to worry about is getting yourself well again. But, speaking of Mr Thwaites...'

Charlotte's eyelashes fluttered evasively.

'Where is he, Aunt Charlotte?'

'Darling! I don't know! He goes...places...' Her aunt's little hands fluttered in illustration of Harold's peripatetic lifestyle. 'Here, there, Christchurch, the goldfields... He has lots of business interests. The bar at the Castledene is only one of them.'

'And how often does he visit the Castledene?'

'Oh, darling!' Charlotte shrugged her shoulders helplessly. 'How can I know that?'

'These other business interests...' Caro persisted, despite her aunt's obvious discomfort. 'What are they, exactly?'

'All visitors ashore!' someone bellowed in the passageway outside and Charlotte brightened immediately.

'There, darling, I mustn't detain you. Now, don't worry about me. I promise I shall be a good girl, and do everything I'm told. Off you go, now, and don't work too hard.'

There was a cursory thump on the door and Mr Matthews leaned into the room. He and Charlotte exchanged a look of utter dislike and then he jerked a thumb over his shoulder. 'Best go ashore now, lass. We're casting off in five minutes.'

'Odious man,' Charlotte remarked to the closing door. 'I'm glad to be seeing the last of him.'

A small prickle of alarm travelled down Caro's back.

'Aunt Charlotte,' she said carefully. 'You do realise why you are going to Auckland?'

'Of course, darling! I'm going to recuperate!'

Caro took a deep breath. 'And you do know who is going to go with you?'

There was a moment of dreadful silence while the penny dropped. Charlotte's eyes widened as her mouth drooped in dismay.

'But, you can't be serious! That little man hates me—he always has! Why can't Leander come with me? I like Leander, and he's far more agreeable company. Oh, Caroline, you can't do this to me!'

''Ere! Enough of that nonsense!' To Caro's huge relief Mr Matthews was at the door again. 'Now go ashore, lass, afore you end up coming wiv us!'

Caro was heartily grateful to escape from the cabin and Charlotte's tearful, reproachful eyes. In fact, she felt tearful herself as she joined Leander and Mr Matthews at the bottom of the gangplank.

'Forget 'er,' Mr Matthews said tersely, for her hearing alone as he enveloped Caro in a rare and very brief hug. 'I'll be back as soon as I got her settled, so don't you fret. You got a good man there, lass. You lean on him and he won't let you down. I'll take care of her ladyship. And you—' he met Leander's eyes '—take care of this one for me.'

'I promise.' She felt Leander's arm around her, warm and strong and supportive. She leaned against it gratefully as she watched Mr Matthews trot back up the gangplank seconds before it was removed. Fortunately, Mr Matthews was not one for protracted farewells, and disappeared promptly below decks, presumably to sort out her distressed aunt.

'I take it Charlotte realised who her chaperon was to be during her convalescence,' Leander remarked.

Caro nodded against his shoulder. 'It's…the most awful misunderstanding. Aunt Charlotte didn't realise that it was Mr Matthews who was going to accompany her. But I *know* I told her that he was the only person who could go with her! I don't know where she got the idea from that it would be *you*, of all people…'

'Ah, well…as for that…' He at least had the grace to look a little embarrassed. 'I'm sorry, Caroline. It just seemed…expedient to let her think that until it was too late for her to refuse to go. You had enough on your plate to deal with without your aunt creating any more problems for you, and we…well, we thought it for the best.'

'*We?* So Mr Matthews knew about this all the time?' So that was why Charlotte had been so amenable. And Mr Matthews and Leander—conspiring behind her back? She shook her head in disbelief. 'And you didn't think to tell me what you were up to? Lying to Charlotte like that! No wonder she was so upset. You have probably set back her recuperation by weeks!'

'I doubt it. I think that Charlotte had envisaged an entirely different form of recuperation with me in attendance for the next couple of months.' He looked over her head to the activity on board the *Lady Clarence*. 'Look, they're casting off. Do you want to stay and watch?'

'No. I have to get back to the hotel,' she said shortly, and turned on her heel. What upset her the most was the rush of pure, mindless jealousy that had surged through her at the thought of Charlotte and Leander together, alone, on the journey to Auckland. It was entirely unreasonable—after all, Charlotte still had no idea that Caro had entered a marriage of convenience with Leander. Moreover, it was a marriage based on nothing more than the exchange of money for a name. Consequently, Leander was entitled to do as he wished. Free to take up with whomever he wished.

On Carlyle Street Leander stepped aside to allow two young women to climb up on to the high wooden footpath. It was an action totally in keeping with his innate courtesy, but Caro caught the girls' demurely covert glances of admiration at her husband as they passed and for the second time in less than an hour a tug of jealousy twisted her insides.

It was her own fault, she reminded herself bitterly. She was getting altogether too fond of him, with his impossible good looks and impeccable manners, and that could only be a major error of judgement. Why, to have let him kiss her last night...

Or rather, she had kissed him. And would have made an utter fool of herself over him, had he not politely withdrawn and wished her a civil goodnight. She flushed, remembering it. What had come over her, to have acted so out of character? As he held the door of the Castledene open for her, her hand brushed against his and, even through her glove she tingled at the contact. Oh, Lord, she was just as likely to throw herself at him today as she had the previous night!

Chapter Eight

As she usually did when she was perturbed, she immersed herself in work and yet more work that day, and found plenty more for Leander to do, besides. News of major gold strikes in the area around the Arrow River in the previous weeks, together with the softening spring weather, was resulting in the daily arrival of hundreds more prospectors at the Dunedin wharves.

Most of the new arrivals made only an overnight camp on the outskirts of the town before setting out on the long, difficult trek to the goldfields on foot. But many of the prospectors were coming from the well-worked mines of California and Victoria, with money in their pocket and a more measured, professional approach to the business of making a fortune. These were the men who spent some time in Dunedin buying the necessary equipment at far more reasonable prices than those demanded out in the distant goldfields. They made inquiries, bought maps, visited the Gold Office, planned the claims they intended making. They also knew enough about the hardships of living for months under canvas in the goldfields to appreciate the civilised comforts of an hotel like the Castledene.

By lunchtime Caro was having to turn guests away, much to her regret. The extra housemaid she had engaged was fully employed laying fires and making up all the beds with fresh linen. The kitchen was a hive of activity as the staff prepared for the first full dining room at the Castledene in months. The skilful cooking of Mr Matthews would be sorely missed, Caro knew, but the new cook, Mrs Mulligan, seemed competent enough.

They were running low on firewood, so she dispatched Leander to charm the wood merchant into making an early delivery. When he returned—with the wood merchant and a dray full of wood, so as to save himself the walk back—she found a dozen other small jobs for him to do. Anything, as long as it kept him out of her sight and, consequently, out of her thoughts.

In fact, so busy did the hotel become, that their paths scarcely crossed over the next few days. Each night Caro would fall into bed at some time close to midnight, utterly exhausted but equally elated at the steadily-filling safe downstairs. With hard work and sound management, the Castledene was making a very healthy profit, indeed!

On Thursday morning she paid the staff wages and all the receipts, and there were still one hundred and five pounds left in the safe. Caro counted the notes three times, barely able to contain her pride. The next repayment to the bank was due the following day. She could pay it, and still have thirty pounds over. Thirty pounds would keep Charlotte and Mr Matthews for at least another month in Auckland. And if there continued to be full occupancy of the hotel, at eight pounds per night, plus what the dining room made, less wages...

'You look very pleased with yourself,' commented Leander as he saw her bending over the reception desk, pen scribbling furiously. She looked up, her face pink with excitement.

'I'm looking forward to going to the bank tomorrow, and giving that horrid banker his money! In fact, I think I'll take it in this afternoon.' She folded the notes inside a sheet of paper with the greatest of care. 'I can't wait to see the look on his face, the pompous old—'

She broke off as a party of four came in the door, looking for accommodation. As Leander escorted them to the last two unoccupied rooms, another party came in and had to be turned away. They were followed by the baker delivering his weekly account, and the clerk of a mining company requesting a booking for a party of six the following week.

It was well into the afternoon by the time she managed to leave the desk for long enough to take a quick bowl of soup in the kitchen. She passed Leander in the dining room, where he was quietly setting the silverware and glasses on the tables for dinner that evening. She stopped long enough to help him straighten a tablecloth on the largest of the tables. It always seemed odd to see Leander performing domestic chores, but he never complained and, in fact, appeared to find it all rather diverting. He seemed genuinely intrigued by the routines of housework, as if he had never seen them performed before. Why, Caro had even had to show him how to clean out a grate and set a fresh fire! Sometimes she had the feeling that such menial tasks were too much of a novelty to him for him to find them irksome.

'I think we might start opening for lunch next week,' she commented. 'I think the demand is there, now that we're having to take bookings for dinner. I wonder if the staff could cope with cooking two meals a day?'

'Mrs Mulligan probably could, perhaps with another maid. Why don't you ask her?' He stepped back and admired the completed tables. 'What do you think of that?'

She followed his gaze around the dining room. It did look splendid, fine enough to rival any other hotel she had ever been in. 'Very nice,' she allowed. 'But what about flowers on all the tables?' She looked at him archly. Flower arranging was the one thing he flatly refused to do, although with his artistic ability she was sure he would be superb at it. She intended suggesting that he learn how to mend linen, just for the pleasure of his response. 'I'll take a walk around the hills this afternoon and see what I can pick.'

'After you've been to the bank?' Leander said absently, straightening a fork. 'Or have you already been?'

She stared at him, suddenly pale. 'The bank? Oh, dear Lord…'

She could see even before she got to the reception desk that the folded envelope with the money was missing. She had left it beside the ledger. Foolish, foolish thing to do! Why, at least two dozen people had passed by the desk today, some of them guests and others tradespeople. Any one of them could have picked it up intentionally or inadvertently…

When Leander came in she was futilely searching on the desk, under the desk, on the floor—anywhere the

envelope may have fallen. Without a word he took her
hands and led her back to the dining room where there
was little chance of their being interrupted. She stood,
shaking in his arms, trying to comprehend the enormity
of what she had done.

'How much is missing?' he asked softly.

'All of it. Everything. I took everything out of the
safe and wrapped it in a sheet of paper ready to take
to the bank. Over a hundred pounds, Leander! Of all
the stupid things to do.' She wrapped her arms around
him and buried her face in his shirt, partly for comfort
and partly to hide her burning face. 'Oh, how could I
have been so foolish?'

'Hush. You were busy. Too busy. Good heavens,
woman, you never stop! At least now I know you're
fallible like the rest of us.' She felt him kiss the top of
her head and she pulled back indignantly.

'You don't mean that!'

To her chagrin he looked amused. 'I do, actually.
Caroline, this could happen to anyone. Yes, it's a set-
back, but it's not the end of the world.'

'It might as well be! What on earth am I to tell Mr
Froggatt? The money's due tomorrow! He'll think I'm
no better than Charlotte, and I'm not, am I? A whole
week's takings, gone, just because of my stupidity…'

He kissed her to stop her tirade of self-abuse and
that was so pleasurable that she almost forgot her misery. When he finally lifted his head she was breathless
and felt decidedly weak at the knees.

'Leander…'

'Don't worry about anything. I'll think of a solution,' he said soothingly. Lulled by his kisses and relieved that she was not having to face this dilemma

alone, it did not even occur to her that a week ago she would have laughed at such a preposterous statement.

That evening there were another twelve pound notes sitting in the safe, paid by departing guests and diners. Leander gathered them up and tucked the wad into the pocket of his jacket.

'It's not a lot, but I'll see what I can do with it.' He brushed the hair back from Caro's worried, flushed face. 'It will be all right, Caroline. Believe me.'

'Believe you?' she retorted. 'How on earth can you say that your going to spend that money in the local bars is going to make everything all right? I'm not a fool, Leander!'

'I know you're not…'

'So why won't you tell me what you intend doing?'

He hesitated. 'Because you would tell me not to do it.'

'Oh, just go, then!' She turned away to wearily climb the stairs to her room. 'You might as well. Twelve pounds is hardly going to make a difference to the fact that we have to default to the bank tomorrow!'

Leander watched her go with far less confidence than he had claimed. She was right to doubt him, but tonight, surely, with so much riding on the stake, he would be strong enough? He took his coat from the cloak stand and pulled it on thoughtfully. It was below freezing tonight, but it was not the outside temperature that was chilling him. If he failed tonight, it would probably be best for everyone concerned if he never came back.

He walked away from the hotel without a backward glance, his footsteps crisp on the ice lightly coating the dirt road. He was too well known in the Castledene bar, but there were bars in the town, around the park area called the Octagon in the heart of Dunedin, that attracted a more transient type of customer and that would consequently be much better for his purpose.

He called in first at the Prince George, one of the quieter bars on a Thursday night. There was only one game in progress, obviously played between friends, with little money on the table. Indeed, it was so quiet that the barmaids were setting up a game of faro among themselves. Further down the street, at the Commercial Hotel, there was considerably more activity, with no less than half a dozen different games being played. One, in particular, looked promising. Four men, miners by the look of them, were playing poker as if the money in their pockets was on fire. There must have been a hundred pounds on the table.

Leander leaned against the bar and returned the landlady's smile. 'Good evening. I'll have a glass of whatever you're having.'

'Double whisky is it, love?' She reached for the bottle but he shook his head firmly.

'No, thank you. I'll have whatever you're having.' He nodded at the glass of amber liquid beside her on the bar. 'What is it? Orange cordial? Lemonade?'

The pleasant expression slid from her rather hard face as she hesitated, then poured him a glass from a jug below the bar. 'Five shillings.'

The cost of a double whisky. Leander paid without comment and took his drink to a table beside the gamblers where he could observe the game inconspicuously. It took him less than three minutes to see that one of the players was cheating outrageously. Despite the drunken conviviality at the table, it was more than likely that his deceit would end in a round of flying fists once the others realised that they had been fleeced. Leander finished his cordial and left.

At the Prince Albert Hotel three games were in progress, all closed games between friends. There were only a few sedate games of dice being played at the Queen Victoria, and none at all at the Grand, but he stopped to observe a very serious game of poker being played at the Empire. Large sums were on the table and it was one of the smooth, fast-flowing games that Leander enjoyed best. His attention was caught by the sure-handed manner in which one of the players dealt the cards. Under the broad-brimmed hat and over the newly grown muttonchop whiskers he recognised Charles Graham, an old acquaintance from the goldfields. Their eyes met for a second in tacit acknowledgment and Leander rose to leave. There was room for only one professional gambler in an hotel.

It was in the Otago Hotel that he found what he was looking for. The bar was crowded, as usual, with a number of groups of men absorbed in games of chance. After persuading the bartender to give him another non-alcoholic drink—orangeade this time, and for a much more reasonable cost of eight pennies—Leander began to slowly make his way around the room.

Most of the men were miners, flush and reckless with newly gained wealth. Having wintered over in the snowy goldfields of Central Otago, bereft of warmth, good food and women, they came to Dunedin determined to have a good time. They were in marked contrast to those miners who were yet to make their fortune, or who had perhaps won and lost several fortunes on the goldfields. Those were the quieter souls on the edges of the room, who nursed a drink for a long time, and watched the noisy merrymaking of the bar with jaundiced eyes.

Leander sat with them awhile. It took all of five minutes to identify which of the poker tables he should join. It took another half-hour of careful observation of the players at that table before he knew with certainty all their small mannerisms, their weaknesses and their level of ability. Most importantly, he was sure that no one was cheating and that none of the players was by any means a professional.

Eventually one of the games came to a rowdy close, with a young player disgustedly throwing in his hand, declaring that the players were all rogues and that he'd be damned if he were to lose his trousers as well as his shirt. As the others all laughed and ribbed him goodnaturedly, Leander picked up his glass and ambled over to the table.

'Evening, gentlemen. Have you room for one more?'

Caro had not enjoyed her evening, but found that the usual busy routine at least kept her mind off her problems. After her guests and staff had retired, she checked that all was clean and tidy in the dining room. In the kitchen, she banked down the fire, gave the breakfast pot of soaking oatmeal another stir, and moved the tins of rising bread dough closer to the heath.

As she straightened up, her back gave a sharp twinge of complaint. She stood for a moment, massaging it absently, wishing that she were not so tired, knowing that the tiredness came at least partly from anxiety. Well, at least she had tried to save her aunt's hotel, although whether Charlotte would ever thank her for her efforts was highly debatable. So much for all her hard work—in the end, all it came down to was money, or rather the lack of money. And to think that behind the stove, through the brick wall, lay the vaults of the Gold Office. Strongboxes full of gold nuggets, all from one of the richest goldfields in the Southern Hemisphere, just feet away from where she stood, virtually bankrupt. The irony of it all made her feel quite ill.

Locking the front door, she hesitated. Goodness only knew what time her husband would decide to return. He would be drunk, of course, and penniless after a night on the town, while *she* had spent the whole evening working and worrying. It would only serve him right if he had to spend the night outside in the frost. Hardening her heart, she pulled the latch across and made it tight. No doubt in the morning, she would find him slumped against the door, hungover and miserable, his useless key in his frozen hand. The image cheered her up somewhat.

And in the morning, he could get his marching orders. She had made a serious mistake, allowing him to take advantage of her momentary weakness and disappear with the last few pounds in the till. If he cared so little about her, about the Castledene, then he could pack the few items of clothing that he called his possessions and go. And, just to ensure that he went, she would even do his packing for him.

His room was opposite hers, but she had rarely had occasion to enter it before. She placed the lamp on the dressing table and looked around her. It was the one room that escaped her vigorous housekeeping but, in the lamplight, it looked tidy enough. In fact, it almost looked as if no one lived in the room at all.

In a cupboard drawer she found a couple of freshly starched shirts, which she laid in the centre of the bed.

A pair of moleskin trousers went on top. The next
drawer held a few items of underwear. She took a deep
breath before quickly placing them on top of the small
pile on the bed. She must not give herself time to think
better of this. Leander was not entitled to privacy, not
given his selfish behaviour. She had to get him out of
the hotel and out of her life.

There was nothing in the next drawer but a few pen-
cils and a large, thin book. She went to lay it on the
pile before realising that it was a sketchbook. Suddenly
intensely curious, she sat down on the edge of the bed
and opened the book.

It was full of sketches of her. Laughing, serious, in
shadow and in light…her face was reproduced on
every page. The competency, the sheer artistry of his
work, took her breath away. How often, she wondered,
had he been watching her while she sat or worked unaware? There was even a full-length sketch of her that
he must have drawn one evening by the kitchen oven.
She was hemming a tablecloth, her mouth set in a tense
line, her forehead wrinkled in concentration as she
plied her needle.

Caro looked up at her reflection in the mirror over
the washstand and rubbed her forehead absently. Her
mother was always telling her off for frowning like
that, saying that the wrinkle that would remain would
give her a bad-tempered appearance through to old age.
Caro rarely looked in the mirror, as a rule—only to
brush her hair and check that her face was clean. Had
she ever passed her identical twin in the street, she
doubted that she would have recognised the similarity.
Now, with Leander's sketches on her lap…

She ran her fingers down the side of her face absently. Was she really as beautiful as the woman in

Leander's sketchbook? All her life people had told her she was lovely, and in recent years, ever since she had entered Sydney society, men had been boringly persistent in reporting the fact to her. Even sweet, jug-eared Frank Benton, with whom she had grown up, had gone peculiar and begun to extol her beauty every five minutes, but then he had fancied himself in love with her. Indeed, more than once it had occurred to her that the state men called Beauty was nothing more than a complete nuisance. She had even considered how pleasant it would have been to be born plain, perhaps too plain to be considered marriageable, so that men would treat her as someone with intelligence and a personality. She had a nose, a mouth and eyes, all of which functioned as they should. Surely that was all that one should ask of a face?

Under Leander's pencil her face was perfect, luminous, memorable. She looked at the mirror, at the sketches, at the mirror again. It was her face, assuredly, but her face reproduced with admiration and tenderness. Maybe even with love. She swallowed hard and closed the sketchbook. Her husband had never irritated her, as so many other men had, with protestations of admiration. His sketches spoke more eloquently than any words could ever have done.

She carefully put his belongings back where she had found them, and then went downstairs to unlatch the front door.

Her sleep that night was restless, punctuated by short, unpleasant dreams that woke her up, perspiring despite the chilly night. At one stage, she dreamed that she was sitting at the dining table with Harold and Aunt Charlotte. Charlotte peered into the custard jug and said plaintively, 'There's no money in this!'

'I'm so sorry,' Caro said. 'I did try…' But then Harold and Charlotte turned into Mr and Mrs Froggatt, and Mrs Froggatt kept complaining that there was no money in the custard jug and no one was listening to Caro…

'Caroline?' Leander's voice was quiet, but a lifeline in such a horrid dream. She looked around the table to try to see him.

'Caroline. Wake up.'

Thankful to be woken, she struggled to sit up, blinking as Leander struck a match and lit the lamp beside the bed.

'What are you doing here?' she mumbled, still caught somewhere between sleep and reality. Slowly, she registered that he was back, it was before dawn, and that he sounded perfectly sober. What had happened?

'This is my room, Caroline. Or it was when I left this evening.' She could hear the amusement in his voice. As the lamp flared she took in the fact that he looked none the worse for wear. Indeed, he looked very pleased with himself.

'I…I didn't intend to fall asleep. I was waiting for you, and…oh, this is most improper,' she flustered. Her blouse had come adrift from her waistband and her hair was all over her face. Fortunately, she had at some stage pulled the eiderdown over her, so at least her bare feet were not on display. She took refuge in attack. 'At any rate, where have you been? Carousing in bars, no doubt!'

'In bars, assuredly, but not carousing.' Too casually, he took his wallet out of the inside pocket of his greatcoat and dropped it in her lap. 'Look inside.'

'And what shall I find? Mothballs?' she could not help saying, even as she noted its considerable weight. She opened it up and her mouth fell open in astonishment. 'How much money is there in here?'

'To tell the truth, I'm not sure.' Leander sat down on the edge of the bed. 'Why don't you count it?'

She did. One hundred and twenty-three pounds, in mixed denominations, were crammed into the wallet, as if in haste. Once she could speak, she waved the wad at him accusingly.

'Where did you get this? You must have stolen it! Oh, Leander, as if we haven't got enough problems…'

'I didn't steal it!' He shook his head slowly, his eyes glimmering with laughter. 'Even the fellows I won it from shook my hand at the end of the game with no hard feelings!'

'You won it?' She looked at the money with no less uncertainty. 'Gambling? Is…that honest?'

Leander looked hurt. 'You make it sound as if I robbed a bank, Caroline. I thought you'd be relieved. Perhaps even pleased. Do you want me to go and give it back?'

'Oh, no!' Instinctively she clutched the money to her breast. 'I am pleased, Leander! Thank you! It solves all our problems, you know that. It's just that…well, when you left last night with the last of the money from the till, I was sure that I'd never see any of it again.'

He shrugged. 'That's not surprising, given my past record.'

There was not a hint of defensiveness in his voice and she looked at him curiously. 'What was different about tonight, Leander? Playing cards is such a risky business…'

'Not when you know what you're doing.'

'And you do?'

'Yes.'

She thoughtfully splayed out the notes across the eiderdown and said slowly, 'So what was different tonight was that you stayed sober.'

'Yes.' He was withdrawing from her emotionally, if not physically, and on impulse she threw her arms around him and hugged him tightly.

'You *are* clever!'

After a moment, he took her arms from around his neck. 'Thank you, Caroline. Now, if you'll go to your own room, I'll bid you goodnight for whatever's left of it.'

She grabbed at his wrist as he stood. 'I…I don't have to go, you know, Leander.'

There was a silence so profound that she could feel her heart thumping uncomfortably in her chest. She almost regretted her words, but it was too late to take them back. Besides, it was true—she didn't want to leave. She wanted him lying beside her, holding her. She wanted to touch him, be as close to him as it was possible to be. And he wanted it too—she could see the desire in his eyes.

Then he looked down and with a deft twist removed his wrist from her fingers. 'There's a simple explanation for this, Caroline,' he said lightly. 'Money is a powerful aphrodisiac, you know, and it's late, and we're alone, and you're patently overcome with gratitude. But let's not do anything rash and jeopardise what is a perfectly good working relationship, hmm? Don't bother about leaving—I'll be perfectly comfortable in one of the armchairs downstairs for the next couple of hours. Goodnight.'

He closed the door carefully behind him.

Feeling thoroughly chastened, Caro sadly climbed off the bed and crossed to her own lonely bedroom. It had taken all her courage to proposition him as she had, but the last thing she had expected him to do was reject her. She was not looking forward to facing him again in the morning.

When she came downstairs at dawn Leander was already in the kitchen, talking to Mrs Mulligan, the cook, as she took the newly baked bread from the oven. Caro hesitated at the kitchen door, trying to gauge her husband's mood. Sitting at the table in his socks and shirtsleeves, with his hair ruffled and the hint of dark rings under his eyes, he looked rumpled and tired—much like herself, in fact.

He looked up and gave her the same composed smile that had greeted her every morning for the past six weeks.

'Good morning, Mrs Gray. A cup of tea?'

She sipped the proffered cup in silence while Leander made light conversation with Mrs Mulligan. So, she thought grimly, they were to pretend that nothing untoward had happened last night. She supposed that that was for the best. Her own husband might have rejected her out of hand but—she felt the thick wad of banknotes in her skirt pocket—at least they were out of debt again. She was longing to ask him how and where he had achieved the seemingly impossible, but that would have to wait for a more private time.

The bell at the reception desk rang and Leander got to his feet. 'I'll get that, Caroline. You look tired.'

Implying no doubt, that she had lain awake throughout the early hours of the morning thinking about him. She rose gracefully, tilting her head pertly at him.

'Thank you, Leander, but I'm not in the least bit tired. Rather, it is you who looks the worse for wear this morning.'

She swept out to the reception hall, to find old Mr Wills, the wood merchant, turning his cap nervously between his gnarled fingers.

'Morning, Mrs Gray. Sorry to come so early, but I was here yesterday, and—' he rummaged in his breast pocket and then thrust out a familiar fold of paper '—I accidentally picked this up off the desk with my receipt book. It looks like a lot of money, Mrs Gray. I haven't opened it. It's all there…'

He temporarily lost the power of speech as Mrs Gray flung her arms around his neck and kissed his grizzled cheek resoundingly.

Chapter Nine

Caro should have been a happy woman.

The Castledene Hotel was now enjoying full occupancy, and eager diners were having to be turned away from the dining room as word spread of the superior food and services to be had there. The newly employed staff had all turned out to be perfectly satisfactory, and Mr Froggatt was now smiling at her when she went to the bank twice each week to deposit the takings. Even the activity next door in the Castledene bar failed to irritate her as it once had.

There had been no word from Charlotte, and Caro did not really expect any; even when healthy, her aunt did not strike her as the sort of person to expend energy on letter-writing, and Mr Matthews—while possessed of a multitude of skills—could not read or write. But short of a shipwreck or a natural disaster, there was no reason why the two unwilling companions would not by now have reached the warm and sunny shores of northern Auckland.

Caro knew that she had much to be proud of. She had done what she had set out to do. She had turned Charlotte's business around and she had—more or less—done it by herself. Even her father would have had to be impressed by her tenacity, foresight and business acumen. As soon as Charlotte was well enough to take over the reins again, Caro could return home, look her father in the eye and demand that she be treated with as much respect as any son would have been.

She had won. She was a success. So why did she wake every morning feeling utterly wretched?

Spring was now well advanced, and most mornings at dawn Caro opened her window to a sparkling clear sky and the scent of blossom. Sometimes the sight of the sunlight on the far hills above the harbour was all too evocative of the countryside around her home farm, and for a while she put the nagging sense of misery down to nothing more than homesickness. Perhaps she had been too long at the hotel, she mused. Accustomed as she was to the wide skies and empty, quiet spaces of New South Wales, the narrow, bustling streets of Dunedin often seemed constricting and staid.

Beyond the hills to the west lay the mountains and the rivers and the goldfields. Fresh air and adventure! Fortunes were being made every day out there—you could not live in Dunedin without being caught up in the excitement. Some men were earning extraordinary sums from gold, and other men—and some women— in setting up in businesses catering to those wealthy entrepreneurs. Every day, it seemed, someone became as rich as they had dared hoped for in their wildest dreams out there in the wilderness. Sometimes it was hard to close her bedroom window and brace herself for yet another day of guests and ledgers and petty problems.

And if the excitement of the goldfields seemed distant and elusive, so too did her husband. Certainly, he was polite enough, but it was the same courtesy that he extended to the guests, the staff and the woman who came to collect the laundry. He seemed biddable enough—he did whatever she asked of him and worked as hard as she did to ensure the smooth running of the hotel. But sometimes, especially at night by the stove when she wanted to talk, it was plain that his mind was elsewhere. And once she found him on the veranda, looking out across the hills, every line of his body tense with frustration. Just like her, he wanted to escape. But, unlike her, she knew he would not come back.

At least, she comforted herself, he had not returned to his old ways. He rarely went out at night now; on those occasions when he did, he returned home apparently sober and subdued. Really, the only complaint she could make about her husband was a lack of attention—and hadn't she herself insisted on that as a condition of their marriage?

The irritation niggled at her, ate at her, until one night, when they had locked up the hotel and were lighting their night candles, she planted herself in front of him and burst out, 'Leander, we need to talk!'

He looked at her quizzically. 'Really? I thought we did that on a daily basis.'

'Please, don't patronise me!' She laid a restraining hand on his arm and was immediately aware of the heat emanating through the light fabric of his shirt. 'We talk about the hotel, and money, but we don't talk…about *us*! And I think we should, don't you?'

With studied care he turned down the paraffin lamp, adjusting the screw so that it glowed with just enough steady light to illuminate the staircase. Anything, she realised, to avoid meeting her eyes.

'There is no "us", Caroline. I've been paid for my services, and I trust I've performed satisfactorily—'

'That's not what I meant,' she interrupted, hurt by his coldness. It seemed that the more she pushed, the more he withdrew. She watched in frustration as he turned and mounted the stairs without a backward glance. Well, if he was content to let the situation between them dangle unresolved, she was not.

The hotel had been dark and silent for an hour when she pulled her dressing gown over her nightdress, tiptoed across the hallway and inched open Leander's bedroom door. For a long moment she held her breath, listening, but she heard nothing. Somehow, she had been sure that he would have been as unable to sleep as she had been.

The moonlight shining between the half-drawn curtains illuminated the shape of Leander lying motionless on the bed. Soundlessly, she closed the door behind her.

'Caro, this is not a good idea,' he said firmly.

'We have to talk, and if you won't stay and talk to me, these are the lengths I have to resort to!' She staged a dramatic shiver and clutched her dressing gown to her. 'Heavens, it's so cold…'

'Then go back to your own room and your warm bed.'

'Your bed's warm,' she said pointedly and very daringly. When he didn't respond she picked up the edge of his eiderdown. 'Move over.'

To her surprised delight, he did. Scarcely able to believe her luck at this lack of resistance, she kicked off her slippers and, primly retaining her dressing gown, slid between the sheets. The narrowness of the bed necessitated some adjustment between the two of them, but after a little wriggling, she had appropriated sufficient space for herself. Their knees and elbows scarcely touched, but their faces were only inches apart on the single pillow.

'Are you perfectly comfortable now?' Leander asked, with little solicitousness in his voice.

'Yes, thank you. I'm feeling much warmer.' She snuggled down under the eiderdown and closer to the heat of his body.

'So am I,' he said wryly. He tried to move back and only just saved himself from falling off the edge of the bed. Caro grabbed him by the waist, both to steady him and in case he thought better of the situation and tried to get up. Across the pillow, in the silver wash of the moonlight, they stared at each other.

'This is most unwise,' he said eventually. 'You shouldn't be in my room, and you most certainly shouldn't be here in my bed. Look, I'll talk to you in the morning, Caroline, I promise. But in the meantime, please go back to your own bed.'

'But you are my husband,' Caro said softly. Under her hand his hip was hard and radiated heat. She moved her fingers up so that they lay over his ribs. Beneath her palm his heart was racing. 'Your bed is not such an unusual place to be, surely?'

'But ours is not a usual marriage.' He firmly moved her hand back to her side of the bed. 'It's a marriage in name only, based purely on a financial transaction. That was the deal, remember?'

'But that was months ago, before I…I got to know you better. Things are different now.' She touched him again, running her fingers up and down his arm, and she felt him catch his breath.

'Caroline,' he said unsteadily, 'what do you want?'

She struggled to answer that. She didn't *know* what she wanted—or rather, it was impossible to put into words. How could she explain the yearning, the compulsion that drove her to his bed, to lie like this beside him, wanting…what? She didn't know. Not exactly.

'I want you to kiss me, Leander.' That would be a start, at least.

He closed his eyes against her moonlit face. 'You're not thinking straight, Caroline. This is a big mistake.'

'I don't see how. I just want a kiss.'

'No, you don't.' He opened his eyes and took in her beseeching expression and soft, parted lips just inches from his own. 'It's not going to end with a kiss, and you know it. Sweetheart, think about this, because this is not a decision to be made lightly! Once you've spent the night with me, there's no going back. No easy end to this marriage, no annulment…'

'Annulment?' she repeated blankly, even as her brain raced to deal with the fact that he had called her 'sweetheart'. Sweetheart! The last shreds of rationality deserted her at the sound of that single word.

'On the grounds that the marriage hasn't been consummated.' He pushed himself up on one elbow and frowned down at her. 'God, Caroline, you've no idea, have you? We can't do this. You don't know anything about me…'

'Oh, tosh! I know everything I need to! And none of it is important!' She took his face between her hands and kissed him, hard and quickly lest he pull away. 'Just love me, Leander!'

For a moment, as she watched his set, rigid expression, she thought he would refuse. But then it was as if a floodgate had broken. With a groan of surrender he sought her mouth, her throat, her shoulders. Her dressing gown was soon discarded on the floor, and Caro was torn between removing her nightgown and assisting Leander in removing his own clothing. Beneath his nightshirt his skin was fascinating to touch, rougher than hers and yet—if the jagged breaths he took when she trailed her fingers over his ribs were anything to judge by—just as sensitive. Eager to discover more she tugged impatiently at his garment, then fell back with a shuddering gasp as his tongue found her breasts.

Lacing her fingers through his hair, she tried not to shriek her ecstasy aloud. Every nerve in her body was concentrated on the harsh lashing of his tongue and when he rolled the hard peaks between his teeth she lost the battle for silence. He rose up to kiss her, thrusting his tongue inside her mouth as if to punish her for her indiscretion. Then his mouth went on its incredible voyage of discovery again, down the line of her throat to trail small fiery bites across her breasts, down in a dangerous, exciting, forbidden foray to her abdomen....

And then he stopped.

She waited, unable to breathe, poised on a knife edge of anticipation.

'Damn!' he muttered against her stomach. 'Damn, damn, damn!'

She pulled him up by his hair until their faces were level.

'What's wrong?' she demanded unsteadily.

He shook his head helplessly. 'I can't...'

'Of course you can! You can't stop now!'

'No. I can't. I can't make love to you.' He slumped back, his arm over his face. 'Oh, God. Now, of all times...'

Caro sat up and pulled his arm away. 'What do you mean, you can't?' she said urgently. 'What is stopping you?'

'I am. I mean I want to, but I can't. Maybe it's the drink... Hell, I don't know... but I can't make love to you. I'm sorry, Caroline, I really am. This... this has never happened to me before.'

The shimmering, intense feelings of a minute before were fast evaporating, leaving her feeling cold, rejected and humiliated. She gathered the sheets up against her breasts and when Leander tried to put his arms around her she shoved him away with the flat of her hand.

'No!'

'Sweetheart... look, this won't last. Let me hold you, please. There are other ways I can give you pleasure, if you let me. Maybe that's a better idea anyway...'

'No!' she said more loudly. 'I don't understand you. I don't understand why you're doing this to me!'

'*I'm* doing this to *you*?' He stared at her in disbelief. 'Do you think I'm doing this deliberately?' With a muttered curse he got out of bed and turned to glare at her, running his hand through his already wildly dishevelled hair. 'Look, you've got to trust me. I can't help this! No man has complete control of his virility! There are just times when... and this is the first for me and...' He saw her blank, uncomprehending stare and his shoulders slumped.

'Oh, Caroline,' he said quietly. 'You don't understand, do you? I'm alone in a bedroom with the most beautiful, desirable woman in the world and I can't... perform. I can't make love to you. I'm so sorry, but... look, can you imagine how that makes me feel?'

Something inside Caro snapped. She swung her legs out of bed and grabbed for her dressing gown. 'That's typical of you!' she said furiously. 'How *you* feel, what *you* want! Well, I've had enough! You can pack your bags and leave, and I never want to see you again!'

'Caroline—' Leander began placatingly, but he was speaking to a slamming door.

When he came downstairs the next morning, she was waiting for him. Arms crossed, her face pale but set, she raised her chin.

'I trust you're packed and ready to leave?'

His footsteps slowed and he came to a stop on the bottom stair. 'Don't be silly, Caroline…'

'Silly? Yes, I suppose I am!' she hissed, only just remembering to drop her voice in case the guests overheard them. 'In fact, you've made me look really foolish, haven't you? But I don't know why I should be surprised—that's something you're an expert at!'

He covered the space between them in three long strides, to take her trembling shoulders in his hands. 'Caroline, just listen to me. Last night…I wasn't prepared for it any more than you were. It's not a matter of looking foolish—I'm the one that feels like the biggest fool on earth, not you! And what happened last night was a private matter between the two of us. No one else is ever going to know…'

She shrugged herself free. 'I don't have to listen to this. Now, I told you, get out! This is my hotel, you were only ever here because of my generosity! You're a worthless good-for-nothing and I want you out! Now!'

She saw his hands curl into fists and for the first time in months she saw anger glinting in the brown depths of his eyes. The knowledge that she had at last provoked him into a response to her own churning emotions gave her a perverse pleasure. So there was a man of passion lurking underneath that mop of blond hair after all. She had never realised before now just how tired she had become of his eternal patience and good manners, his consideration and charm. She wanted him hurt and angry, as angry as she was right now!

She was disappointed when he shook his head and said simply, 'I'm not leaving you, Caroline. I can't.'

'Oh, but you can! It's a simple enough exercise. See that door there? All you do is put one foot in front of the other until you've walked through it and down the street!'

'I can't go. I promised Mr Matthews that I'd stay.'

Caro felt the last vestiges of self-control slipping away. So, that was why he was staying, was it? Not due to any feeling or attachment to *her*! Seemingly of their own volition, her fingers grasped the vase of flowers and hurled it at him. He ducked in time, unfortunately, and the vase shattered on the wall behind him, leaving him only a little splattered with water.

'*Get out!*' she managed through teeth so clenched together that it was hard to speak at all. At last, he got the message. With one last, impassive look, he turned and climbed the stairs again.

The guests had managed to put up with various peculiar noises and slamming doors through the night, but the sounds of raised voices and smashing glassware at six in the morning was too hard to ignore for some. Mr Potts, a surveyor with the Victorian Mining Company, certainly felt that he had to date exercised the patience of a saint, and that matters had gone quite far enough. Pulling on his dressing gown, he drew himself up to his full five foot and went to the head of the staircase. The manageress of the hotel, a young matron he had hitherto thought to be of demonstrable good sense, was standing staring at a wet mess of glass and flowers on the stairs. The silly woman was making no attempt to clean it up—why, any guest might inadvertently stand in it and do themselves damage!

He noisily cleared his throat. 'Mrs Gray, I must protest…'

The rest of his sentence died, stillborn in his throat, as she looked up at him. In a face as set and white as marble, her eyes glittered with a ferocity that Mr Potts took to be certain insanity. Without another word he scuttled back to the comparative safety of his room.

By the time Leander came downstairs again, she had regained sufficient composure to greet him civilly enough from behind the registration desk.

'I've taken this—' he raised the small leather carrybag in his hand '—from Charlotte's room. It didn't seem to be needed.'

'That's perfectly all right, Mr Gray,' she informed him, taking pride in the coolness and steadiness of her tone. 'I won't charge you for it. However, the crystal vase broken this morning was worth at least a guinea, so I have deducted it from your wages. Eight weeks, at one pound a week…'

'So much? I'm flattered you think me worth even that,' he said even more frigidly.

'It's what I would pay any other hired labour. And, of course, I wouldn't want your lack of funds to hinder your departure to somewhere as far away from here as possible.' She held out an envelope. 'Six pounds and nineteen shillings. You can count it if you wish.'

'No, you're honest about money, even if about nothing else in your life.' He put the money in the breast pocket of his coat and extracted a note from the same place. 'And if you ever need me—when you need me—you can contact me at this address.'

Caro took it from him, screwed it into a tiny ball and threw it away. 'Goodbye, sir. I can't say it's been a pleasure and I can only hope that I shall never see you again.'

The expected retort never came. Without a word he picked up his bag and walked out of her life. Good riddance, Caro thought. He's been nothing but trouble from the start. Now I can get on with my life, doing things my way. This has been the best decision I've ever made. It was a refrain she had to repeat incessantly to herself, all that long, dreadful day and through the interminable dreary night that followed.

Chapter Ten

As Caro was to find out, the pain did not get any better. Indeed, if anything, each passing day brought more sharp reminders of how integral Leander had become to her life at the hotel. The public were by and large pleasant to deal with, but those who were not seemed to become even more demanding, and without her husband's soothing influence and good humour, there were several unpleasant incidents with drunk or abusive guests.

The situation was not improved by the sometimes unhelpful attitude of the staff. Clean towels not laid out in a guest's room, a broken glass left on a table, silverware less than pristine…all the small things that the staff would once have attended to immediately were now left undone. Usually it was faster to correct the error herself and then point it out to the servant involved, but the extra work added hours to an already long day and, besides, the mistakes would only be repeated the following day.

At first she had put her staff's lack of enthusiasm down to simple ill-discipline, but a conversation she overheard one morning, a week after Leander had left, explained much.

She had been in the pantry, counting provisions, when there came the crash of silverware being tipped with force on to the kitchen table.

'There just ain't no pleasing her, Mrs Mulligan!' That was the kitchenmaid Kate's whiny little voice. 'All yesterday I spent, cleaning all this, and she tells me to do the whole blimmin' lot again! As well as change all the tablecloths, 'cos she reckons they're not clean, either! I dunno. No wonder her husband's shot through. Couldn't put up with her ordering him about every minute of the day. Why, I'll bet even in bed she'd have to be on top...'

Mrs Mulligan's throat-clearing reached paroxysmic levels and a horrified silence followed. By the time Caro had pulled herself together enough to walk back into the kitchen the only occupant was Mrs Mulligan, head bowed diligently over the bread she was kneading.

Not for the world would Caro have shown her hurt, but Kate's comments echoed in her mind for days afterwards. The staff might respect her, but they had liked Leander, and, now that he had gone, they were not inclined to do anything more for her than the mere essentials required by their employment.

To avoid the accusing eyes at the hotel, she escaped on whatever pretext came to hand. An account to be paid, an extra order to be made, and she would cram her hat on her head and hurry out the door. Once outside she would walk for miles, usually bypassing the prettily set-out garden of the Octagon to stride along the foreshore, or up on the hills above the harbour.

Otago Harbour, whether whipped by light breeze or

heavy gale, was always dramatic, a moody roll of colours reflecting the sky, and white-tipped waves. The salt spray on her face was the perfect excuse for her eyes to water, and at least there was no one to see. By the time she returned to the hotel, exhausted and emotionally wrung out, she would have regained sufficient composure to carry on with her work.

For six long, bitter weeks she existed—she would not have called it living—while the warmth of summer turned the hills around Dunedin a vivid green, and the fortunes of the Castledene Hotel inched out of the red and into the black. All Caro's hard work and attention to detail were at last paying off, but there was no joy in it for her any more.

Then, one sunny Thursday morning she paid the wages and accounts and tallied up what was left in the till; there was enough to clear the loan from the bank and with ten pounds to spare.

She had done it. Against all the odds, she had won. This moment was testimony to her fortitude and good business sense. Why, she had even gone through the mockery of a marriage to achieve this success. As she folded the money neatly inside an envelope, she reflected how flat victory tasted when there was no one to share it with.

At the bank Mr Froggatt came out of his office to shake her hand.

'Well done, Mrs Gray! I knew your husband would do a sterling job, turning the hotel fortunes around the way he has! Please give him my best regards. I haven't had the pleasure of seeing him recently?'

'He…he is visiting other business interests in the goldfields,' she responded calmly enough. How adept she had become at lying recently! 'But I shall pass on your good wishes, Mr Froggatt.'

'Please do.' He eyed her consideringly, his head to one side, and for a dreadful moment she wondered if the whole charade was writ large on her face. 'How is your aunt, Mrs Gray? Still in Auckland?'

'Yes, she is, and making a good recovery.' Another lie—she had not heard a word from either Charlotte or the nursing home she had been sent to.

'Good, good. When Mrs Wilks is more recovered….there is still the matter of the five thousand pounds this bank has advanced to her to be resolved.'

Caro thought she was going to be ill. Somehow she said the correct pleasantries and made it back on to the street, but she couldn't remember how. She walked away, putting one foot in front of the other, like a machine. Five thousand pounds. Five *thousand* pounds. He had mentioned it before, of course, but somehow Caro had only focused on the thousand she had needed to get the Castledene up and running again. Now that the hotel was trading solvently again, it was a certainty that the loan could be paid back. It would only take— say—a year to eighteen months…

At the end of Castle Street she stopped and looked at the hotel, as if once more seeing it for the very first time. It was a grand place, a fine place, surely as fine an hotel as any to be found in the colonies. She had sacrificed months of her life to this building, and for what reason? Out of some misguided loyalty to her aunt?

No, it hadn't been loyalty, but her own stubborn pride and arrogance that she, Caroline Morgan, was the answer to all Charlotte's problems. It had mattered not one whit that Charlotte could not have cared less about the hotel. Instead, Caroline had been so carried away with her own cleverness and conviction that she knew all the answers that she had created her own prison, here on Castle Street. Her own private prison, with all the time and loneliness required for her to serve out her sentence.

A sudden longing for her home and family seized her and it took all of her resolve to blank it out of her mind. She was being fanciful, that was all, and self-pitying. There was work to be done, so why was she standing outside here in the sunlight when there was linen to be sorted, and menus to choose and paperwork to be done? She rubbed absently at the pounding in her forehead. But first, a quick lie-down in a dark room with a damp cloth over her eyes.

Little red-headed Kate was waiting for her in the foyer, wringing her hands and bobbing up and down in anxiety.

'Miss! Miss! There's a man, says he wants to see you soon as you got in, miss! I put him in the dining room, miss, 'til you got here.'

Caro opened her mouth to say that she was too tired to see anyone, but the distress on the girl's face was too real to be ignored.

'What sort of man?'

Kate's little hands wrung even harder. 'Dunno, miss! Sort of…important? Like he…like he owns the place!'

Harold Thwaites. Caro could feel her headache intensify by the second. She had almost managed to forget about the horrid creature for the past few months. For a moment she thought about running upstairs to the sanctuary of her room, but doubtless he would not regard it as such. Oh, well, now was as good a time as any to demand rental from him, while her head throbbed so badly that she could not care less about hurting anyone else's feelings.

Without removing her hat, she walked through into the dining room. Harold was lounging at one of the bare dining tables, his heavy legs stretched out before him, the pungent small cigar in his fingers overwhelming the familiar dining-room scents of beeswax and cut flowers. To her rage he was scanning her ledger book.

She marched up to him and held out her hand. 'That is mine, sir. You have no right to look at it!'

'Good morning, Mrs Gray.' He got lazily to his feet, dusting off the cigar ash from his jacket as he did so. 'How nice to see you again.'

'The ledger, Mr Thwaites. It's mine.'

He sighed and gave her a beatific look. 'I think not, Mrs Gray. Please sit down and let me bring you abreast with events.'

Aware that Kate in the foyer and the staff in the kitchen were actively listening in on their conversation, Caro hesitated for only a moment before seating herself on the far side of the table.

She had forgotten how much she detested this man and everything about him, from his carefully manicured nails and waxed moustache to the fact that not a speck of dust was ever allowed on his highly polished boots. Doubtless he spent an inordinate amount of time before mirrors every morning, because the image he chose to present to the world was of paramount importance. She did not trust him one inch.

'I do have some happy news for you,' he said at last, when it became clear that Caro was not going to break the heavy silence. 'About your aunt.'

'Is she well?'

He spread his fingers and studied his nails with a

slight frown. 'She is improved, certainly. As to her being *well*, I can't say. It will be a long road to recovery. However, I had the opportunity to visit her in Auckland and…well, perhaps it was the change of scene, or climate, or perhaps her improved health… Who can say? But your aunt was finally persuaded to make me the happiest man on earth, Mrs Gray. I do hope that we have your blessing?'

She stared at him blankly. 'Blessing? For what?'

'For our marriage, of course.' He laughed at her expression. 'I managed to convince her that she had mourned poor old Jonas for long enough. We were married last week, at her bedside. So, I suppose, that now makes me your…uncle. Well, that's a thought, isn't it? Mind you, I've yet to congratulate you on entering the same felicitous state. I asked the staff after your husband, but couldn't get a straight answer from any of them. I take it he is still here?'

Even in her state of shock, Caro knew not to let on that she was alone. 'But Mr Matthews—' she began after a stunned silence.

'Took it very well. Offered us his congratulations and has decided to return to Sydney. He asked me to let you know. He said there was no point in returning here, now that you're a married woman with a husband to care for you, and that it was high time he returned to Australia. Nice chap, I thought. Very fond of you, isn't he? But he seemed very keen to return home after all these months.'

Caro had never felt more bereft in her life. No Leander, and now no Mr Matthews. She could scarcely credit that he and Harold had got on, but Mr Matthews would certainly have been only too pleased to have given over the care of Charlotte to someone else. And why would Mr Matthews not have returned to Sydney? He was devoted to her parents, and would be keen to let them know that their eldest was married and settled in Dunedin. Knowing her father, it would be only a month or two before he stormed south to interrogate her husband. Oh, it was more than she could bear thinking about!

The clink of teacups brought her to her senses, and she realised that Kate was placing a tea tray on the table before them. She managed a quick, tight smile at the girl's thoughtfulness and leaned back in her chair, easing fingers that ached from having gripped the edge of the table.

She waited until Kate had left the dining room before saying slowly, 'So now that you're married to Aunt Charlotte, you own the hotel.'

'I do, although as you know, it's just a formality, really, because Charlotte and I have been business partners for years. All it means now is that we can run the hotel and the bar jointly. I know that my dear wife has run this part of the business into the ground, and I also know that you've done a sterling job turning it around. But my wife's debts are now my business. Thank heavens I can afford to keep the dear woman in the style to which she wants to be accustomed.' He laughed benignly. 'But please don't think that I don't appreciate everything you've done for Charlotte. We owe you a huge debt of gratitude, and you and your husband are more than welcome to stay on for as long as you wish, of course. But...well, there really is no need now, is there?'

'I suppose not, no,' she said woodenly. He gave a nod of satisfaction and turned around to toss the stub of his cigar into the unlit fireplace. He missed but seemed not to care that the smouldering butt landed on the hearth rug.

He couldn't have cared less about the hotel, and it was no longer her place to do so, either.

She packed her bags in less than five minutes. The twenty pounds she kept locked in her dressing table would either keep her until she found another job or take her back to Sydney. She was going to have to make a decision either way very soon. But the decision was made for her when Kate scratched timidly on the door and thrust a crumpled piece of paper at her.

'Beggin' your pardon, Mrs Gray, but I kept this. Don't know if you want it…'

Caro took it in silence and smoothed the paper flat. Written in Leander's fine, sloping hand were the words 'The Lake Hotel, Queenstown'.

Given her employer's uncertain temper, Kate had fully expected a telling-off for her temerity, and so cowered back when Caro flung her arms around her and then pushed a pound into her hand as a thank-you.

'It was like there was wings on her heels,' she later reported to Mrs Mulligan in the kitchen. 'She sort of glowed and ran down the stairs with her bag, all happy like. She must love her husband after all, Mrs Mulligan. An' I always thought she were a mean cow, an' all.'

'Even mean cows fall in love, Kate,' the cook said prosaically into the pot of soup she was stirring over the fire. 'Well, it's for the best, I suppose, though I reckon we've exchanged one hard taskmaster for a worse one, if you ask me. I don't like the look of that Mr Thwaites one bit.'

Chapter Eleven

From his bed, on the first floor of the Lake Hotel, Leander had an unparalleled view over Lake Whakatipu to the aptly named Remarkable mountain range beyond. The ice-fed lake was an extraordinary blue, the mountains—still topped with the remnants of winter's snow—were spectacularly perpendicular. He still couldn't quite believe it was real. If he had seen a landscape of such a scene hanging in a gallery, he would have dismissed it as the fantasy of a second-rate artist.

He closed his eyes against the late-morning sun slanting through the open window. It was time to get up, he supposed, although he felt entitled to a lie-in after the arduous journey from Cromwell the previous day. Cromwell, Cardrona, Dunstun…he had visited them all and a half-dozen other mining towns besides, spending just a night or two at each. Extremely profitable nights, too—there was a small fortune in the saddlebag under his mattress. But he never gambled in Queenstown; it was the only place in the goldfields that approximated to anything like a civilised town.

While its origins were those of a gold town, Queenstown was now the centre of the new and thriving farming industry, possessing as it did the advantage of relative accessibility from Dunedin. It took a week of travel through the flat hinterland to Kingston, followed by a ferry ride across the lake, as opposed to the more direct route to the goldfields involving days of tortuous and frequently perilous travel through rivers and across mountain ranges. Rather than the itinerant lone males that made up the bulk of the population of gold towns, Queenstown largely consisted of families. There were schools, churches, a constabulary and even a newspaper office.

There was a quiet and order here that appealed to Leander just as much as the breathtaking scenery. This was the place he came to whenever he needed to rest and sketch and think.

Although it was a pleasure to be gambling with miners again—and by now he knew how to pick his games and his places—he never played against drunks or cheats or desperate men. He himself never cheated and, these days, he never played drunk. In fact, he had been sober for close on two months now.

He yawned and stretched out luxuriously. It got hot on these Central Otago nights, and, as he had long since dispensed with wearing a nightshirt, the crisp linen sheets felt wonderful against his skin. He was enjoying the sensual side of living again and the abstinence from drink had done him no harm at all.

Turning teetotaller had been effortless, in the end. If ever he was tempted to take another drink, all he had to do was recall the look of hurt on his wife's face on that last, humiliating night in Dunedin. The remembered shame of his impotence was more than enough to keep him sober and, for the first time in a year, he felt fit and rested and healthy. Too healthy, he thought wryly as he noted his body's usual response to wakening. It was the other sort of abstinence that was so much harder to take.

Turning his head on the pillow, he stared into the bright blue eyes of the young woman lying beside him. 'Good morning, Molly,' he said after a moment.

'Morning, lover.' She kissed him swiftly on the mouth and then retreated back to her side of the bed, her mouth curved in a wicked smile.

There was another, longer silence.

'Molly, why are you in my bed?'

She gurgled deliciously. 'Why, Mrs Watkins told me to bring up your hot water, and there you were, fast asleep and looking all lonely in this great big bed. And, I thought, he'll be wanting some company when he wakes up, so here I am!'

'Well, I appreciate your thoughtfulness,' he said carefully, not wanting to hurt her feelings. The last time he had been in the goldfields, over a year ago, had been the worst time of his life, and he had spent very little time sober. He had made several mistakes in those months, and Molly had been one of them. It was not her fault, and it was not fair for him to reject her out of hand now. 'Look, I'm sure I told you last month that I married a young lady in Dunedin…'

'Oh, sure you did!' she laughed and leaned over to caress his cheek. 'Oh, I do like you without all that hair, lover. You look ever so handsome. Come on, give us a kiss.'

He evaded her eager mouth. 'Molly, I'm a married man!'

'So where's the missus, then?'

Leander rolled over and out of bed to stop her from

seizing his most sensitive parts. Despite his struggles to get away from Molly—or perhaps because of them—he was now in a state of high arousal. Wrapping a towel around his waist, he retreated to the far side of the room. He had to admit she looked delectable, sitting up in bed wearing nothing but a transparent chemise and a smile, but he was a changed man. He told her so.

Molly smiled slyly. 'And I'm a changed woman. See?' She hauled the chemise over her head and lay back against the pillows, her voluptuous, brown-tipped breasts bobbing invitingly. 'Notice the difference?'

'Oh, God,' muttered Leander. He hauled on his trousers—his shaking hands were not the only impediment to doing that—and risked a foray to get his shirt from the chair beside the bed, only just managing to stay out of reach of Molly's hopefully clutching hands. His boots were under the bed, which made them far too risky to collect.

'Well, it's a lovely day,' he said with forced brightness as he looked out of the window in a vain attempt to divert her. 'Look, the ferry has just docked. There's bound to be new guests arriving any minute—won't Mrs Watkins be needing you?'

'Oh, the old hag can shift for herself. I've got needs of me own.' Molly pouted. 'Come on, Leander, you never used to be so shy!'

'Molly, I told you—I'm married. So please leave. Now!' To avoid looking at her all-too apparent charms, he was staring fixedly out of the window. The ferry was an old whaling vessel, capable of carrying a hundred passengers and as many heads of stock. There was the usual range of passengers disembarking—miners, farmers, travelling salesmen…and a tall, statuesque blonde standing uncertainly by the pier, becomingly but familiarly dressed in a dark blue travelling suit and bonnet. Leander wasted a good minute trying to ensure through squinted eyes that it was, indeed, Caro. He expelled his breath in a long hiss of frustration.

'Look, Molly, get out of my bed! My wife's here, and I'm going to go down to the wharf and meet her.'

'Of course it's your wife,' Molly crooned, almost falling on to the floor trying to grab him as he made an unsuccessful foray on his boots. 'Oh, you didn't used to be this difficult to get into bed! Don't you remember the time down by the lake, when you said you wanted to paint me, and when I took me clothes off you painted me all over in—'

'Molly! For God's sake!'

'And then there was that time I tied you to the bed, and you got so excited the bed fell apart and all the hotel guests came to see what the commotion was—'

'Out! Now! This minute!'

Giving up on his boots, Leander ran downstairs, tucking in his shirt as he did so. Fortunately for his bare feet, there were raised wooden platforms in front of the shops lining the main street, and it took a only a minute to race down to where Caro was asking directions from one of the farmhands unloading cattle from the hold of the ferry. She turned her head at his approach and, as always, her loveliness took his breath away. He stood staring at her, for once incapable of speech, scarcely able to believe that not only was this incredible beauty his wife, but that she had spent at least the last week following him here. She was smiling, too, that cool little self-possessed smile that was so uniquely hers, even as her eyes warmed him with their affection.

'Good morning, Leander,' Her eyes dropped to his bare feet. 'Do I take it that you are down on your luck again?'

'No, far from it. I...I was in such a hurry to see you that I didn't wait to put my boots on.'

'Really?' She raised her eyebrows mockingly.

'Really. Oh, God, how I've missed you...' And with one step he covered the space between them and pulled her to him, kissing her hungrily until she laughed and flung her arms around his neck.

'I've missed you, too! Oh, do stop, people are staring!'

'Do you care?'

'No,' she whispered into his neck, holding so close that he could not see the tears in her eyes. She had never felt such an overwhelming sense of rightness as she did in his arms. But passers-by were staring and, very reluctantly, she pulled away at last. 'Are you still staying at the Lake Hotel? Can we go there now?' she whispered, suddenly shy.

Leander hesitated. By now, surely, Molly would have looked out the window and seen him with his wife, but by the time she dressed and left his room... Desperate as he was to possess his wife, he decided to play it very, very safe.

'How about a cup of tea first? You must be tired after all that travelling. How long did it take? A week?'

'Just six days—the roads were very good. And I stayed at Kingston last night, so there's only been the ferry trip this morning,' she assured him. 'I'm not in the least tired, honestly. Your room...'

'It's still a long way to travel,' he said firmly, picking up her small travel case. Taking her by the arm, he propelled her in the direction of a large, pleasant-looking tearoom on the lake front. 'A cup of tea will be just the thing to restore you.'

'But you have no shoes,' she pointed out, flustered and laughing at the same time. Running out in his bare feet to meet her was an impetuously romantic thing to do, but one could hardly enter a public place in such a state. Besides, all she really wanted to do was sink on to a bed with him and finally be able to put an end to all the long weeks of loneliness and frustration.

'Life in the goldfields is a great deal more informal than in town,' he assured her. 'No one's going to mind. And I'm sure you could do with a cup of tea—I know I could.'

In fact, a cup of tea was the last thing she wanted just then, but she thought it would not do to appear too eager, so she allowed him to pull her along beside him. Inside the tearoom the proprietor, a pleasant-faced, middle-aged man, welcomed them, quite oblivious to Leander's bare feet.

'Mr Gray! How nice to see you back in Queenstown again! A pot of tea for you and the lady?'

'This lady is my wife, Mr Jones,' Leander told him, and Caro thrilled to the pride in his voice.

'Well, well, well. A recent happy event, I take it?' Mr Jones boomed, shaking Leander's hand warmly. He turned to Caro and the wide smile slipped for a second as he frankly stared at her. 'Well, well, well,' he said again, as if his vocabulary had temporarily deserted him. His eyes slid questioningly to Leander and back again.

'Tea, please, Mr Jones?' Leander said pointedly, and the proprietor gave himself a little shake.

'Of course! Please, come this way,' Clearly flustered,

he took them to a window table and hurried back to the kitchen.

Caro thought his behaviour was a little odd—but then, perhaps, no odder than the fact that her husband had bare feet tucked out of sight beneath the lace tablecloth. Impulsively, she slipped her hand into his. In the week since she had left Dunedin she had lived only for the moment, refusing to dwell on their last, bitter fight, frightened to think of what his reaction to her arrival might be, driven only by the imperative to see him again.

And now, here she was, holding his hand as if they were lovers of long standing. He might be in his shirt-sleeves, barefoot, unshaven and tousle-haired, but he was still infinitely desirable. How could she have forgotten just how handsome he was? He smiled at her and she felt her insides become liquid.

Leander turned her hand over and began to trace light, intricate patterns on her palm. She tried to stop her hand from trembling.

'So tell me, Caroline. What brings you here?'

She had practised her reply to this inevitable question. 'Why, I thought it would be amusing to visit the goldfields,' she would say, accompanied by a light laugh and a shrug. 'I got bored with the hotel and wanted to travel before returning to Sydney. What a surprise to see *you* here…' That was what she *should* have said.

Instead, she swallowed hard and whispered, 'I missed you.'

His eyes lit up and he brought her hand to his lips. 'I missed you, too. God, Caroline, you have no idea how much I missed you.'

'I think I have,' she said shakily. 'I didn't mean

those things I said to you, and I'm sorry I charged you for the vase when I was the one who threw it, and—'

'Ssh,' he said softly, shaking his head. 'That's all in the past. This is now. It's a new beginning in a new place. We're allowed to start afresh here, you know.'

'Are we?' Her breathing seemed suddenly terribly constricted by her stays. 'And how do we do that?'

'I'm looking forward to showing you how very, very soon,' he said against her fingers, and the heat of his breath against her skin and the sensuous promise of his words sent a jolt of pure desire through her. The arrival of their tea saved her from having to give him a coherent answer.

'How's Charlotte? Have you heard?' He released her hand and sat back, putting on a show of polite social conversation for the benefit of the waitress as she arranged cups and saucers before them.

'She…she's well,' Caro began and then stopped, reluctant to tell him yet about the real reason she had fled Dunedin. She would tell him about Charlotte marrying Harold when she was sure they were friends again. No, when they were more than friends; when they were lovers, husband and wife in the truest sense of the word. They would probably talk about it in bed, and he would make her laugh about it as he always did…

'I'm pleased that she's on the mend. And have you had any word from Harold Thwaites?' he asked, as if reading her thoughts.

'Thank you,' Caro addressed the waitress, and busied herself picking up the teapot. 'And—good heavens—a whole plate of sandwiches. Just as well I'm hungry!'

'Well, eat them all up, then,' Leander said and

grinned wickedly. 'You're going to need all your energy later.'

She found it close on impossible to eat anything after that promise, and so she simply drank two cups of tea and nibbled on a single sandwich while Leander ate the rest. The tearoom was beginning to fill with customers; mostly farmers' wives, she guessed, in town to do some shopping and have lunch.

'It's a much bigger town than I had expected,' she confided to Leander over her teacup. 'I had expected a rough sort of mining town, but this is quite civilised!'

'Compared to all the other canvas towns out here, this is a metropolis,' he agreed. 'I think the difference is that when Queenstown's gold ran out, the farmers moved in, together with their wives and children. And where you have women, you have civilisation.'

She fought back a surge of jealousy at his words. Of course there were other women out here, she had known that! But she had heard that men still outnumbered women in the goldfields by forty to one, and Leander had only been here for a matter of months… There wouldn't have been another woman, surely? Not when he had been so patently delighted at her appearance in Queenstown?

She drew little whorls on the tablecloth with her teaspoon and said with studied casualness, 'And what have you been doing out here? Here it is the middle of the day and you look as if you've just woken up. Do you have a job? Some form of gainful employment?'

'Me? A job?' He laughed out loud. 'You should know me better than that, Caroline.'

'Oh. But you're not…?' She scowled as he nodded ruefully and shrugged.

'That's how I earn my living. I know you disapprove, but gambling is a lucrative business. Especially out here.'

'Really?' She concentrated on keeping the teaspoon pattern even. Getting out to the goldfields had been unexpectedly expensive, and—if the truth be known— she had barely enough in her purse to cover afternoon tea. 'And…just how lucrative would that be?'

He didn't answer, and when she looked up he was studying her in amusement, a teasing smile twisting the corners of his mouth. She flushed and looked away, realising that he knew her far too well.

'Money is important,' she muttered defiantly.

'Money is boring,' he said softly. 'Let's go to bed.'

They walked across the road to the hotel in silence, Leander carrying her suitcase, Caro with her hands held tightly before her. She followed him through the side door and up the stairs. At the door to his room he put down the case and turned to her.

'You're sure about this, Caroline? There's no going back from this.'

'I'm sure,' she whispered. 'I've never been more sure about anything in my life.'

'Coming from you, that's quite a statement,' he said unevenly, and bent to kiss her. She gave a little sob of pleasure as her mouth opened under his, and she pressed herself hard against him, wanting him with a shocking desperation.

'Not out here, sweetheart,' he said, snatching his breath between kisses. 'I suppose I should carry you over the threshold or something…'

'Takes too long,' she muttered, pulling at the buttons on his shirt. 'Just open the door.'

Freeing one hand from under her jacket, he wrestled with the door handle and kicked the door open. They

staggered inside and Leander pressed her against the
wall as he shut the door with his foot. There was no
space between them for Caro to continue opening his
shirt, so her hands dropped instead to his belt, anxious
as she was to uncover whatever it was that was pushing
so excitingly against her thighs. As her fingers brushed
over him, he made a sound at the back of his throat, a
sound of impatience and desire and loss of control that
thrilled her immeasurably. There was no thought of
modesty now; when he pulled back far enough to drag
up her skirts she assisted him with alacrity, her hands
trembling uncontrollably.

Over the harsh sound of their breathing she heard a
muffled squeak.

Breaking free from Leander's mouth, she peered
over his shoulder to the bed, where a very pretty, rus-
set-haired young woman was sitting, clutching the
sheets to her naked bosom, her eyes and mouth as wide
as saucers.

Sensing Caro's frigid withdrawal, Leander turned to
look behind him.

'Oh, hell!' he muttered.

Caro felt her world fall apart. With a strength she
would never have thought herself capable of, she thrust
him away so hard that he hit the foot of the bed and
nearly fell backwards on to it. The girl on the bed automatically put out a hand to steady him and it took
all of Caro's self-control not to rush over and slap both
their faces.

There was a very long silence.

'Caroline, this is not what it looks like,' Leander said
unsteadily. 'You've got to let me explain…'

'Oh, do I, indeed?' she said icily, wrapping her arms
around her shoulders so as not to betray their trem-

bling. 'You have an explanation for why this…this *person* is in your bed? Let me guess, now. This is the wrong room, perhaps? Or maybe this is the maid, come to make the bed, and she decided to take a little nap, and take her clothes off while she was at it?' She stopped as Leander and the girl on the bed began nodding hard in agreement. 'That's *it*?' she demanded incredulously. '*That's* your explanation?'

'That's pretty much what happened,' Leander said tentatively, and the girl on the bed, obviously very close to tears, nodded even harder.

'It's true, missus. He told me to get out, but I thought he was joking, so I fell asleep waiting for him to come back, and—'

'Oh, shut up!' Caro snarled, turning on her. 'Shut up and get out. No, don't bother dressing, just get out!'

'Caroline,' Leander began in a conciliatory tone.

'And you shut up, too!' she hissed. 'I'm not going to stand here and listen to a whole pack of lies from you.'

His mouth thinned at that and he unwisely compounded his sins by showing his temper. 'This is not my fault. I *told* her to leave as soon as I saw you get off the ferry—'

Caro's hand slapping against his mouth silenced him.

'You bastard!'

'Yeah.' Molly flung a corner of the sheet over her shoulder, toga-style and glared up at him. 'You deserve that, and more besides. That's her picture downstairs, isn't it? Aw, how could you? Your own missus? You *are* a rotten bastard!' And she smacked him with equal velocity on the other side of his face before exiting the room with surprising aplomb.

For a long moment they stared at each other and then, as Leander opened his mouth to speak, Caro shoved him with all her force out the door, slamming and locking it loudly. Then, with legs that could barely support her, she dragged herself over to the bedside chair and sat down, heavily.

What a fool she had been. All these weeks of missing him, of wondering what would have happened if she had acted differently, of imagining him thinking of her, longing for her...just as she had been longing for him. She had risked everything to come to find him in Central Otago: her pride, her independence and the last of her money. And now to find that, all this time, he had been lolling around in bed with that...that *floozy!*

A single, long red hair lay on the pillow. With a shudder of distaste she got up and began systematically stripping the bed, rolling the remaining polluted sheet up into a bundle for washing. So what if her husband had turned out to have the sexual habits of a rabbit? When he brought his next conquest up to his room— no doubt in a matter of hours—at least he and his *amour* would be met with nothing but a bare mattress. And even *that* was too good for them! She seized the edge of the mattress and hoisted it off the bed.

A saddlebag slipped to the floor.

Not the most original of hiding places, Caro thought, as she picked it up and opened the side flap. The idiot deserved to lose his money, if that was the best he could come up with. However, at first glance the packet she pulled out was too big to contain money—it was carefully wrapped in a square of canvas, and she took it to be his painting materials. She took one corner and shook it violently.

A cascade of bank notes fluttered gently to the floor.

Sinking to her knees, she ran her hands through the paper, wondering how much there was; typically, Leander had not bothered sorting the money into denominations. She started counting, but there was still a huge pile left after the first thousand. Then, she remembered to look in the other side pocket of the saddlebag, where there was an identical packet.

Eventually she sat back on her heels, her head reeling with figures. Four thousand, three hundred and sixty-two pounds, exactly. An absolute fortune and all of it, she had no doubt, ill-gotten gains from the gambling tables. The lazy, good-for-nothing philanderer had been here for seven weeks, and already he had more money than she had ever seen in her life. And she, who had worked so hard and risked so much, had no more than a guinea left in the world. Oh, but life was so unfair!

With sudden resolve she counted out two hundred pounds and folded them neatly inside her reticule. She was entitled to it, surely, after the humiliation of this afternoon. Now she could return to Dunedin and take the first ship back to Sydney, back to her family, back to the life of comfort and security she had always known. No one need know about what had happened here, or her disastrous marriage…

Except for Charlotte and Mr Matthews. Mr Matthews, at least, would feel bound to enlighten her parents as to what she had been up to in New Zealand. Besides, it was a fact that the truth always seemed to catch up with you one way or the other. Her marriage of convenience, which had seemed such an ideal solution at the time, was going to be an albatross around her neck for the rest of her life. She could never be single, carefree Caroline Morgan again.

She tried to cheer herself up by reflecting that at least she had not made the mistake of consummating her marriage, although not for lack of trying. She could always get it annulled, as had been her original plan, and be free once again. No longer bound to a man she detested.

And as the said detested man was no doubt still on the other side of the bedroom door, that brought her back to the immediate problem of how to get out of Queenstown. The stairs were out of the question—he would stop her and make a scene. Worse, he might demand his money back. The window, however, was a possibility, opening as it did on to the first-floor veranda. She pulled it open and, pulling her skirts over her knees, climbed out.

It was a twenty-foot drop down to the main street below. Not an impossible feat by any means, especially if she made a rope from the bedsheets. However, with dozens of people on the road at any time, it would have to be a very public feat. Already the sight of her standing there on the veranda was attracting attention. One man had stopped in his tracks in the middle of the road and was staring at her, open-mouthed. As he called over a companion to join him, she beat a hasty retreat, embarrassed by his rudeness.

It was no good. Even if she waited until night, when it was quiet, Leander would be bound to hear her. Besides, if one wanted to avoid weeks of travelling, the ferry was the only quick way out of Queenstown, and he would easily find her if she tried to board tomorrow.

Tense with misery, she huddled on the chair, rocking back and forth in an agony of indecision. She needed to leave and she needed to leave with money. And it rather looked as if the only way she could do that was by being pleasant to her husband.

Caro didn't think she could bring herself to do that.

Chapter Twelve

The shadows were lengthening when she at last opened the door. Stretched out at ease at the top of the stairs, Leander looked up from the book he was reading.

'Good evening,' he said politely.

'You're still here.'

'So it would seem.' He closed the book with deliberation, turning down the corner of the page to mark his place—a practice Caro had always thought was odious. 'Are you hungry?'

She hesitated, but then thought there could be no harm in confirming the obvious. 'Yes.'

'I've ordered dinner for seven o'clock. Would you like some hot water to wash before that? Do you need me to show you where the outhouse is?'

'I am perfectly capable of finding my way around.' She flounced past him, down the stairs. Afterwards, being in no hurry to return, she wandered down to the lake edge afterwards to ask what time the ferry for Kingston left the next morning. The news that the first departure of the day was at six pleased her. Leander would most certainly still be sleeping soundly at that hour, and it should be no trouble at all for her to quietly slip out, now that she had money in her purse again.

She returned to the hotel bedroom to find a spare, tired-looking woman making up the bed with fresh linen. A jug of hot water steamed gently on the wash-stand beside a pile of towels. As she stood uncertainly in the doorway the woman stood up, brushing her hair away from her face with the back of her hand.

'Mrs Gray? I'm Mrs Watkins, the landlady. Your husband asked me to set the room to rights and…' Her voice trailed away as she took in Caro's appearance. Caro automatically checked that her dress was straight and wondered if she had a smudge on her nose.

'Mrs Watkins?' she ventured after a moment, as the landlady continued to stare. 'Is everything all right?'

The woman shook herself and began to briskly thump the feather pillows into shape. 'Everything's fine, Mrs Gray. I just think your husband has some explaining to do, that's all.'

So she knew. No doubt all of Queenstown knew about Leander's amorous habits. Caro squared her shoulders. She was not prepared to be an object of pity, however blatant her husband's indiscretions.

'You will understand then, Mrs Watkins, why I couldn't possibly stay in this room.'

The landlady nodded. 'Right enough. Your husband asked me to put you in the room next door. There's fresh linen and hot water waiting for you there, and Mr Gray took your luggage in there himself but ten minutes ago.'

What was he up to? Caro checked the next room. It was as pleasant as the first room, and as ready for oc-cupation. Beside the bed a bowl of lusciously pink pe-onies glowed in the last of the sun. She touched the petals lightly with her fingers, wondering who had been responsible for the thoughtful gesture. Leander knew how much she loved flowers.

Her stomach contracted painfully and she remembered that it had been a long time since her last decent meal. She might as well take up Leander's offer of dinner, if he was paying for it; she didn't have to talk to him, after all, and she could simply ignore whatever lies tripped so easily out of his mouth. It must be close to seven o'clock now, and she was going to have to hurry if she wanted to wash and change before dinner.

Should she bother dressing up? After a moment's hesitation, she opened her valise and carefully took out the beautiful, pale green evening dress, wrapped in tissue paper, that she had concocted from a number of Charlotte's discarded gowns. Spreading it out on the bed, she was relieved to see how well it had travelled. With her hair pulled up and perhaps fastened with one of Charlotte's diamante broaches, she would look very well, indeed, and hopefully much better than Molly wearing nothing but a sheet. Dining with her husband was going to be an ordeal, but she might as well show him what he was missing out on! She turned to take her toiletry case out of the valise and stopped.

Her reticule. Surely she hadn't put it inside the valise? No, she clearly remembered leaving it on the floor beside it. Then she had gone downstairs, and Leander had…

'Looking for this?' her husband inquired lazily and she looked up to see him lounging in the doorway, her reticule swinging between his fingers.

'That's mine!' she said automatically, a split second before she registered the fury glittering in his half-closed eyes.

'It is. But what's inside it is mine.' He tossed it to her. 'Or rather, what *was* inside it.'

'You had no right to look inside my purse! I was entitled to that money!'

'Entitled?' He walked in and closed the door behind him. Caro gulped and moved behind the bed. She had never realised before how tall he was. 'And in what way were you entitled to it, Caroline? If you were my wife in more than just name, I might consider sharing my money with you—or I might not. I don't have to, after all. But you're not my wife. You've *chosen* not to be my wife. You're not my business partner, you're not my employee, you've not made me a loan…' He shrugged. 'So, Caroline Gray. Tell me *why* you feel entitled to two hundred pounds of my money.'

She gripped the bed-end with both hands, and the chill of the metal steadied her. 'I…I came all the way out here in good faith, Leander. I wanted to be with you! I wanted to start again! And you…you were with that trollop…'

'Molly is not a trollop,' he said tersely. 'She is a very nice girl that I slept with before I was married to you—'

'So you admit it!'

'*Before* I was married to you,' he continued, each word bitten out with chilly precision. 'I did a lot of things before I got married, none of which seemed to matter a damn to you when you hired me as your husband. To become hysterical over them now seems somewhat hypocritical, don't you think? I never asked you about your background when I accepted your offer. I agreed to our bargain because I needed money. It was only later that I realised that I cared for you. I cared about what happened to you. Do you really want to throw all that away, over something that you *think* happened here? Because nothing did happen here. I've not been unfaithful to you, Caroline.'

She stood uncertainly, wondering if he was, indeed, speaking with a relentless logic or if it simply seemed that way because she so desperately wanted to believe that the things he was telling her were true. They *had* to be true. He couldn't say the things he was and meet her eyes the way he was—unwavering, unblinking, intense… She was being mesmerised, she thought helplessly, like a rabbit caught in the stare of a snake. Or a professional gambler.

Just in time she stopped the abject apology about to leave her lips. 'I know what I saw,' she said coldly. 'A naked woman, in your bed, waiting for *you*. Don't you dare try to convince me otherwise. I am not stupid.'

'Aren't you?' he said shortly.

'No. What if it had been me in another man's bed? Would you have accepted the sort of explanation you're trying to give me?'

Just for a second his eyes blazed and then, to her huge relief, a look of amusement softened his face. 'You're right. I wouldn't have believed it, either. No matter how innocent you were.' The sound of a door being quietly closed in the hallway reminded both of them where they were and he lowered his voice. 'But it would seem to me, Caroline, that I'm more committed to this…this marriage of convenience than you are. Why the hell you came all the way out here to be with me, I don't know. You seem to want the sexual benefits of a marriage, but not the emotional closeness, the sharing, that marriage means.'

'You're a fine one to talk,' she broke in, her face scarlet, 'when just one minute ago you were resenting the paltry hundred pounds I took from your saddle-bags!'

'*Two* hundred pounds.'

She tossed her head. 'I thought you said money wasn't important.'

'It's not.'

'So why won't you share any of your money with me?'

Anger flickered again in his eyes. 'Caroline, until you learn that *sharing* does not necessarily refer exclusively to money or possessions, this marriage doesn't stand a chance. You're a strong woman, and you're used to getting your own way. That can be great fun in bed, but when you start treating me like some paid underling, fit only to do your bidding, I'm afraid I lose all enthusiasm. This is a partnership, Caroline. Not a business with you in charge and me in paid employment.'

Caro sank down on to the bed. 'You make me sound so mercenary,' she said in a small voice. 'But you're wrong! I'm not like that at all...'

'Yes, you are,' he said gently. 'And I know you very well, Caroline. But I don't think you know me.'

She opened her mouth to argue, but the truth of his statement struck her like a lightning bolt. How many occasions had there been in the past when he had given her the opportunity to ask about his past and she had wilfully ignored it? Intent on maintaining what she had regarded as a strictly business arrangement, she had refused to show anything other than complete uninterest in her husband's past.

Leander looked down at his wife's bowed head, fighting the impulse to kiss away the tears glimmering under her eyelashes. 'Caroline,' he said after a very long moment, 'let's talk about this after we've had dinner. I'll come back in fifteen minutes, shall I?'

After he had gone she sat motionlesss, blindly staring at the wall. How could things have changed so much? Leander was only supposed to have supplied her with a name and financial respectability. She had never wanted to see him again. Then, he became simply an extra pair of hands about the place. Just when had he become the centre of her universe?

She had made the wrong choice of man, obviously. But was it a bad choice? She shook her head at that. Leander was too beautiful, too talented and clever to ever be a bad choice for any woman. She thought of Molly, of Charlotte, of prune-faced Mrs Froggatt, of every woman who had ever met and been charmed by Leander. But he was married to *her*, and she could either drive him away and into the arms of other women, or make her marriage work.

'I choose to make it work,' she said loudly to the empty room, and it was as if a load had suddenly lifted from her shoulders. She moved over to the washstand and poured the water into the wash basin, scarcely registering that it was now cold. Dinner was going to be interesting.

He was waiting for her at the foot of the stairs, dressed in a dark suit she had never seen on him before, but which emphasised his lean elegance. She noted his lack of a cravat and wondered if she was perhaps too formally dressed, but then decided that the open admiration in his eyes was worth it. He took her hand as she reached the bottom stair and raised her fingers to his mouth.

'You look absolutely beautiful. Quite ravishable.'

'You mean ravishing.'

'No, I don't.'

She nodded coolly and took her hand back, determined not to be provoked. She had already convinced herself to approach tonight with an open mind. If, indeed, Molly's appearance in her husband's bed was as innocent as he claimed, the least she could do was listen to him and try to resurrect what there was left of their marriage. Besides, she wanted the two hundred pounds back.

He picked up a large wicker basket and offered her his arm.

'Shall we go?'

She hesitated before accepting his arm. 'I thought we were going to have dinner now?'

'We are. Mrs Watkins has packed us a picnic dinner. I thought we could eat it down by the lake. I have a blanket, so you won't spoil that beautiful dress.' He looked down at the uncertain expression on her face. 'We do need to talk privately, Caroline, if we are to sort things out between us.'

Ah, but there was a difference between being private, and being perfectly isolated, with her estranged husband. But he smiled beguilingly, and tugged on her arm and—wisely or foolishly, she could not tell—she went with him down to the lake.

They walked along a path away from the township, to a small, rocky outcrop on the very lakefront. While the sun had already disappeared behind the towering Remarkable Range, the air was still and warm and held a strange, lingering glow.

'The twilights here in summer last for hours,' Leander explained, when she commented on it. 'In another couple of weeks—around Christmas—we'll only have darkness for around four hours. It's really very pleasant.'

'So this is not the first summer you've spent in Central Otago,' she surmised, helping him spread the blanket over the ground.

'It will be my second summer here.' He took her hand and helped her sit gracefully on the ground, as if he knew that her too-tightly laced stays made that manoeuvre difficult. She silently cursed the vanity that had made her pinch in her waist to such an uncomfortable degree, but at least it had the effect of keeping her sitting straight-backed and avoided the impression that she welcomed any change in the formality between them.

He opened the picnic hamper and revealed the many delights inside. Crusty rolls, still warm, with butter and cheese to accompany them. Small lamb pies, a medley of vegetables in aspic, a dish of tiny meringues joined with cream and even a basket of early but perfectly ripe strawberries.

'And to wash it down with, a bottle of Mrs Watkins's finest ginger beer,' Leander announced, pulling out two wine glasses. He pulled the stopper out of the stone bottle and sniffed the contents with a grimace. 'For which I apologise.'

'I'm sure it will be delicious.' She accepted a glass. 'Had you asked for champagne?'

'No, I hadn't. I haven't drunk alcohol in months, Caroline.' His eyes met hers squarely. 'I realised that the price was too high to pay.'

She recalled, all too vividly, the occasion on which he had reached that realisation, and her face flamed at the memory. 'Do you miss it?' she surprised herself by asking.

'The alcohol? No. I feel better, I can think straight, I even draw better. Everything is clearer now.'

'So—why did you start?'

He was silent for so long that she thought he had either not heard her or was choosing to ignore the question. But at last he sighed and settled back against the blanket. Overhead, pale stars were struggling for visibility in an opaque sky.

'When you're the youngest son of a titled family,' he began slowly, 'and you know you will never have any hope of inheriting, you don't have a lot of choices. You can go into the army or into the church, and neither of those appealed in the least. I was hopeless at my lessons, so there went any chance of a government post. All I really wanted to do was enjoy myself and draw—or scribble as my family called it.

'I ran off to Paris when I was twenty and spent two marvellous years there, learning how to draw and paint, and it was there I started to drink too heavily. But even living the life of a starving artist in a garret costs, and eventually I had to go home again. My family had had enough of me by then, so I was given a ticket to the farthermost colony and told not to bother coming back. I'd always been good at cards, and out here I got all the practice I needed to become very, very good at it. I spent my nights gambling and drinking, and eventually one just took over the other. When I ran out of money I went to Dunedin to winter over and…well, it was all downhill from there. I suppose I just didn't see the point in…well, *anything*.'

Caro sat and thought that through. 'I don't feel in the least bit sorry for you, you know,' she said eventually and Leander laughed.

'I don't expect you to. I've spent my life doing exactly as I pleased, when I pleased, and to hell with everyone else. Eventually, of course, I had to pay the price for it. But just at this moment, under a starry Otago sky, with the most beautiful woman in the world next to me and a bottle of Mrs Watkins's finest ginger beer in my hand, I don't feel in the least bit punished. Quite the opposite, in fact.'

It was the nicest compliment Caro could ever remember receiving, but she resisted the urge to reach out to him, reminding herself that he really was impossible, and possessed of no redeeming features.

'So, you really are an aristocrat?' she asked, intrigued.

'I am, for what that's worth.'

'Well, I suppose that explains why you are utterly useless at looking after yourself and holding down a job. I expect you had servants to save you from having to lift a finger when you were growing up. And you really don't have a title?'

'My eldest brother gets that. I'm a plain Mr.' He looked at her in mock apology. 'Sorry.'

'Oh, don't worry about that.' She waved a hand in airy dismissal. 'I think titles are pretentious and unnecessary. But your family—don't you miss them?'

'No more than they would be missing me. They are all very nice people, and I don't deserve them. I'm quite happy without them.'

'But to leave behind wealth and position…'

'And all the strings that go with it. That's the beauty of coming to a place like New Zealand, don't you see? No one knows you, there are no expectations. You can be—you can *become*—anything you like. Your mistakes, bad as they may be, are at least your own.'

'But your parents must worry about you, Leander, and wonder what trouble you've got into—'

'Like your parents?' he shot back. 'Caroline, my family asked me very nicely but very firmly to go away and leave them alone. From what I gather, you left your family in a fit of pique, so you can hardly preach to me about filial duty.'

'I suppose not,' she allowed after a moment.

'Besides—' he rolled over and took her hand '—I think my parents would very much approve of you. Not only do you have character, you're by far the most beautiful of their daughters-in-law.'

'Am I?' she asked coyly.

'Oh, yes. There's a tendency to chinlessness in my family, and as my brothers have mostly married women with buck teeth, I have very unfortunate-looking nieces and nephews. My mother breeds lurchers, and she knows a good blood-line when she sees one. She'd take one look at you and order me to start reproducing immediately.'

'*Leander!*' Caro gasped between giggles, clutching her corseted sides to stop the aching. 'No wonder they asked you to leave the country! You *are* horrible.'

He kept her alternately amused and appalled throughout the rest of dinner and, by the time they packed up the remainder of their meal, she felt completely at ease in his company and far happier than she had been in a long time. Hand in hand, they strolled along the shore to the twinkling lights of Queenstown. The sky had by now darkened to purple, but by starlight and a sliver of the moon they could see their way perfectly.

Caro gave a sigh of contentment and leaned her head against Leander's shoulder as they walked.

'It is so beautiful here. Have you tried painting it?'

'Many times, but even if I capture it on canvas, it always looks too incredible to be real. I've decided to stick to pencil sketches and stop insulting Nature.'

She smiled against his arm and said, without thinking, 'How long are we staying here?'

'We?' he queried gently. 'So you're not planning to clean out my wallet again and run off?'

She stiffened. 'It was scarcely taking your last penny, Leander. You have thousands of pounds there! Why don't you put it in the bank, where it's safe, if you are so concerned about it?'

'A large deposit like that, in a small town like this, would be remarked upon, and I don't think it expedient to let people know too much about how I make my living and how much of a living I make.' He looked at her askance. 'And you didn't answer my question.'

They had spent the entire evening talking about everything but Molly and the question of Leander's lack of fidelity. By now, however, she was very inclined to believe him; he was so open about so much of his life that it was almost impossible to think of him lying about something so important. But there remained the problem of money. Caro did not enjoy poverty, and did not think she should endure it when her husband was so flush with funds. She withdrew her arm from his on the pretext of adjusting her jacket and did not replace it.

They returned to the hotel in silence, and outside her bedroom door he bent and kissed her forehead. 'Goodnight, Caroline.'

'Goodnight, Leander.' She watched him go back down the stairs, presumably to return the picnic hamper to Mrs Watkins. He could have at least tried to talk her into going into his room with him, she thought. Perhaps he intended coming to her later? But she rather thought that the kiss he had deposited on her forehead was too brotherly for that.

An elderly man, smelling of strong liquor, began making his way a little unsteadily up the stairs. He tipped his hat to her automatically.

'Evening, miss.' His steps slowed to a halt and his face under the battered felt hat furrowed as he peered at her. ''Scuse me, miss, but don't I know you?'

'I don't think so. Good evening to you.' She quickly stepped inside her room and shut the door. There was no lock on it, unfortunately, but she pushed her travelling case against it, so that she would at least have notice if someone attempted to enter during the night. What strange men there were in this town! she mused, as she undressed. There were enough women around, surely, for them not to gawk so obviously at a new arrival.

She slipped between the sheets and lay staring at the ceiling, running the evening's conversation with Leander through her mind. Was he telling the truth, or was she simply desperate to believe him? She ran her thumb back and forth across her thin gold wedding ring—recalling that it had been the cheapest she had been able to find—and wondered why she was so determined to save her marriage. What kind of marriage was it, after all? A sham, a paper marriage of convenience... Then she thought of Leander, of his humour and kindness and occasional flashes of common sense. Of how he cared for her and supported her. And of how, at this moment, he was probably lying in bed, just a wall away. She wondered if he was thinking of her.

Was he also remembering that afternoon? Her shamelessness, the way she had all but dragged him across the road and up to his room to ravish him? If only Molly hadn't been there, everything would have been perfect. By now, she would have been a wife in every sense of the word. She would be lying next to Leander, knowing all the mysteries of what happened between a husband and a wife, ecstatic or perhaps disappointed…

No, she decided firmly. Never disappointed, not with Leander as a lover. She recalled the odd, secret little look her parents would exchange sometimes in the evening, prior to calling it an early night. Had her mother ever felt like this about her father? It was an appalling thought, but did explain her own existence and that of her sisters.

Would she ever have children with Leander? She began to think of them—fair-haired, obviously, with either her blue eyes or Leander's brown—when she shook herself out of her absurdity. What *was* she doing? Planning a lifetime with a man whom that very afternoon she had been convinced was bedding every woman in Otago! And yet…

'Oh, Caro, you stupid girl,' she whispered into the darkness. 'You've gone and fallen in love with him.'

She had always detested her younger sisters' sentimental discourses on love, dismissing them as little more than infatuations but now, in the grip of just such a passion, she wished she had not been so quick to sneer. She was guilty of precisely the sort of irrational acts for which she had so roundly condemned others. Instead of sensibly returning to Sydney and immediately filing for divorce, she had spent her last few pounds coming all the way out here to see him. She had let her heart rule her head, and that was a foolish, foolish mistake because now the balance of power had shifted very firmly in his favour.

She needed money of her own. Leander's talk of the need for honesty and trust and sharing in a marriage was all very well, but sentiment was not going to pay the bills should he lose all his money on the tables one day. Besides, without money she was going to be completely reliant on her husband and his whims, and the very thought of that was intolerable.

A surge of male voices in the bar below broke into her reverie. The bar must be doing a good trade, she thought absently, and then her head cleared. Customers needed serving. If she could run an hotel, then surely she could run a bar successfully? Mrs Watkins had looked weary and overworked, and if Molly was the type to fall asleep in guests' beds, she did not deserve employment; Caro was sure she could outwork her any day of the week. She turned over, thumped her pillow into a comfortable shape and prepared for sleep. First thing in the morning, she would go downstairs and ask for a job.

The rising sun had turned the tips of the Remarkables burnished gold by the time she awoke. After washing and dressing, she stood by the window for a while, wondering at the way the light shimmered on the dark blue water of Lake Whakatipu and how the stark brown contours of the ranges softened in the brilliant dawn. The sight was so heart-wrenchingly lovely that she found the breath catching in her throat. It took the arrival of the early-morning ferry at the dock to remind her that time was slipping away.

There was no sound from behind the door of Leander's room as she passed on tiptoe, and she assumed that he was still asleep. Confirmation that he was sleeping alone came when she met Molly, bearing jugs of hot water, at the foot of the stairs.

The maid coloured brightly and managed a bob. 'Missus.'

'Good morning,' she responded coolly and went to pass, but Molly remained firmly in her way. Caro eyed her warily. Molly was a remarkably pretty girl, and the thought of her and Leander together was physically painful. 'What do you want?'

'I…I wanted to tell you, missus, that…well, nothing happened yesterday,' Molly said hesitantly. 'We used to, afore…well, afore he came back to Queenstown and said he was married now, and couldn't no more, and…it was me what got into his bed and he begged me to get out but I didn't believe him when he said he was married and then I fell asleep and—'

Caro held up her hand. 'Please don't continue, Molly, I don't want to hear it. I've discussed this with Leander, and I have decided to forget the matter. If, indeed, what you say is true, then I trust it will never happen again.'

Molly sniffed loudly, her huge blue eyes bright with unshed tears. 'It won't. Oh, I was ever so embarrassed…'

Caught unexpectedly with sympathy, Caro almost smiled. 'You weren't the only one, believe me.'

'I s'pose not.' Molly sniffed again and then regarded Caro askance. 'Funny thing, though. You're not anything like what I thought he'd choose to marry.'

Forgiveness of her husband's ex-mistress was one thing, but allowing her to indulge in personal comments was quite another. Caro inclined her head, said an abrupt good morning and walked on. To her shame, however, she stopped around the corner, out of sight and peered back up the stairs to see just where Molly was taking that hot water. It was, she saw to her relief, to the room across the hallway from Leander's room.

She found the way to the bar room with no trouble and let herself in, wrinkling her nose as she did so at the pervading smell of spilt alcohol and stale tobacco smoke. It was, she decided, much to the same standard as the Castledene bar, which was the only other public bar she had ever entered. There was a wide wooden bar, and groups of tables at which men could sit and drink and gamble in comfort. A large fireplace would provide comfort in winter and welcome ventilation in the height of summer. The light in here was dim, due to the patterned window-glass, but she supposed at night the room would be light and cheerful.

The wooden floor looked reasonably clean, and she was pleased that Mrs Watkins ran the sort of establishment that was swept out at the end of the evening. There were rows of glasses set out on the wide bar in readiness for the evening's customers, and she moved over to pick one up to check its cleanliness.

Dust motes hung in the rays of sunshine slanting through the unfrosted glass of the upper windows. On the wall behind the bar the gilt frame of a large painting glittered, momentarily blinding her. She stepped forward, blinking, to peer up at it.

The oil painting was of a young nude, reclining on an unmade bed. One of her outstretched arms lay beneath her languid head, the other rested casually over her breasts. Her slightly upraised knee and the rumpled sheets saved her from complete immodesty, and it was far from being the most explicit portrait of a nude that

Caro had ever seen. Rather, it was the way the woman lay and the expression on her face that made the painting so outrageously erotic.

She looked as though she had woken from a sensuous dream to find her lover, naked and aroused, standing by her bed. Her eyes were shining with desire and not a small amount of mischief. The smile on her parted lips was eager, but self-assured. Her fingers were extended in invitation, ready to touch and stroke and explore. The artist had caught her at the very moment of surrender, just as she was about to open herself up to her lover. A wanton, uninhibited mistress, supremely confident in her own sexuality. A Venus welcoming her Adonis.

A Venus with Caro's face, hair and body.

Even with no one else to witness her shock, she felt herself flush hotly. She didn't need to check the artist's signature at the bottom of the painting to know who was responsible for it. How could he have done this to her? Every man who had ever drunk in this bar would have gazed at her, at her naked body, her face caught in wordless passion… No wonder men in this town stopped and openly stared at her! They had all—hundreds of them, perhaps!—seen her as intimately as any lover.

Yet Leander had never seen her naked, a small voice of reason reminded her. He had touched and kissed her, certainly, but only in the dark. How could he possibly know what she looked like? She studied the painting more closely, as pangs of suspicion and jealousy gnawed at her.

At last she released her breath. No, it definitely wasn't her. Her husband had painted her face on the body of someone completely different. No doubt it had been Molly who had lain there like that and let him paint her so intimately…

Except that she would swear that it wasn't Molly's body, either. The breasts were smaller and higher, the legs and waist were longer. But if it wasn't Molly's, whose was it?

The only thing that Caro knew about works of art was that they were useful things to hang on the wall, but even she could appreciate that this was a good painting. It was better than good. Leander's brush had captured all the lush curves, the play of light, the satiny texture of the skin. The woman in the painting was so skilfully drawn that one almost expected her to be breathing. And she was *beautiful*. Whatever Leander's motives for painting her, whatever inspiration he had drawn upon, every brush stroke was a sincere compliment to its subject. She could only be sorry that Leander had chosen such a public place to demonstrate his admiration.

She stepped back to view it from a greater distance and nearly jumped out of her skin as she met the solidity and warmth of another body behind her.

Leander put his hands around her waist before she could spin around. 'Well, you haven't run screaming from the room,' he observed softly into her ear. 'Or are you looking about for something to throw at me?'

'Both courses of action appeal,' she said coolly. She stood rigid beneath his hands, neither melting into his touch nor moving away. 'No wonder every man in Queenstown has been staring at me so peculiarly. How *could* you, Leander? Depicting me like that, without a shred of modesty, for every miner in Central Otago to see. And that's not even my body! Who did you get to model for you?'

'No one.' He bent his head so that his words fell warm and soft on the back of her neck. 'The only model I used was my memory of you. That's you as I imagine you to be under your clothes. Soft and sensuous and smooth…'

'Then you have an incredible imagination,' she snapped, pushing his hand down as it began to wander up from her waist. Much as she wanted to believe him, she wasn't sure that she did. 'What I don't understand is why. Why here, in this place?'

He lifted his shoulders. 'I arrived here with very little money. I needed to pay for my lodgings, and a stake to start playing with, and Mrs Watkins thought a portrait of Venus over the bar would be a great drawcard. If I'd known that you were going to arrive unannounced…'

Caro turned around, her eyes narrowed. 'How much?'

'I beg your pardon?'

'How much did you get paid for it?'

He hesitated. 'Two hundred guineas.'

'I see,' she said neutrally, and looked back up at the painting. 'Two hundred guineas.'

There was a long silence while Leander held his breath, waiting for the inevitable outburst. It didn't come.

'You're not as angry as I thought you'd be,' he said eventually, trying not to sound relieved. When he had painted the portrait, over two frenzied days of loneliness and frustrated desire, the last thing on his mind was that he would soon be standing here, beneath that same painting, trying to justify it to its subject.

Now it was her turn to shrug. 'Because at least you made a reasonable amount of money out of it. I would have been absolutely furious if you'd sold my portrait for anything less.'

She twisted around in his arms and gave a short, rueful laugh at the stunned expression on his face. 'Which makes me no better than you, does it?'

He expelled his breath slowly. 'No. It makes you a great deal better than me. Whether you knew about it or not, I should never have used you as a model. I was thoughtless, selfish and unwise—'

'But you're also a gifted artist,' she broke in. 'Even though you have taken considerable artistic license; the body in that painting is not even remotely like mine.'

'Really?' he said in dismay, and she cuffed him lightly for the look of profound disappointment on his face. Then she kissed him for his talent and the extraordinary compliment he had inadvertently paid her. And then she kissed him again, for the pure pleasure of it.

'Mr Gray! And…Mrs Gray?' The landlady stopped short in the doorway. She put down her bucket and mop to plant her hands on her hips. 'I rent out rooms for that kind of thing, you know.'

The amusement in her voice took the sting from her words, and Leander and Caro stepped apart with a smile.

'That's a point,' he mused, looking at her askance. 'What are you doing down here in the bar, Caroline? And at such an unsociable hour.'

She was reluctant to tell him in front of Mrs Watkins that she had come in search of bar work, and so retorted, 'Why, I was looking for you, of course. I thought you might well still be in here, sleeping off the excesses of last night.'

'Excesses? Stuff and nonsense,' interrupted the landlady stoutly. 'Why, Mr Gray don't even touch the hard stuff now. Last year—well, that was a different story. But since he married, it's nothing stronger than lemonade, is it, lad? Not like some husbands I could name. My, but you two make a good-looking couple. It's nice to see you settled at last, my boy.'

She reached up and pinched his cheek fondly before turning back for her bucket and mop with a sigh. Leander smiled so beatifically that Caro was hard put not to burst out laughing.

'Ah, yes, Mrs Gray, you're a lucky woman.' Mrs Watkins rested on her mop and surveyed the painting hanging over the bar. 'Except for that, of course. Lovely painting, but I think he should have painted another face on the lady, don't you?'

Caro sobered abruptly.

'You're absolutely right, Mrs Watkins,' Leander said contritely. 'So you will understand why Caroline and I will be leaving as soon as possible. I'd like to spare my wife any further embarrassment here in Queenstown.'

'I'll get the girl to pack you a decent lunch, shall I?' Mrs Watkins began to move towards the kitchen door. 'And where do you think you'll be heading to?'

Leander and Caro looked at each other.

'Your choice,' he said.

'I'd like to go to Arrowtown,' Caro said without hesitation. It was where the biggest new finds in the goldfields were being reported. Dunedin had been abuzz with the news when she had left and the gold town's remoteness and reported beauty made her eager to see it.

'Good choice,' he said. 'I was there last month, so it's not too soon to return.'

She frowned. 'What do you mean?'

'There'll be a whole lot of new faces at the gaming tables by now.' He grinned at her disapproving face. 'I might as well ply my trade while we're travelling, Caroline.'

Chapter Thirteen

Before they left Queenstown, Caro insisted that the ill-gotten fortune in Leander's saddlebags be banked at the Union Bank, where he admitted to having an account. She deposited all the money save for fifty pounds, which she thought to be ample for their purposes.

'Fifty pounds!' Leander looked up from the camp roll he was packing on his bed. 'That's a ridiculous amount, Caroline! That puts me out of all the big games—'

'Which means that you have less to lose.'

'And we'll only be able to stay at the cheapest hotels—'

'There's no sense in wasting money on accommodation. I don't mind sleeping on the ground, if need be.'

'And by the time we buy a couple of horses—'

'We'll walk. Much healthier, and think of the money we'll save.'

With an expletive that was fortunately too indistinct for her to catch, he seized his camp roll and stormed out of the room. Half an hour later, wondering where he was, she wandered out onto the street to find him adjusting the stirrups of two very nice-looking chestnut horses.

'I told you, it will be cheaper to walk,' she said grumpily, but without much heat, as she walked forward to fondle the ears of the nearest gelding, which was already carrying a side-saddle. The horse moved away in order to mouth her hand enquiringly and she drew a deep, appreciative breath of the special, warm, grass-and-sweat smell of horse. Like no other scent, it reminded her of home, of the farm, of her beloved Summer that she had sold to a Sydney horse trader—albeit a highly reputable one—in order to fund her trip to New Zealand. Who was riding him now? She swallowed hard on a bitter wave of homesickness. What stupid, irresponsible things she had done to demonstrate her independence.

'They're nice animals,' she allowed at last, by way of making peace.

'We need decent horses. It's a very long way to anywhere from here.' Leander stepped back to check that the stirrups were even. 'We'll not be at the Arrow before dark, now.'

'Does that mean we have to spend the night in the open?'

'Probably. We're leaving it rather late in the day. Unless you want to spend another night here in Queenstown.'

She was envisaging herself spending a cold night huddling on a mountain side with only a horse and a husband of uncertain temper for company, when she became aware that she was the object of keen observation by a company of miners across the road. Tugging on her bonnet strings in a futile effort to hide her face, she muttered, 'I don't think I have any choice but to leave today, thanks to your inconsideration. For just how much longer do you intend holding us up?'

His mouth tightened in anger but he turned and walked back into the hotel without a word, presumably to pay the bill. Across the road, the group of miners were debating whether to approach her, and she desperately hoped that he would not be long. The second chestnut, convinced that his stable-mate was being fed, leaned over to snuffle hopefully for a treat, and she was seized with the strongest desire to be on horseback again. The sun-washed hills rising steeply behind Queenstown promised escape and adventure, and suddenly she could not wait to be gone.

When Leander returned, it was to find her already mounted and with a familiar battle-light in her eyes. 'Come on, slow coach. Or do you need a hand up to mount?'

A slow smile lit his face. 'I know which way to face on a horse.'

'Oh, really? Well, let's see.' She turned her horse and lightly touched her heels to its flanks, thrilled by the animal's eager response. Within seconds Leander was riding alongside her. She fought back an exultant laugh. So he knew a good horse when he saw it and he could mount swiftly. But could he really *ride*? They rode side by side at a sedate canter up Ballarat Street and through the miners' camp beyond, the horses tossing impatiently at the bit as they caught their riders' excitement.

At home, in New South Wales, Caro had habitually ridden in a split skirt on a man's saddle over the farm. But after not riding for so many months, even the discomfort of wearing a corset and petticoats on a side-saddle could not distract from the sheer joy of being on horseback again. Common sense told her to pace her horse for the long journey ahead, but the horses were so fresh that they needed little encouragement to race each other up into the hills to the north.

After half an hour, in a much better temper, Caro drew rein and turned to look down at the lake below. It glimmered in a large, wavering semi-circle between the mountains, the bluest blue imaginable. Beyond, the mountain ranges stretched as far as the eye could see, promising limitless opportunities for adventure. She had never thought to see anything so beautiful in her life. Mind you, she thought as she leaned forward to pat her horse's neck, every scene in the world was improved when viewed between the pricked ears of a horse.

'This has got to be better than walking.' Leander spoke her thoughts aloud as he wheeled his horse around to stand beside her. Under the broad brim of his hat she was pleased to see that his eyes held their old, teasing sparkle.

She held her face up to the clear, golden light, rejoicing in the heat. 'It's such a beautiful day. And it's wonderful to be riding again. You—' she took a deep breath '—you were right to hire the horses.'

'Of course I was right.'

'Well, you have to admit that you usually aren't,' Caro said indulgently. 'I mean, you have about as much common sense as you do money sense...' Her voice faltered as she registered the look on his face. There was a very long and uncomfortable silence, broken only by the sound of tearing grass as the horses took advantage of the break to graze.

'Caroline, can you tell me how much money you have in your possession just now?'

'Not enough. I never have enough money,' she feinted.

'So who was it who paid for the horse you're sitting on?'

'And who picked you up from the gutter and gave you a home?' Caro retaliated, stung by the unaccustomed insult.

'Who talked the banker into giving you enough money to keep the hotel going? Who won enough money at the tables to keep the Castledene from going under a second time?'

'And who was it who…who…' Half-furious and half-amused, Caro broke off and shook her head. 'Oh, this is pointless, Leander! That's all in the past…'

'Then leave it there, for God's sake.'

For a moment she debated with herself, then decided—for perhaps the first time in her life—that she was engaged in an argument that she was likely to lose. 'All right, I will. For now.'

He seized her rein when she would have turned away. 'Listen, Caroline. Just now, I'm the one holding all the cards. Remember that next time you want to throw a tantrum over how I spend my money.'

She fought back a smile. She rather liked it when he was being masterful.

'So, you hold *all* the cards?'

He leaned back in the saddle and gave her a long look, that swept from the top of her bonnet to her boots and which dwelt for what seemed like an inordinately long time on the patch of skin exposed by the open neck of her blouse. She was blushing furiously by the time he met her eyes again.

'Perhaps not *all* the cards,' he conceded with a smile that melted her insides. 'But a word of warning, my lovely wife—if one card is all you're holding to your… er…chest, then you'd better make damned sure it's a good one.'

'Oh, it is,' she assured him, touching her horse's flanks with her heels and sliding into a smooth trot. 'A very good one,' she threw over her shoulder.

He drew alongside her. 'Ah, an over-confident beginner,' he mused. 'I shall look forward to collecting my winnings.' He nodded to the hills beyond.

'We're going over there today. We'll follow the lake around to the Kawarau River, and then follow the Arrow River up to Arrowtown. If we keep up a good pace, we'll get there by dark.'

But it was not the day for speed. After the initial burst of enthusiasm, the horses were content to amble along in the sunshine, and neither Caro nor Leander was of a mind to hurry them along. They forded swift, shallow, pebbly rivers and tracked over high, rolling hills, golden with knee-high tussock grass. The air grew warmer as they travelled inland, until the brown mountains began to shimmer in the midday heat.

They met many others on the route, some commercial travellers with drays and mule packs, a couple of family groups with small, tired children strapped to their parents' backs, but mostly gold prospectors laden with swags, picks and pans. A few were travelling back to Dunedin, but most were headed inland to stake claims at a dozen places along the Shotover and Arrow Rivers. By and large the greetings were genuine and sociable, but on three occasions Leander limited himself to a curt nod of response to a called greeting and sped up their pace until they had passed the other travellers. After a good look at such men, Caro decided that this was prudent behaviour—she was fairly sure she could spot a horse thief when she saw one, and the tired, covetous eyes on her chestnut gelding were enough to make her touch her heels to the horse's flanks and follow Leander's lead.

They stopped in the heat of the afternoon beside a river crossing, where a party of travellers hailed them with an invitation to join them for a mug of tea. It was an extended family group, with a half-dozen children splashing in the shallows of the river, under the watchful eye of the adults. The tea was hot and strong and very welcome, and the children were ecstatic with the oat biscuits Leander produced from Mrs Watkins's picnic lunch.

Leander went to sit with the men as they discussed masculine affairs in the shade of the trees, and Caro was drawn into conversation with the women making damper and feeding the children around the fire. There were three of them, all sisters-in-law, accompanying their husbands to the goldfields. The family had walked all the way from Dunedin, with only three packhorses between them.

''Tis a long way,' the eldest of the women agreed, and gave her a grateful smile when Caro grabbed a toddler about to teeter into the river shallows. 'But I've walked further before now, when we were travelling between the fields in Victoria. Still, you've got to go where your man goes, don't you? And maybe this time he'll be lucky and get a digging where there's money to be made.' She stood up to ease her back and Caro saw with a pang of sympathy that she was heavily pregnant.

'Fine lookin' man you've got there,' another of the women observed with a nod to where Leander sat with the other menfolk. Her eyes flickered over Caro's flat stomach and she added with barely concealed resentment, 'You've not been married long, I take it.'

Not long enough to lose your figure and your looks and your hopes, was what she meant. Caro's sympathy was swiftly turning to guilt at her unemcumbered and relatively wealthy status. Cries of delight from the children as Leander shared out the contents of Mrs Watkins's packed lunch gave her the excuse she needed to make her way back to her husband's side.

'You're very quiet,' Leander observed as they set off again over the hills, leaving the travel-wearied family behind them. 'Is something wrong?'

Caro sighed. 'Those poor women, walking for weeks over this country, carrying their children and everything they own on their backs! And here am I—'

'Comfortably mounted on horseback, complaining about the cost and wanting to walk,' he finished for her and smiled. 'Why don't you go back and offer them one of the horses?'

She drew to a halt, a thoughtful frown on her face. 'Maybe I should at that.'

Leander stared at her in genuine amazement. 'Good heavens. Is this really the hard-headed woman of business I knew back in Dunedin? The woman who can do accounts in her head and who knows the cost of every item of expenditure down to the last penny? The woman who believes in the virtues of thrift and hard work? The woman who—'

'Oh, all right!' she broke in, touching her heels to

the gelding's flanks. 'I just thought... Oh, never mind. I'm not going soft, if that's what you're suggesting.'

'No, I don't think you're going soft. I rather suspect you've been that way all along, but never wanted to show it.' He reached across and took her hand as they rode side-by-side. 'They'll be in Bannockburn by nightfall, Caroline, and the mining's good there at the moment. Within the month the children will have shoes on their feet and food in their stomachs and a roof over their heads. They'll do very nicely there, believe me. The journey out will have been worth it.' He sat back in the saddle. 'Unless, of course, the men of the family decide to drink it all away in the bars.'

'Or lose it to you over the gambling tables,' she said tartly.

'I'll make a point of avoiding them, just to keep you happy,' he promised.

They continued at a leisurely pace, but by evening they were still some miles from Arrowtown.

'Another hour, I think,' Leander said. 'Then we'll have to find an hotel. The better ones will be full by now, although I suppose we can always share a room...'

It was not a hard decision to make. They turned off the track and headed east over the hills until they found a sheltered valley with a small stream running through it. There were no signs of recent human habitation, which was reassuring—bushrangers were by no means unknown in the goldfields, although there had been no reports of any recent attacks.

They made camp within minutes, both being well used to sleeping out under the stars. Leander took a billycan down to the river and returned some time later with water and an armful of firewood. His shirt clung to his wet skin and his hair was slicked close to his scalp. He looked cool and relaxed, with a glow that came from more than exposure to the sun. Caro looked up from the fire she was coaxing from the brushwood and wiped a grubby hand across her perspiring forehead. Although the sun had disappeared behind the hills some time ago, the ground radiated heat beneath her knees and she felt hot, tired and uncomfortable.

'You've been in the stream,' she said enviously.

He smiled and tossed her a towel from his saddlepack. 'Your turn. There's a small pool about a hundred yards downstream. Deep enough to sit in, if you can stand the cold.'

Oh, to be a man. In Australia she had had a wardrobe full of appropriate clothes for the outdoors: light, hardwearing, comfortable shirts and split skirts that kept her cool and allowed her complete freedom of movement. But here… She thought of her heavy dress, her layers of petticoats, her stays, her stockings, all to be taken off and then pulled back on over wet skin. It would take an age, when all she wanted was cool water and air on her skin. She sighed and got to her feet.

'I won't be long.'

He read her expression accurately and kept holding the towel when she would have taken it. 'Be as long as you like, Caroline. There's just you and me here. No one else.'

'But I can't…'

'Can't you?'

Well, she could, she supposed, as she took the towel and walked down to the stream. She found the pool he had described and, after checking that she was out of Leander's sight, she swiftly pulled off all her clothes and lowered herself into its icy depths with a series of small yelps. It was utter bliss to feel the day's dust and sweat wash away. She took a deep breath and submerged her head under the water, erupting seconds later with a gasp of exultation. She had never felt so clean and so cold in her life.

Shivering, her feet sliding on the flat, grey pebbles, she walked back to the bank where she had left her clothes and vigorously towelled herself dry. By the time she had buttoned up her chemise, however, she felt perfectly warm again. Her dress and the hated stays lay ready to put on. After contemplating them for a moment—and the possible consequences of not wearing them—Caro folded them up and carried them, together with her boots, back to the campfire.

Leander took in her changed appearance with a smile, but wisely made no comment. 'I've made tea and damper,' was all he said. 'And there are apples to follow.'

It was the best meal she could ever remember having. Food always tasted better outdoors and here, in the still warmth of an Otago twilight, Caro thought even plain water would have tasted like nectar. She fed their apple cores to the horses tethered nearby and came back to sit cross-legged by the fire.

'Now,' she said. 'I'd like you to teach me how to play poker. And please don't tell me it's not a fit game for young ladies! I want to know how you make money out of it.'

He hesitated for a second and then shrugged. 'All right.' He pulled a case from his saddledpack, and extracted one of several packs of cards from it. She watched with interest as he shuffled them, the cards appearing to fly from hand to hand with extraordinary speed and grace.

'Are they marked?' she asked.

'Certainly not!' he retorted, deeply offended. 'Only amateurs use marked cards. How do you know about such things as marked cards, anyway?'

'Well, how do you always manage to win, then?' she wanted to know.

'I don't always win. Sometimes I choose to lose.' He spread the cards out before her and then scooped them up with one fluid motion. She realised he was showing off. 'And sometimes I just meet someone better than me. That's what makes poker the best game of all. There's an element of chance, but there's a much greater element of skill.'

'So, what is a "poker face"?'

He laughed, rather condescendingly, she thought. 'Something you'll never have, Caroline. Right, so what shall we use for a stake?'

'A what?'

'A stake. Something I win and you lose. Do you have any money?'

'You know very well that I haven't!'

'Well, then. We'll have to use matches. Ten each. See how long you can hold on to them.'

She lost them all in the first game, but she didn't mind. The rules were surprisingly simple, and she quickly realised what Leander had meant about skill being more important than luck. It took all her concentration to control her reactions to a good or poor hand, and it was hard to try to remember the cards that passed through the game, but after an hour of fast play she began to gain in confidence.

'Had enough yet?' Leander asked, as he handed back her matches yet again.

'Not yet.' She picked up the cards and began to shuffle them with what looked like extreme clumsiness after Leander's lightning speed. 'I think I'm beginning to understand this game.'

She lost the next game, but only just. Leander raised his eyebrows in surprise.

'Beginner's luck.'

'I don't think so,' she said confidently. She had begun to watch him closely as he played, had noticed the tiny frown that denoted a poor hand, the way he blinked a little faster when he was bluffing. She schooled her own features into rigidity so as not to give him the same advantage over her. A short time later, she won her first game.

Leander shook his head disbelievingly and gathered the cards. 'A fluke. I don't know how you did that.'

She merely smirked and beat him again. He won the next game and then yawned rather loudly. 'Well, that was interesting. Time to call it a night, I think.'

She sat upright and blinked as she realised that they had been playing for hours. Now, only the faintest light lit the sky and they were having to rely on the firelight to see what they were doing. 'You're only saying that because I'm beating you,' she said accusingly.

'I'm saying that because I'm tired and I want to go to sleep. And besides,' he added patronisingly, 'you've only won a couple of games. Hardly a winning streak, Caroline.'

'One more game,' she demanded as he went to rise. 'Just to prove to you that I can beat you and that it's got nothing to do with beginner's luck!'

He sighed. 'All right. One more game. But I'm bored with matches. How about something different?'

'Such as?'

'A kiss.'

'A kiss?'

'Yes, a kiss. One kiss. And then we'll call it a night.'

Caro didn't mind one kiss at all. In fact, she would not have minded playing for even higher stakes. However, she rather liked the idea of kissing Leander. Or even of making him wait until a time of her choosing for the kiss…

'One kiss it is.' She shuffled the cards one last time and dealt them.

It was getting hard to read his expression in the firelight, but it was not impossible. Sure enough, he began blinking again, and she knew she had him.

'Full house,' she said triumphantly, laying the cards out one by one before him. He stared down at them, an odd expression on his face. He was patently not used to losing, she thought with pleasure. 'Come on, Leander. Show me your hand.'

Slowly, he did. 'Royal flush.'

She frowned at it for a full thirty seconds. 'You can't have,' she said incredulously. 'You were bluffing!'

'How do you know I was bluffing?'

'Because you were…' Her words trailed away as she saw the gleam in his eyes. 'Oh, you…you *bastard*! You were pretending all the time! Weren't you!'

He fell backwards laughing while she huffily gathered up the cards and returned them to the cardcase. She did not think she would be demanding another game of poker with him in the foreseeable future. When he had recovered sufficiently to sit upright again, she crossed her arms and glared at him.

'That wasn't fair.'

'That's poker. Now, about that bet we had…'

'Oh, the kiss. All right then.' She leaned forward so that he could kiss her.

He leaned back. 'No. I'm going to have to think about this. Lie down.'

'What?'

He reached over and pulled her bedroll closer. 'On that. Lie down.'

She moved over to sit on it, but was not about to lie down. 'I thought the forfeit was just a kiss,' she protested.

'It was. It is.' He grinned and in the firelight he looked almost wolfish. 'But I didn't say where.'

'Leander…!'

Very, very gently he touched the tip of her nose. 'It could be here, I suppose. It is a very pretty little nose. Or—' his finger dropped to outline her lips '—here. But then that's so *conventional*, don't you think? And we're neither of us that.'

She held her breath as his fingers and his gaze dropped to her shoulders. 'Then there are these, or your arms. Lovely arms, I've never seen them before. I feel quite deprived. Or there's always here.' His fingers trailed across the tops of her breasts revealed by her chemise. She shut her eyes on the sight of his long brown fingers on her skin but could not stop a small whimper of desire escaping from her lips. She felt the warmth of his breath on her face as he moved closer.

'Yes, there would be nice.' His voice was a whisper, stirring the fine hairs by her ears, sending a constant, electric thrill through her entire body. 'I might decide on that place, after I've looked at the other options.'

She felt him move and then he was running his

hands over her ankles, holding the fine bones assessingly. Her eyes flew open.

'Leander!'

'Very pretty, but your feet are not as clean as they should be. That's what comes of walking about barefooted.' Her giggle was stifled as his hands moved up to stroke her calves. 'These are nice and clean though. Perhaps that would be a good place. Although maybe a little cold. It feels warmer up here...'

'Leander!' Almost helpless with horrified laughter, she only just managed to pin her chemise down to her sides as his hands began to part her knees. 'Now stop it! This is not fair!'

He looked affronted. 'Are you reneging?'

'No, I'm not! But...I didn't expect this.'

'Oh. So, do you want to negotiate the terms of your payment?'

She smoothed her dress down to her ankles. 'If we can.'

'Very well then. *You* kiss *me*.'

She considered that option, her head tilted. 'That sounds more reasonable.'

'In a place that I choose.'

It took the span of mere seconds for her to work out where that was likely to be. With an exaggerated sigh she lay back on the bedroll and made herself comfortable. 'Kiss me, then,' she said to the emerging stars above. 'But please don't take so long. I'm getting cold.'

'Oh, dear,' he said solicitiously and, lying beside her, he pulled up the blanket she was lying on to cover her shoulders. But she knew it was not the slight chill in the air that was making her shiver. 'Now, where were we?'

'Oh, for heaven's sake, Leander, make up your mind!'

He sighed. 'I wish it were that simple, but with a whole body to choose from, and only one kiss… Well, I don't want to waste it.'

She glared at him. 'Perhaps I should put a time limit on this.'

'I know what,' he said suddenly. 'We'll do it mathematically. Forget the extremities, and work out the centre. That's it.' He traced a line with the tip of one finger down from the base of her throat, down between her breasts, down to her midriff. 'There.'

'There?' She could scarcely breathe. His fingers rested on her stomach, warm and invasive.

'There. It's the logical place.' He leaned back on one elbow and frowned down at her chemise. 'Now for the next decision. Do I unbutton your chemise down the front, or do I simply lift it up?'

Wordlessly, she sat up and pulled the whole thing off with one abandoned movement. Then she lay back, feeling her nipples tighten in the cool air and the almost intolerable tension in her abdomen. Leander shakily let out his breath.

'Now there's a bit I hadn't noticed before. I think *that* might be the place for me…'

With a sound that was half-snarl and half-gasp she seized his shoulders and pulled him down to lie beside her. She rid him of his shirt and trousers with the same speed that she had tossed off her chemise and then rolled on top of him.

'Now kiss me!'

His hands covered her hips as he held her heat and wetness over him. 'On the mouth it is, then,' he said against her lips. 'How very conventional.'

* * *

But surely there was nothing conventional about what happened after that, she thought dazedly as she lay beneath him later. Somewhere between the laughter and the kisses and the caresses he had slipped into her body as naturally as if he belonged there, and the slow, surging rhythm between them had become fast and then frantic, erupting into a shattering climax that left her feeling weak and satiated. It had taken minutes. It had taken a lifetime.

With the greatest effort she raised a hand to brush Leander's fringe from his damp forehead. He was hot and slick with sweat, and she could feel his heart pounding against her breasts. He lifted himself away from her and she sighed with regret as she felt him leave her body. He ran his hand down to her hips to draw her over to face him, and she slowly obliged, her limbs like lead weights. They lay with their faces inches apart, gazing into each other's eyes.

'Do you know, I don't mind losing to you as much as I thought I would,' she said, when she was able to speak coherently.

He gave a laugh that was more of a gasp. 'I'm glad it wasn't too unpleasant.' Cupping the side of her face he kissed her with a tenderness that wrung her heart. 'I found the experience quite tolerable, too.'

Suddenly shy, she buried her head in his shoulder, listening as the heavy thud of his heart slowed to its normal beat. All she wanted just then was to sleep, with his arms and his scent and his taste surrounding her.

'I love you, Leander,' she said drowsily, as her eyes closed.

'I love you, Caroline,' he whispered into her hair. She fell asleep with her lips curved into a satisfied smile.

Chapter Fourteen

'Caroline, wake up.'

Her eyes fluttered open and then closed again. 'Let me sleep, Leander,' she muttered. 'I'm so tired.'

'I'd like to, but I can't. Come on, wake up.' A light but persistent hand on her shoulder was shaking her. With a sigh she rolled over and opened her eyes to a pale blue sky streaked with pink.

'It's so early.'

'True, but we've had company already.'

That had her eyes wide open. 'What? Who?'

'A party of miners came by about fifteen minutes ago. I managed to discourage them from staying for a mug of tea, but they're not likely to be the only travellers through this morning. I think it would be a good idea if you got dressed.'

She sat up carefully, pulling the blankets around her tightly. Freshly washed and dressed in a clean shirt and moleskins, Leander squatted beside her, a mug of tea in his hand. He frowned as she winced.

'Are you all right? I'm sorry, I wasn't as gentle as I should have been last night.'

'Oh, nonsense, I'm fine,' she said as brightly as she

could manage, although in truth she ached. 'Are the miners still here?'

'No, they've gone on down the valley. I've warmed you up some water to wash with. I'll go down by the stream while you dress, just to make sure we don't have any other visitors. I'll call out if anyone's coming.'

She was grateful for his consideration in giving her privacy. There was dried blood on her thighs and pulling on her clothes made her aware of muscles she never knew she had. That was odd, when she had felt nothing but unadulterated pleasure the night before. She watched Leander walk back to their campsite, so tall and lean and elegant even in his rough clothes, and she felt a pang of lust pierce her groin. Ache or no ache, she could not wait until to repeat the experience.

He stopped before her and gave her a slight smile, but beneath his blond fringe his brown eyes were concerned. 'Are you sure you're all right?'

She suddenly realised that he was far from certain of her reaction. With a laugh she flung her arms around his neck and kissed him with all the exuberant passion of a well-loved woman. 'I'm better than all right. I'm wonderful! And you're wonderful! And life…well, life is just…'

'Wonderful,' he finished with her and relief lit his face. He held her close. 'Thank you, Caroline. That was quite a night.'

She nuzzled his shirt happily. 'I can't wait to be alone with you again, Leander! Tonight, in a bed, together…'

'Hmm,' he said cautiously. 'We'll be in Arrowtown tonight.'

'In an hotel, surely?' she said blankly.

He grimaced. 'In an hotel, hopefully. But there are no places as grand as the Castledene, and we might not be alone. There are precious few places to stay on the Arrow, and beds are at a premium. We may have to share.'

Caro stared at him, her mouth agape. 'But…! I don't want to share my bedroom with a total stranger! I'd rather sleep outside, under the stars again…'

'With a few thousand miners for company?' He gave her a wry grin. 'I'm sorry, sweetheart. It's hardly honeymoon country, is it?'

A shouted greeting from the river parted them and Leander went down to speak to the lost-looking young prospectors who were laden down with mining paraphernalia and waving a map hopefully in their direction. Caro picked up her now-cool mug of tea and sipped it thoughtfully. If privacy was not going to be easy to come by, then they were going to have to be inventive. She smiled unseeingly at the tussock-covered hills now glimmering gold in the early sunshine. She had always loved a challenge.

The glorious weather did not last—dark clouds were milling over the hills by the time they reached Arrowtown. It had taken but three hours, and that was with the delay of being forced to follow a plodding mule-train along the river track. There was no point in Caro and Leander allowing their energetic horses to overtake—there was a steady stream of drays, laden donkeys and equally heavily laden miners walking in the opposite direction.

Caro caught her breath as the track widened into Arrowtown. Steep hills cradled what once must have been a most picturesque valley. But any trees that had once grown had long since been cut down for firewood, and you could no longer see the Arrow River as it wound its way back into the hills. Instead, a vast sea of canvas roofs and humanity covered the valley floor. She turned to Leander in amazement.

'I had no idea! I've never seen anything like it!'

'Nor will you again, I'm sure. Only a goldrush can set up a small city overnight.' He reined in and leaned forward in the saddle to study the few dozen wooden structures proudly standing above the canvas lean-tos and tents. Saloons, gambling halls, theatres, a handful of hotels and a couple of general stores hastily erected to service the massive influx of miners. 'Looks like the Miners Arms has gone—probably burnt down. We'll try the Victoria.'

It took a while to pick their way around the tents and the campfires, but there were not as many people around as she had at first thought. 'They're out on their claims,' Leander explained when she commented on this. 'Wait until they're all back tonight. You'll not be able to get a horse between the bodies, then.'

The Victoria Hotel looked to offer only the most basic of facilities, but the landlady was perfectly respectable. Unfortunately, she could offer them not so much as a space by the fire to sleep that night. She referred them to the Apollo Hotel, some fifty yards away, but Leander came out of there shaking his head. 'Not a hope. That means we'll have to move on. We can't risk sleeping rough near the town.'

'I don't mind. You would if you were by yourself, wouldn't you?' she asked.

'I would and I have, but I wouldn't risk it with a woman,' he said rather curtly and swung back into the saddle. 'As you've no doubt noticed, there are very few women around, and you're already causing more than enough interest.'

She had noticed, but felt completely safe with her husband riding beside her. Asleep at night surrounded by strange men would be quite different, however, and she certainly wasn't that foolhardy.

'You did want to stay for some games, though, didn't you?'

'There are other towns. If we get going now, we can be at Cardrona by tomorrow afternoon. Unfortunately—' he glanced at the black clouds overhead '—we're going to get caught in a downpour. We'll have to get under shelter soon.'

'Where do you usually do your gambling?' she asked, falling in beside him as he nudged his horse back the way they had come.

'A couple of places. Over there, in the Billington, mostly.' He pointed out a brightly painted building ahead of them. It looked clean, and it looked substantial.

'Does it have bedrooms?' Caro asked.

He dropped his arm and looked at her in amusement. 'Yes.'

'Then can we see if they have any vacant rooms?'

'Oh, they'll have vacant rooms all right, but we're not staying there.'

'Why not?' She reined in her horse, forcing him to stop and wheel back to face her. A large drop of rain bounced off her nose.

'Because they rent the rooms by the hour, Caroline, that's why.' He clicked his tongue in exasperation as a couple of drops fell on his head. 'Come on.'

'Oh, for goodness' sake!' Caro snapped, as the rain began to fall in earnest. 'One hour or twenty-four, what does it matter?' She wheeled her horse around too quickly for him to seize her rein and rode at a trot to the entrance. By the time Leander caught up with her, she had tied the reins to the hitching-post and walked inside.

It looked much as she expected a gambling hall to look—a bar, rows of bottles and glasses behind, and tables and chairs neatly set out. All perfectly clean and quite respectable-looking. Overhead, the rain pounded ferociously on the tin roof.

'Excuse me,' she called over the racket of the downpour to the burly man wiping glasses at the bar. 'Are you the manager?'

'I am.' He put down his cloth and stared at her quizzically. 'What can I do for you?'

'Nothing,' came Leander's firm reply behind her. 'Nothing at all. Caroline…'

She shook her arm free from his grip. 'We need a room. Do you have one free?'

'Caroline…'

The manager looked vastly entertained. 'They're all free this early in the morning. How long were you wanting one for?'

Caro flashed him a quick, grateful smile. 'Just tonight.'

'All night?'

'All night,' she confirmed. 'And we don't want to share it with anyone else.'

'Fair enough.' He gave her a gap-toothed grin and looked past her to where Leander was—for once—quite lost for words. 'Cheer up, mate. If the lady wants to make a night of it…'

'Would you like to tell the lady how much it's going to cost her?' Leander said from between gritted teeth.

'Ten shillings an hour,' the manager said merrily.

'You mean a *night*, of course,' Caro corrected him. 'Well, that's a little on the steep side, but I suppose that's only to be expected with the demand for rooms. Do you have stables? We have horses that will be getting very wet. Leander, would you go and fetch the saddlepacks? And if you could show us to our room?'

A roll of thunder boomed across the valley and shook the Billington to its foundations. Leander waited. The manager opened his mouth and then shut it again.

'Certainly, madam. This way.'

The room he showed her to was clean and perfectly presentable, with clean linen on the surprisingly large double bed. When Leander brought in their saddlepacks and closed the door, Caro turned to him with an arch little smile.

'You have to admit that this is much better than riding around in the rain, trying to find shelter, Leander. And this is perfectly comfortable. I don't know why you made such a fuss.'

His mouth was twitching as he put their saddlebags on the floor. There was no chest of drawers in the room, which struck her as odd, and she said so to him.

'You're quite right. Do you notice anything else unusual about this room?'

There was a washbasin and towels, a chair, and a standing mirror facing the bed. She shook her head. 'It looks perfectly normal to me.'

'Why don't you lie down on the bed?' he invited her silkily.

Somewhat warily, she removed her boots and did just that.

'Oh,' she said. He joined her and together they looked up at their reflections in the large circular mirror over the bed. 'What a very strange place for a mirror,' Caro said after a while. 'Why would you want to lie in bed and stare up at yourself all night?'

'It depends on what you're doing all night. Or rather, what someone else is doing to you.'

Realisation dawned at last with an almost audible thud. Caro sat bolt upright, her face scarlet. 'Oh, goodness! This is a...'

'Yes.'

'And that man thought I was... And you were...'

'Yes.'

She burst into a fit of giggles and collapsed back on to the bed. 'No wonder you were so upset! Oh, Leander...' She looked up at him with tears of laughter sparkling in her eyes. 'I'm sorry!'

'You won't be laughing tomorrow morning when you get the bill for the room, young woman,' he warned her, getting up to lock the door as he spoke. 'I'm going to have to do well at the tables tonight if we're not going to leave here as paupers.'

She flung out her arms and legs and stared up at the recklessly abandoned pose of the girl in the mirror above. 'Now you're the one being boring about money,' she purred. 'Why don't you come back here and start getting your money's worth?'

They made love while the rain hammered on the roof and the thunder rolled around the hills, drowning out the sounds of their pleasure. Hours later, as dusk began to fall, Caro fell back against the pillows, utterly sated. Despite her bravado, she had thought the mirror over the bed might be a little embarrassing, but in fact she had found it riveting to watch her joy reflected. And as for Leander...

'Don't you have any shame?' she teased him, as he pulled away the sheet she would have pulled over herself.

'Shame? Don't know the meaning of the word.' He lay back, one hand behind his head, the other absently teasing the tips of her breasts. 'God, you're lovely. I'm going to have to paint you like this.'

'You've already done that!' she laughed and pushed his hand away. 'And look at the trouble it caused…'

'No, I want to paint you like *this*,' he said, suddenly serious. 'All flushed and tousled and satiated, with your mouth swollen from being kissed, and *here—*' he touched her and she gasped '—here, where I have loved you…'

'Leander…' she whispered.

A boisterous male shout and accompanying high-pitched female giggle from the bar room made them both start. Leander sighed, and stretched and then rolled lazily off the bed. 'We'd better get dressed and have something to eat before the action starts. Are you coming to watch me play?'

'If you don't mind, I'd like to,' she said in surprise. 'But I didn't think you would want me to come with you.'

He looked at her in mock reproof. 'I want you where I can keep an eye on you, Mrs Gray. Besides, you're probably safer at my side than shut away in this room. This is going to be an interesting evening.'

It certainly was that. The rain had lessened to a damp mist, so after they dressed they left the saloon to buy food. The camp was crowded now that dark had fallen, and they had to pick their way carefully between tired, already inebriated miners, and heavily painted women on their way to work in the bars and dancehalls. They found a man selling food beside a cooking fire and ate hot, roasted mutton served between thick slices of fresh bread, standing out in the open air. The food was delicious, the people around them were enjoying themselves, the man she loved was beside her… She was so happy that she found herself laughing for no other reason but that life was absolutely perfect.

Later that night, in the smoky, crowded saloon, she watched Leander effortlessly win hundreds of pounds at the tables. She pulled up a chair behind him—he had warned her that if she moved elsewhere the other players would assume that she was checking their cards—and wondered at the amount of money thrown carelessly on the tables. The most grizzled, grubby-looking miner could reach into his pockets and toss handfuls of crisp notes, fresh from the Gold Office coffers, into the games. There were different games—faro, whist, poker and any number of dice games going at the tables—but poker was by far the most popular. It had, Leander told her, been brought out by the American miners from California to Victoria, and then on to Otago—the game moving as swiftly across the Pacific as the gold hunters.

She felt not the slightest bit of awkwardness at Leander's shoulder, as there were dozens of other women in the saloon, serving drinks, moving from one man's knee to another, coaxing whatever money they could for a drink or a kiss.

And then there was the steady procession of painted ladies disappearing down through the doorway into the back of the saloon with customers. They would reappear some thirty minutes later, with the women looking rearranged and the men looking eased. Despite the fact that Leander had locked their room, and that the landlord had hung a 'Do Not Disturb' sign on the door handle, she still went to check it several times.

She fetched Leander several glasses of ginger ale from the bar during the evening at his request. It came in a whisky glass, it looked like whisky, and certainly he acted as if it was, indeed, whisky as he drank it through the night. But he was stone-cold sober at midnight when he deliberately lost the last two games and then leaned back in his chair, shaking his head ruefully.

'You've cleaned me out, gentlemen. I'm calling it a night.'

His pockets were filled with hundreds of pounds from earlier games, but none of the other players minded that as they protested and jibed at him goodnaturedly. They all shook hands and then the miners settled down to continue their play, their faces intent, Leander already forgotten in the excitement of a new game.

He took Caro's arm. 'Always leave 'em smiling,' he said in her ear.

Back in their room, lying on the bed, he watched Caro avidly counting the money. 'Three hundred and sixty-two pounds, eighteen shillings and threepence,' she said at last. 'As well as six American dollars and this.'

He squinted through the dim light cast by the single oil lantern at the object she held up. 'A nugget.'

'It's not very big, is it?' She peered at it dubiously. 'Should you have accepted it? Is it legal tender?'

Leander yawned. 'Solid gold. Worth almost as much as all that paper. Come on, Caroline, put away the filthy lucre and come to bed.'

His eyes closed and within seconds he was fast asleep. Caro quietly tidied away the money and readied herself for bed, but she doubted that she was going to be able to sleep. For one thing, the racket through the thin walls of the saloon was far too distracting, and for another, the sight of Leander so easily earning a hundred pounds an hour both excited and disturbed her.

She washed her hands and face and then lay down beside her husband. In the dark reflection of the overhead mirror, Leander looked utterly at peace in his deep sleep, and she looked worried. Automatically, her hand went up to smooth away the frown that her mother always warned her about. She made herself smile, instead. Her reflection smiled back and for a second it was Charlotte, a younger, tousled-haired Charlotte in the mirror.

With a gasp, Caro covered her mouth with her hands. Had Charlotte ever lain like this, in a brothel, with a naked man beside her, gloating over quick and easy money? No matter that the man was her husband— Charlotte had had at least four of those. But this was no way to live, day to day, profiting from the greed of others. Her parents would be horrified if they knew…

She recalled how her father bred his best sheep and horses, weeding out the undesirable traits, breeding those traits he wished to keep. She recalled Leander's horrible joke about his mother and her lurchers. What if wantoness was hereditary? What if she turned into another Charlotte? Living only for the moment, craving love and money and losing her self-respect in the pursuit of both. Becoming nothing more than a puppet, a doll for men to toy with and then discard.

She was beginning to understand the probable cause of the long-ago rift between her parents and Charlotte.

Far from resenting being rejected by Charlotte in favour of his father, Ben—that most upright and righteous of men—would have been appalled at his father's choice. And if Charlotte had tried to ensnare Ben with her practised charms... It was no wonder that her parents and Charlotte had not communicated amicably in years.

Oh, but she, Caro, did not want to turn into another Charlotte! She turned to study Leander's sleeping face. She loved him and she could now not do without him. But what if he was entirely the wrong sort of man for her? In Australia, in that long-ago time of her innocence, she had vaguely planned to marry one day a man similar to herself in outlook, values and work ethics. Instead, she had married Leander.

It took little effort to dredge up the memory of jug-eared Frank Benton's earnest face as he pleaded with her to marry him. Perhaps she should have. It would have been the sensible thing to have done. Her parents would have been delighted with her. She could manage Frank effortlessly—she always had done—and she would have been her own mistress. She would have been respected, privileged, secure under her own roof, with thousands of acres of farmland to call her own. There would have been no ecstatic couplings, of course, no dangerous abandonment of thought and morals and consequences. Why, poor Frank would have been shocked to the core at the things Leander had encouraged her to do these past two nights...

As if reading her dark thoughts, Leander turned in his sleep and slid his arm across her waist. 'Sweet Caroline,' he muttered drowsily.

Sin was so hard to resist.

* * *

The saloon was silent just before dawn, when a series of loud moans was audible through the bedroom wall. Caro was awake in an instant, thinking someone was being harmed. But the moans and gasps continued, together with a steady thumping sound, and gradually Caro understood that she was listening to another couple's most intimate moments. Horrified and embarrassed, she met Leander's eyes across the pillows.

'Do I sound as loud as that when…?'

'No, she's acting. No man's that good at this hour of the morning.' He closed his eyes again.

'Oh, this is terrible!'

She stuffed the sheet into her mouth to stop from giggling in mortification, and Leander was laughing at her when the moans abruptly stopped. Then there was a slap and a short, swiftly ended scream.

'*That's* not acting,' Leander said softly. He swung out of bed and was out the door in seconds. There was the mutter of voices, a couple of loud thumps, and then the sound of an outside door opening and closing. A minute later, he rejoined her in bed.

'What happened?' she hissed frantically.

'Peace has been restored.' She waited for him to elaborate, but he gave every sign of going back to sleep. She shook him, hard.

'Leander, what happened? You went out there with no clothes on!'

'None of us had any clothes on,' he said drowsily. 'But only one of us ended up outside in the horse trough.'

'So what happened to that…that female making all that noise?'

'The lady is fine. Quite safe.' He nestled close and pressed his lips against her shoulder.

'I wouldn't have called her a lady, Leander.'

'Mmm?'

'That woman, next door. She wasn't a lady, she's… she's a…'

'A woman in need of assistance then. It's almost dawn, Caroline. Let's catch some sleep.' He closed his eyes and within seconds his regular, light breathing told her that he was, indeed, asleep.

Outside she could just make out muffled grunts and the sound of squelching footsteps as someone walked past the window. Then there was silence.

She should not have been surprised by Leander's gallantry, she thought. He had been the only man to come to her rescue when she had blundered into the Castle bar, and his immediate response to Aunt Charlotte had been one of great kindness, although he had seemingly instinctively known her for what she was. The gallantry, the courtesy and the reluctance to pass judgement on anyone were bone-deep in him. Perhaps it was the result of being reared in what sounded like a life of immense privilege, perhaps it was the result of having been plunged from a life of luxury to a life on the streets. But, most likely, it was just him.

'Oh, Leander,' she whispered and pressed a careful kiss on his forehead. 'I am a lucky, lucky woman.'

Chapter Fifteen

She was not sorry to leave the Arrow later that morning.

She had not liked the leer on the face of the saloon manager as she paid him his ten shillings for the night's accommodation. She had not liked the smell of stale beer and cigarettes that seemed to cling to her clothes and hair even after they left the saloon. And she especially had not liked the half-dressed floozy who came running out, just as they were about to mount their horses, and flung her arms around Leander.

'My hero!' The voice might be gin-soaked, but the gratitude in it was real. 'You were wonderful. How can I thank you?'

'My pleasure.' Leander managed between the enthusiastic kisses being showered over his face. 'I hope you're not troubled again…'

'Not after the seeing-to you gave him,' the floozy said adoringly. Her hand slid downwards. 'You're not leaving, are you?'

'Yes, he is!' Caro broke in venomously, but the woman took not one whit of notice as Leander extricated himself from her clutches.

'Come and see me again, darling,' the floozy cooed, and patted him on the bottom as he swung on to his horse. 'When you've got rid of madam here—' she winked '—then I'll show you how grateful I am.'

'Grateful, is she?' Caro burst out when they had ridden well out of earshot. 'I'll bet she's crawling with goodness-knows-what disgusting diseases! Poxy old... cow!'

Leander looked genuinely shocked. 'I didn't think you knew words like *poxy*,' he said mildly.

'And as for you—how dare you stand there and let her paw you! You were enjoying it, weren't you?'

'Hardly...'

'Well, I didn't see you fighting her off, Leander! How could you do that to me? You should have left her to sort herself and her customer out last night. Now, if you ever go back there, she's going to be all over you showing her gratitude...'

'She will never have the opportunity. Besides,' he pointed out reasonably, 'it was you who insisted that we stay there. If you'll recall, I was most strenuously against it.'

'Not strenuously enough!' she stormed. 'You should have stopped me!'

'It would take a braver man than me to do that.'

She bared her teeth at him. 'You are not spineless, Leander. In fact, you never do anything you don't want to. And if you ever, ever, ever go back to that place and that woman...'

'I won't.'

'If you ever do, I'll...I'll...' She ran out of breath and Leander waited with interest while she regained it. The horses ambled alongside the river track, oblivious to the turmoil raging in Caro's heart. She had not a

jealous bone in her body, or so she had thought, but
seeing Leander—*her* Leander—being fondled by a
grateful tart was more than she could bear.

'There's an amazing view from that hill,' Leander
said after a while. 'I'll race you to the top, and if you
still feel the same way when we get there, you can push
me off the cliff.'

'It's a deal,' she said, touching her chestnut's flanks.

By mutual consent they stayed away from the gold
towns for a few nights, meandering instead along the
valleys, riverbeds and hilltops of Central Otago. Caro
came to love this country. Queenstown had been almost
ethereally beautiful, but the rolling hills, covered with
rippling tussock grass, hiding small, sapphire-blue
tarns, were equally breathtaking. Otago was every
shade of gold and brown, with the sturdy backbone of
the mountain ranges rising steeply to curve against the
bluest, widest sky imaginable. It was a sight that Caro
wanted to gather to her heart and hold there forever.

'Why can't you paint it?' she said in exasperation to
Leander one afternoon, as he sat sketching a group of
miners who were setting up a long wooden sluice on
the Shotover River. 'All this colour, all this beauty!
How can you just draw *people*?'

'I can't do landscapes,' he said almost absently, his
eyes narrowed against the sun. His pencil flashed
across the sketching pad with sure, precise movements.
'I never get the colours right.'

'There was nothing wrong with the colour in the
portrait you did of me.' She threw herself down beside
him and peered over his arm. On the paper the scene
was coming to life under his pencil. With just a few
strokes Leander captured movement, effort, exhaustion,

the intensity on the tired men's faces. His talent never failed to astonish her. If only he were to make use of it! 'You could sell landscapes, if you did them,' she went on sullenly. 'People always hang landscapes on their walls. You could do them if you really wanted to.'

'But I don't want to,' he said, not even glancing in her direction.

She didn't know if she had hurt his feelings, and she didn't want to know. They sat in silence until Leander finished his sketch and went down to thank the miners for allowing him to capture their likenesses. Caro stayed sitting, tearing at a single strand of tussock grass in frustration. Why did he never do what she wanted him to do? Why did he always have to cross her at every point? Her father was the only other person in her life who had resisted her efforts to organise him, and she had run off and left him thousands of miles away in New South Wales. What on earth had possessed her to marry a man just as single-minded and determined as herself? She wanted a compliant man, a man who would cater to her every whim and who would openly acknowledge her intelligence and common sense.

It was something that niggled at her frequently during the long, sun-filled days, threatening at times to overwhelm even her pleasure in the spectacular scenery around her. She knew it had much to do with her relative inactivity—she needed to be busy and organising people, and this enforced idleness was unnatural to her. But Leander did not seem to understand or notice her frustrated outbursts. Or he chose not to.

There were the nights, though. The short, warm, tussock-scented nights when they hid themselves from the

world in an isolated valley and made endless love in
the starlight. They understood each other, then. She
adored learning how to arouse him, exhaust him, and
then arouse him again. Every inch of his skin was familiar territory to her, as hers was to him, and there
was infinite pleasure in its touch, taste and scent. He
was tender and passionate and strong, and she treasured
all the words of love he whispered or gasped or even
shouted in the throes of lovemaking. But in the bright
light of day the friction remained between them, unspoken but very real.

They spent Christmas Day in Cromwell, in a charming stone hotel. They toasted the New Year with a hundred other miners at the Dunstan Hotel. They swam in
snow-fed pools high in the mountains and listened to
the echoes of their shouts bouncing across the Remarkables. Several times they had to leave the track
hurriedly to make way for the Gold Coach as it thundered along its circuit of gold towns and Dunedin, accompanied by a dozen hard-faced military men carrying rifles in their hands. Caro clung in utter terror to a
swinging rope bridge across the raging Shotover River
and Leander filled sketchbook after sketchbook with
images of mining life.

He played a couple of games in whatever town they
found themselves, netting hundreds of pounds each
night. Their bank account grew steadily.

One magical night they lay silently staring at the
Aurora Australis as a multitude of brilliant lights
played across the broad sweep of sky. Caro lay with
her husband's hand in hers, for once completely content with her life.

The next morning she woke and stretched luxuriously. It was another beautiful day and Leander was

already up, breaking eggs into a frying pan for breakfast.

'Mmm, that smells wonderful. I'm so hungry,' she announced and sat up. Her head began to spin and she waited for a moment before standing up. A wave of nausea rolled through her.

'How many would you like?' Leander asked, flipping the eggs expertly. The smell of cooking oil was too much to take. She dropped to her hands and knees and retched violently into the tussock, again and again. At last she sat back and he squatted beside her to tuck her hair back behind her ears.

'Damn, that was fast,' he said softly.

Caro laughed shakily. 'I can't imagine why I did that. I'm never ill. It must have been that stew we had last night, although it tasted fine…'

She caught the strangest look on his face—regretful, almost sad. 'I'm fine now,' she assured him. 'Really.'

'Good. Here, rinse your mouth out with this.' She took the mug of water he gave her and obediently swilled her mouth out. Already she was beginning to feel herself again, but she still didn't want any eggs for breakfast.

Leander took the mug from her and went back to rescue the eggs from burning. 'Caroline,' he said carefully, 'when was your last monthly course?'

'I really can't remember, and I'm not sure it's a subject I want to discuss,' she spluttered, suddenly shy about such things.

'Are you usually regular?' he persisted.

'Well, yes…'

'And you haven't had a course since I met you in Queenstown six weeks ago.'

'So what?' she demanded. 'I would have thought that would be a convenience to you, rather than something to be concerned about. Are you trying to tell me I'm pregnant?'

'It's a possibility.'

'Well, I'm not! I can't be! I...I don't choose to be!'

He made no answer but tipped her cooked eggs on to a plate and held it out to her. And then he brought her a cup of tea when she promptly threw up again.

By mid-morning she felt perfectly well, and the matter was not referred to by either of them again that day. That night he made love to her with unaccustomed gentleness and, when he left her, his hand rested for a moment on her belly. I am not pregnant! she thought fiercely as she nestled against him for sleep. But the nausea gripped her the next morning and the morning after that.

On the fourth morning, when she was comfortably ensconced in a deep featherbed in the Clyde Hotel, her husband woke her with a mug of tea and a plate of plain, dry toast.

'Eat this before you get up,' he instructed her. 'The landlady swears it to be the best remedy she knows for morning sickness in early pregnancy.'

'I am *not* pregnant,' she snapped, 'and I don't appreciate you telling complete strangers that I am. This is just a mild stomach upset, that's all.'

He sat back with a sigh. 'Eat your toast, there's a good girl.'

'And don't talk to me as if I were five years old!'

Leaner had had enough. 'You're not five years old,' he agreed savagely. 'You're twenty-two and a married woman who also happens to be pregnant. Don't you think it time that you accepted that fact?'

'I'm not—'

'You are. You just don't want to be. Can I ask why?' She couldn't answer that, and turned her head away. Slowly, he expelled his breath.

'It's because you can't walk out when you're tired of playing at being married, isn't it? Because now—for the first time in your entire, selfish life—you've got to think of someone else for a change.'

'Oh, go away and leave me alone,' she muttered.

He left.

By the time they returned to Queenstown, early in February, she felt perfectly well again. But there was no sign of her monthly courses. Instead, her breasts were tender and swollen and she was either giddy with happiness or tearful. Some nights she could not bear Leander to touch her and he had begun to sleep in another room whenever they stayed in an hotel. Although she missed his warmth and physical presence beside her when she woke in the night, pride and resentment kept her from going to seek his company. The thought that this might be the pattern of the rest of her life secretly horrified her, but she seemed unable to make the effort to change anything between them.

She left him by the lake one afternoon to take a long, strenuous, solitary walk up into the hills above Queenstown. On the top of a hill overlooking the lake she curled up into a ball of misery and cried her heart out. She was pregnant. She hated her husband. She wanted her mother. She wanted to go home.

At last there were no more tears and she rested her

swollen face on her knees to stare moodily across the great valley. Far below her, Lake Whakatipu lay serene under the hot, late-afternoon sun. Not a breath of wind stirred the long grasses around her. A drowsy twittering from some ground-bird was the only sound. The absolute stillness slowly soothed her heart and at last she began to feel much better.

The innate practicality that never completely deserted her began to reassert itself. Perhaps she was being too hard on Leander; he was probably as worried about their future as she was. She should sit down together and talk things over with him and together they should decide what to do. It wasn't as if they were paupers, after all—there was plenty of money in the bank if she should manage to persuade him to return to New South Wales with her. Perhaps her father would have relented, and would accept Leander—well, he would have to now, wouldn't he? Although for the life of her she could not imagine Ben and Leander ever having anything resembling a sane conversation. They had nothing in common apart from their stubbornness. Apart from her, of course.

Perhaps it would be best after all if they did stay in New Zealand, but not as they were living now. The nomadic lifestyle was beginning to pall after two months, and she was beginning to long for a roof over her head that did not change every few nights. Leander would have to give up living off the cards, too—that was no occupation for a family man. She could buy a business, she supposed, and put Leander to gainful employment in it. But the idea of her husband behind a desk was not one she could readily bring to mind. He was not, nor ever would be, a businessman. Money came and went with alarming ease from his talented fingers—he simply did not regard it as important enough to worry about. People mattered more to Leander. People and colour and the beauty of the world around him. That was why he spent so much time paying homage to those things on paper and canvas. It was the one aspect of her husband's character that she found hardest to accept. It was also, she admitted to herself, one of the things that made her love him.

There was so much to discuss. Suddenly very tired, she began to rise to her feet but she staggered as her head reeled. Her heel caught in the hem of her skirt and she fell, rolling over and over down the steep hillside until at last she fell hard against a large rock. Leander, alarmed by her lengthy absence, found her an hour later. His face tight, he carried her back to the hotel. By the following morning she had miscarried.

The local doctor was kind but pragmatic. It had been very early days, he told her, and there was no lasting damage done. She could resume her marital duties within a couple of weeks. Before he left, he patted her hand consolingly as she lay white-faced and silent on the hotel bed.

'This time next year you'll have a baby in your arms, Mrs Gray. Don't you worry about that.'

Leander paid him and saw him off, and then came to sit beside her.

'Go away,' she said coldly.

He ignored her to brush the hair tenderly off her forehead. 'Caroline, he was right. There will be another baby, another time…'

'I don't want another baby! I didn't want this one and it's dead. I'm never having another one. Can't you understand that?'

His hand stilled. Her grief and guilt and anger were plain in every word she spoke, but he had no idea how to get through to her.

Over the next few days he kept trying to talk to her about it, but each time she cut him off, refusing to acknowledge that he had any part in what she had been through. All she could do was hide her face and cry, shaking off any effort he made to touch her. There was no point, she raged at him. No point to anything. Why didn't he just go away and leave her alone? As she sank into depression so the pain and loss festered between them, making them strangers to each other. They barely spoke to each other. Leander fought a silent battle with the urge to take refuge in the bottle again. Caro was so lost in her misery that she would not have cared if he had.

The only thing they did manage to agree on was to take the ferry to Kingston and, back in Dunedin, to go their separate ways. It was all done with great civility and a minimum of conversation. They went to the bank together, drew out all the money in their account and divided it up equally between them. Outside on the footpath, they faced each other.

'I'm going to the Castledene, to see if there is any news of my aunt,' Caro said quietly. 'Then I will go back to Sydney.'

She had grown thin these last weeks. Her eyes were huge in her narrowed face and her hair had lost its sheen. He wanted to take her in his arms and kiss away the new lines of strain appearing around her eyes, but he did not dare touch her any more.

'I'll go to an hotel, too,' he replied. 'Probably the

Regent, on London Street. If you should ever need me…'

'I won't.' She bent her head to avoid looking at the pain on his face. He seemed so much older and harder now, nothing like the laughing young man she had first fallen in love with. 'We can divorce each other for desertion after five years. It's best if we don't have any contact, don't you think?'

'Caroline.' Her name left his lips in no more than a whisper, but she stopped, her head still averted.

'What?'

'How did we ever come to this?'

'It's for the best, Leander,' she said steadily. 'Goodbye.'

He watched her slight figure walk swiftly down the road in the direction of the Castledene, her shoulders bowed. She'll be all right, he told himself. She has plenty of money to keep her safe, and within a month she'll be back with her family in Sydney, forgetting that any of this ever happened. That I ever happened.

And as you for, old chap… A very pretty young woman caught his eye as she passed him and smiled. He smiled back. The world was full of pretty women. There were places to go and games to play. Life was a game of chance, after all, and everything could turn on a single card. Fortune was a fickle mistress…

And his wife was almost out of view. For only a moment Leander hesitated, and then he slung his bag over his shoulder and set out to follow her, his long legs easily closing the distance between them. Just to check that she was all right, mind, he told himself. She was still too frail to be let loose wandering around Dunedin.

He stopped at the end of Castle Street and watched

as she tried the door of the Castledene. It was locked, as was the door of the bar. He shared Caro's puzzlement at that. She went back to the front door, knocked and waited. On the second floor, a curtain moved and then was still.

Eventually Caro picked up her bag and Leander retreated to the musty depths of the corner drapery, where he took an inordinate amount of interest in a length of grey serge material. When he looked out again, it was to see her threading her way through the foot traffic up Princes Street. She turned directly into the Royal Hotel.

Good choice, Leander approved. Quiet, respectable, safe. He waited a quarter of an hour before he went in.

The youth at the reception desk looked rather dubious when the tall, fair-haired stranger asked that he be notified of any movements of the hotel's latest guest, but the man persisted in writing out his own address on a card.

'For your trouble,' he said smoothly, and the lad's eyes widened at the sight of a month's salary crossing the desk.

'Thank you, sir. Thank you kindly.' The five-pound note disappeared into his jacket pocket with alacrity. 'You can trust me to make sure she's safe and well, sir.'

Chapter Sixteen

Caro slept almost solidly for a week. She took her meals in her room, and left it only for short, solitary walks along the waterfront. Several times she returned to the Castledene in the hopes that someone might be there, but she was always disappointed. The nice young man at the reception desk in the Royal Hotel told her that he had heard that the owner had closed it down.

'Mr Thwaites?' she asked, and he nodded.

'That's the name. I hear tell he's gone to Auckland. His wife's up there, I believe.'

That explanation made perfect sense, but it seemed odd to Caro that a lucrative source of income like the Castledene bar should simply have closed for business. She made inquiries at local land agents, but none of them knew if the hotel had been listed for sale. She resorted to writing a long-overdue letter to her aunt, addressed to the boarding house that had been her last address. Then, worn out by all the activity, she went back to bed.

The second week, she went shopping for new clothes, which cheered her up immensely. Leander, watching her flit from shop to shop from the other side of the Octagon, thought the bright new colours most becoming.

The third week, she made another futile trip to the Castledene. On the way back to the Royal Hotel she stopped off at the shipping office and enquired about booking a trip back to Sydney. She noted the prices and times, thanked the clerk kindly, and then walked slowly back to the hotel. She did not know what was keeping her here, she thought in exasperation. Dunedin in late summer was a pleasant enough place, but it was not home, and there was always the worry of bumping into her husband on the streets, although she was fairly sure that he would have returned to the goldfields and the cards by now. But once she left Dunedin, it would be the last link she would ever have with him, and for some inexplicable reason, she found herself reluctant to break that link.

Back in her room she opened the sketchpad she had inadvertently packed with her own things when they had separated. There were several dozen sketches in it, none of them what she would have considered among Leander's best, but all of them very good. There was the one he had done of Mr Matthews, in the Castledene Hotel's kitchen. He had so exactly caught the older man's grumpy expression that Caro laughed aloud. Mr Matthews would appreciate it, she was sure, but perhaps she should have it framed first.

There was a small art gallery she had noticed on her walks around the Octagon, and she took the drawing of Mr Matthews with her the next time she passed.

The shop bell rang when she entered, but no one came to the counter. She stood for a while, waiting for service, noting as she did so the piles of paper and bits of frame that lay tumbled upon the counter. There were some attractive paintings for sale hanging on the walls and in the window, but there was a general air of neglect about the shop. Dust lay over everything, the floor needed sweeping out and some of the tickets had fallen off the paintings on display.

She got tired of waiting and called, 'Shop!' Still there was no answer.

Leaving the sketchpad on the counter, she went exploring. Down a narrow backroom lined with framing materials and out into a backyard she tracked the sound of a small hammer tapping away. An elderly man, a frame in one hand, a hammer in the other and with a mouth full of nails, looked up at her in surprise.

'Oh. Sorry, miss. Were you waiting in the shop?' he said when he had spat out the nails.

'Yes, I was,' she said brightly. 'I have a picture I'd like framed.'

'Certainly, certainly.' The old man put down his hammer and searched around for his glasses, finally finding them under a sheaf of papers. 'Sorry about this, I don't like to keep people waiting.'

'Don't you have anyone to help in the shop?' she asked as he led the way back to the shop counter. 'You could lose business working so far away in that backyard.'

His wrinkled old face suddenly lost all animation. 'My wife used to take great care of that side of the business. Wonderful lady she was. But she died last winter.'

'Oh, I'm so sorry,' Caro said softly. 'How terrible for you.'

He accepted her sympathy with a philosophical shrug. 'We had close on forty happy years together, which is more than most people get. My sons tell me I should close the business up, stay home and take it easy, but I like my work. It's not going to be easy.' He held up Leander's sketch. 'I say, this is jolly good! But it's unsigned. Who is the artist?'

'Oh, just an acquaintance of mine,' she said swiftly, uncomfortable at the memories that the sketch exhumed. 'He's not a professional.'

The old man looked unconvinced. 'Is he local, miss?'

'No. He's English, and I don't know where he is now.' She dragged her eyes away from the sketch. 'How long do you think it will take you to frame it for me?'

He frowned and rubbed his ear uncertainly. 'I'm behind in my orders, you see, and…well, it might take as long as a month.'

'A month!'

He nodded resignedly. 'Perhaps you should take it somewhere else, miss. There's a good framer just off the Octagon, down Harrop Street, just before you get to the Town Hall. I'll write down the directions for you, shall I? Now, where did I put my pencil?'

She watched as he scrabbled through the piles of papers and frames on the front desk, his old face pinched and miserable. A glass paperweight came perilously close to falling off a stack of what looked to be order sheets and she caught it just in time.

'Why don't you get someone in to help you?' she burst out. 'Mr…?'

'Willoughby, miss. James Willoughby.' He gave her a rueful smile. 'Good help is hard to find, miss…?'

'Mrs Gray.'

'Mrs Gray,' he nodded with a gentle courtesy that

had Caro liking him even more. 'And to be honest, I'm so far behind in my orders now that I couldn't afford help even if I could find it. My sons are right, I suppose. This is not a business for an old chap like me to be running single-handedly. Ah, here we are.'

With a triumphant flourish he pulled out a stubby pencil, only to send a small framed picture crashing to the ground.

'Oh, dear,' Mr Willoughby said, surveying the broken glass that covered the floor with dismay. 'Mr Purvis was coming in today for that. Or was it tomorrow?'

He looked as if he were about to burst into tears. Caro resisted the impulse to give him a comforting hug—there was something much more practical that she could do for him.

'Mr Willoughby,' she said, putting her reticule down on the one corner of the desk that was not covered by disorderly papers. 'May I offer you a suggestion?'

She started work that very afternoon, purchasing an apron to put over her smart dress before she tackled the dusting and washing. Mr Willoughby remained very unsure.

'I really don't know if I can afford to pay you,' he said worriedly, as she began to sort the order sheets from the bits and pieces of timber on the front counter. 'And everything is such a mess...'

'It won't be in an hour or two,' she promised him with a sudden, brilliant smile that seemed to him to light the dingy shop. 'And, as I've told you, you don't need to pay me anything at all until the business is back on its feet again and you can afford to. Now, why don't you go and repair Mr Purvis's print while I get this tidy?'

In fact, it took days before the shop front was to Caro's liking. Once the counter was tidy, and the orders were organised and the bits of framing returned to the workroom, she dusted everything thoroughly, gave the floor the best scrub it had had in years, and cleaned the front window until it sparkled.

Mr Purvis came in for his print, and half a dozen other customers came in to ask if their framing was completed. She dealt with them firmly but charmingly, sending them all away happy with her promises of satisfaction within the week. To ensure that they were not disappointed, she joined Mr Willoughby in his workshop after she closed the shop that evening.

'Mrs Mills wants that series of landscapes ready by Thursday, Mr Willoughby,' she told him, pulling him away from a portrait that she knew would not be needed for several weeks. 'I've put the framing sample she chose on top of them. Then, if you could do the small watercolour for Miss Smith for Thursday afternoon?'

Far from resenting her ordering him around, he seemed most relieved to have a firm direction to follow. Caro suspected the late Mrs Willoughby had spoken to him in much the same way. He was a gifted craftsman, and his work was faultless, but he was not a man for paperwork and orderliness. She thought of Leander with a sudden pang.

'I shall put the kettle on the stove for another cup of tea, shall I, Mr Willoughby?' she offered, and he nodded absently, his hands already moving swiftly as he measured the landscapes and selected the backboards. He began to hum a little song from well before her time and she smiled to herself. It was nice to be busy again.

Within the week, however, she was becoming dangerously close to boredom again. The shop was positively gleaming, the workshop was a model of efficiency, and Mr Willoughby was almost on top of the backlog of work. She had prepared all the accounts, chased up two bad debtors and banked the week's takings. She had written new tickets for the dozens of pieces of artwork hanging on the walls and in the window, but had not sold a single one. The only customers to come in were those wanting framing or restoration work done and, while there was a steady stream of such people, there were not enough to keep tedium from creeping in.

Mr Willoughby was right, she thought. There really isn't enough business in this little shop to pay two wages. It was just as well that she had no need of the small sums that crossed the counter each day for the framing work. She was heartily grateful for the opportunity to put her energies to good use, but she knew the lack of profitability worried Mr Willoughby.

The solution came one afternoon when a large, pompous gentleman in his middle years strode into the shop, opening the door so violently that the little bell on top looked to be in danger of falling off.

'Where's Willoughby?' he demanded without preamble.

She met his glare calmly. 'Mr Willoughby is out at the moment,' she replied, although in truth he was taking his mid-afternoon nap in the comfortable chair at the far end of the workroom. 'May I be of assistance?'

'Yes. You can help me take my paintings down and package them up for me. Carefully, mind you. I don't want you damaging them.'

She moved to block him as he reached up to remove a seascape from the wall. 'Who are you, sir?'

He glared down at her from his greater height, the hairs in his nostrils twitching superciliously. 'George Everett's the name. You'll have heard of me.'

'I can't say that I have,' she responded politely, although she now recalled seeing the signature of G. Everett on some of the more pedestrian oil paintings on the walls.

'Well, then you damned well *should* have! Six *months* I've had these paintings hanging here, and I can't see a single one that's been sold. It's not good enough, I tell you! There's no excuse for it!'

'Perhaps no one wanted to buy them,' she suggested.

He seemed to become even larger, if that were possible. 'Are you being impertinent?' he boomed.

'No, sir. There is no need for me to be,' she said steadily. 'Would you care to show me which paintings you want to remove from the premises?'

He obviously did not trust her to touch his precious paintings, but stalked around the shop removing them himself and placing them with reverent care before her to package up. The five he took were, without exception, the most nondescript of the paintings on exhibit. Caro busied herself with some figures on a piece of paper as he blew imaginary specks of dust off the paintings and patted them tenderly with a handkerchief.

'What are you doing, girl?' he demanded after a mo-

ment. 'I told you I wanted these parcelled up and ready
to be removed!'

She looked up at him with a smile. 'I'm just calcu-
lating the cost of the framing for these paintings. You
will want to settle your account before you take them
out of the shop, won't you?'

His jaw dropped. 'You…you little hussy! How dare
you? I'm the one who should be charging Willoughby
for displaying my art! He's the one who has had the
privilege of having them in his shop all these
months…'

Caro tapped the top painting with the end of her
pencil. 'That's gold gilt on that frame, so—let's see—
that's five pounds, plus three…' She ran her pencil
down the column and did a quick calculation. 'Sixteen
pounds. Shall we say fourteen for a bulk order?'

'Bulk order?' His boom was reduced to an impotent
croak and she thought his eyes were going to pop out
from his head. *'Bulk order?'*

She stood up straight and stared him down.

After what seemed an interminable length of time he
called her a name that made her flinch and then he
pulled a crumpled note from his waistcoat pocket and
threw it at her.

'Damn you! I'll not set foot in this poxy hole again!'

It was a ten-pound note, so she let him go when he
gathered up his treasures and stormed out. He did not
shut the door behind him, and as she went to do so,
she heard the crash of splintered wood and more bellowed expletives outside the shop next door. She closed
the door and stood and laughed aloud at the empty
shop. Oh, that had been fun!

She went to check on Mr Willoughby, who was still
dozing peacefully in his armchair, and then she made

herself a cup of tea. She drank it while she studied the spaces on the walls where Mr Everett's paintings had so recently hung. She was rather pleased they had gone, as the other, better paintings stood out to advantage. Still, none of them had sold in the two weeks she had been working there.

That night, in her hotel room, she opened Leander's sketchbook again. There were dozens of sketches there, some in ink and some in pencil. The ones of herself she set aside, but she selected her favourite of the Otago scenes. There were miners at rest and at work, their faces grimy and tired or laughing with the exultation of a find. There were saloon girls sitting outside to rest their weary feet, grimacing in the sun. There was a single prospector, laden with all his worldly goods, walking along the river, his shoulders bowed but his face hopeful. And behind all the characters peopling Leander's work was the broad sweep of the mountains and the sky. To look at them was to be there.

She sat and studied them for a very long time, realising that she had been wrong to try to stop him from capturing all that life and energy on paper. And, surely, it was wrong to keep these drawings hidden in a sketchpad under her bed?

Leander never bothered to sign any of his work, and she knew enough to know that an artist's signature was important. The next morning she practised on a piece of scrap paper until she was satisfied, and then she signed all Leander's sketches with a flourish. He wouldn't mind, she told herself resolutely, firmly setting aside any qualms at such forgery. But there was an odd intimacy in so closely tracing the signature of her husband and that did unsettle her.

'Mr Willoughby?' She put the sketches beside him when he stopped for his morning tea. 'I was wondering if you could frame these for me. I don't know if there is any demand for this sort of work, or what prices we could ask, but I thought we might put them on the walls to replace Mr Everett's masterpieces.'

He chuckled and drew the sketches towards him. 'Thank you again for dealing with that man, my dear. He is such a conceited bully that I was always a little afraid of him. And, of course, his talent comes nowhere near his high opinion of it. Ah, more sketches? From your amateur acquaintance, are they?'

He studied each sketch intently, saying nothing. Caro stood and watched him in growing nervousness. She was no judge of art work, she knew. Perhaps it was the subject matter and the artist himself that was important only to her. Just when she would have stepped forward and gathered the sketches together with a deprecating remark, Mr Willoughby looked up and cleared his throat.

'Remarkable,' he said unevenly. 'Just remarkable. It's…it's just like being there, isn't?' She nodded, too relieved for words. Mr Willoughby picked up the sketch of the single miner, his hands shaking slightly. 'The composition of this, the control… My dear, this artist is no amateur.' He looked at the signature and then at her. 'Same surname as yourself, I see.'

'My…husband.'

He had long since come to understand that her absent husband was not a topic for discussion and so he did nothing more than raise his eyebrows a fraction. 'I shall frame these with pride,' he said. 'And then we shall see what the buying public think of them.'

With great trepidation Caro chose a sketch of a group of miners around a campfire by the Shotover for display in the window. The flamboyant oils and water-colours that hung on the walls could take the heavy, ornate gilt frames that were so in vogue at the moment. For Leander's delicate, evocative sketch Mr Wil-loughby had chosen an equally elegant and understated plain black frame and pale grey matting. Her heart beating wildly, Caro placed it carefully on the stand in the front window. Then she went outside to look at it.

She had feared that it would look small and insig-nificant through the glass and was relieved to see that it didn't. Standing alone, it caught the eye immediately, a small jewel in a perfect setting.

'Oh, how lovely!' A woman stopped beside Caro. 'Most unusual. I have a son in the goldfields,' she added chattily. 'That looks just like he describes it in his letters. Why, to look at that, it's almost like being there, isn't it?'

Caro responded politely and returned to the shop, her nerves thrilling at the immediate response to Leander's work.

It was only an hour later when the first buyer came through the door. He was a prosperous-looking man, who asked to see the sketch more closely. She obliged by fetching it from the window for him. He studied it at arm's length and then nodded.

'Perfect. I want this hanging in my bank, so that the employees will be able to look at it and remember where their wages come from. Who's the artist?'

'An Englishman,' she said quickly. 'A new artist.'

'Hmm. Well, he's good. Very good. Do you have any other work by him?'

She hesitated. He hadn't asked the price and she didn't want him beating her down with a bulk purchase. 'There are other sketches, but they're being framed at the moment.'

'I'd like to see them when they're done. Same subject? Good. I'd like a set.' He laid down the sketch and reached inside his jacket. 'Now, how much are we asking?'

She took a deep, deep breath. He was clearly determined to have it, and she could always haggle over the price.

'Thirty pounds.'

He didn't even blink, but extracted the money from a filled wallet and laid it on the counter. 'A sound investment, I think. Would you wrap it up for me please, young woman? And when do you think the others will be ready for viewing?'

She sold another two by the day's end, for the same amount, and one of them was still needing to be framed. Mr Willoughby was delighted.

'Well done, Mrs Gray!'

She looked at the ninety pounds in her lap and shook her head in disbelief. 'Such a lot of money for three little drawings! But of course there's your commission to come out of it, and the framing costs…'

Now it was his turn to shake his head. 'Certainly not, my dear. Not when you've been working so hard to turn this little business around, and for not a penny of wages! It is I who owe such a debt to you. No, keep it all, although I do think you're probably underselling them. People are always prepared to pay a great deal of money when they see real talent. Mind you, you can demand even more when the artist is deceased, of course—rarity value, you could call it. I take it the artist is not…deceased?'

'No, I don't think so. I hope not,' she muttered. This was not her money, after all. It was her husband's talent that she was selling here. She folded the money neatly and stood up. 'Do you mind if I go home a little earlier than usual, Mr Willoughby? There's an errand I must run this afternoon.'

The Regent Hotel, he had told her when she had last seen him, but when she called there, the clerk at the reception desk told her that the gentleman had left a week ago. 'But,' he went on, just as her shoulders began to sag, 'he did leave a forwarding address.'

She left the hotel, clutching a card in a palm that was inexplicably clammy. For one dreadful moment she had feared that he had left Dunedin or—much worse—had somehow fallen on hard times and gone back to living rough. But the address the clerk gave her was but fifteen minutes' brisk walk away, and in a respectable area of the town.

She found the address she was looking for, in a quiet avenue pleasantly lined with trees. His house was a rather charming small cottage, surrounded by a once-well-tended garden that was only just starting to get out of control. She stood for a moment at the front gate, trying to gauge from the look of the cottage just who Leander would be living with. A family? A landlady? Or even—and she had to face the possibility—another woman? It took considerable courage to walk up the overgrown path and knock on the door.

She waited.

It was pleasant out on the veranda in the evening stillness. Bees droned lazily around the honeysuckle that climbed around the veranda posts. Large, crimson roses bowed their heads in the heat, releasing their soft, powdery scent.

She knocked again. 'Hello?' she called.

Not wanting to give anyone a nasty shock, she turned the handle and opened the door as loudly as she could. 'Hello?' she called again, but she could tell that there was no one to hear her even as she spoke.

There was little furniture in the house, but she knew that Leander lived here. His paintings filled the two front rooms of the house, propped up against the walls, or set on easels. It was the colour that struck her at first. A riot of blues, greens and every shade of gold, the colour of the Otago goldfields. He had claimed not to want to paint in colour, but she could see that he had painted from his sketches and then drawn on his memory for the colours. And he had done that with breathtaking accuracy, with energy and joy, showing his love of the scenery in every brushstroke.

There were people in all the scenes—there would always be people in Leander's work—but they were not the main feature. It was the Otago mountains and hills that drew the eye and made Caro's heart turn over in her breast with delighted recognition.

She moved from painting to painting, scarcely able to breathe for excitement. The paint was still wet on one painting and she stood before it, her hand covering her mouth as she studied it. It was of her, and she remembered him sketching it all too vividly.

They had made love rather recklessly in the broad light of day, and Leander had seized his sketchbook and pencil, demanding that she pose for him. He had

looked infinitely desirable, sitting crosslegged and naked, with the sketchpad on his lap and a look of fierce
concentration on his face. She had pulled faces and
twisted this way and that while he scolded her, until in
the end he had given up and left his sketching to join
her in the tussock grass.

Now it was as if she were Leander, gazing down at
her as she lay back, teasing him, in the warm Otago
tussock under the midsummer sun. The pale cream of
her skin, the gold highlights of her hair seemed a part
of the grass on which she lay, as if she had somehow
been magically born by the earth beneath her. It was
far less erotic, but painted with no less of a loving
hand, than the portrait of her as Venus that hung over
the bar in the Lake Hotel.

She turned at the sound of footsteps through the
kitchen door and the smell of turpentine. Leander had
obviously been painting without a shirt, and was in the
process of removing paint from his arms and hands
with a rag. He stopped short in the hallway as he saw
her standing in front of her portrait. He looked tired,
he looked older, but there was a look of elation on his
face that she knew came from a successful day working
on his art. He leaned against the doorway and watched
her, a small smile on his lips.

'These are very good,' she said at last, when it was
clear that he was not going to speak until she did. She
motioned at her portrait. 'Especially that.'

'Thank you.'

'I had a little trouble finding you. Have you bought
this house or are you renting?'

'I've bought it. I need somewhere quiet to paint.'

'It's…charming. I'm pleased for you.' She took an
unsteady breath and pulled out the wad of money from

her reticule. 'I've come to give you proceeds of the sale of three of your sketches. I hope you don't mind, but it was good money.'

A slight frown marred his forehead. 'Thank you.'

'I won't sell any more, unless you want me to. But these—' she indicated the canvases '—are wonderful. If you want to sell them...'

Her voice trailed away. He said nothing.

'Well, I must be going,' she said with all the brightness she could force into her voice. 'I'm pleased to see that you're well, and working...'

She turned swiftly and walked straight into the doorjamb. As she reeled back, holding her nose, Leander's hand was there to steady her.

'It's all right, it's just a little nose bleed. Does it hurt?' She nodded. 'Here, hold this over it to stop the bleeding and I'll go and fetch a handkerchief.'

But the cloth he gave her had turpentine on it, and her eyes began watering even more. By the time he came back with a clean handkerchief her face was covered with blood and green oil paint, and her eyes were streaming.

'Not one of my better ideas,' he apologised, removing the offending cleaning rag. He pinched her nose carefully with the handkerchief and then checked. 'There. It's stopped bleeding. Although you do have the most startling green moustache.'

'Do I?' she choked, caught between tears and helpless laughter.

'Oh, Caroline,' he said softly. With infinite care he leaned forward and very softly kissed her lips. She closed her eyes and clung to him, dizzy with relief and longing. He felt her collapse and caught her arms. 'Are you going to faint on me?'

'I need to lie down.'

'All right,' he said, worried. 'The bed's in here…'

'With you.'

There was a rumble of laughter from deep in his chest as he bent to pick her up. 'If you're sure it will help…'

It helped. They made love very slowly and carefully, as if testing each other's boundaries for the very first time, and then they lay close together, talking of all the things they should have said long before. They talked long into the night, before they got up and ate all the bread and fruit that Leander had in the house. Then they went back to bed and loved again. Sometime before dawn, between the loving and the laughter, they fell asleep wrapped in each other's arms.

Chapter Seventeen

'I should go to work,' Caro fretted. 'I can't let Mr Willoughby down.'

'It's Saturday,' Leander protested. 'He won't expect you in, surely?'

'I work a half-day today. I should go in.' She was standing at the table, dressed in one of Leander's shirts, cutting slices from a loaf of still-warm bread he had bought off the baker's boy minutes earlier. 'I've put another of your sketches in the window, and there are bound to be more inquiries about it. When you're in business, you have to keep the customers satisfied.'

'What about me?' Leander put his arms around her and held her close. 'Don't I deserve to be kept satisfied as well?'

She laughed and pressed back against him. 'You're easy to satisfy, Mr Gray.'

'Oh, but I'm not. Can't you tell?' His hands moved up to cup her breasts and she put down the knife, no longer trusting herself to cut straight. 'Why don't we go back to bed and work on your customer skills?'

'I really should get dressed and go…'

'Get dressed in yesterday's clothes? With the oil

paint and the blood all down the front? Whatever will your Mr Willoughby make of that?'

'I would have to go back to my hotel and change—'

'By which time it will be almost closing time. Come on, sweetheart, Mr Willoughby will be able to manage without you for a single morning, I'm sure.' He ran his tongue lightly down the curve of her neck and she shivered in delight. 'Pleasure before business, Caroline. The first rule of a happy marriage.'

She chuckled and handed him a piece of bread to keep his energy up. 'I'm beginning to believe you're right. Although it's the sort of thing Charlotte always said. I hope it's holding true for this marriage.'

He bit hungrily into the bread. 'Which marriage?'

'Her marriage. To Mr Thwaites. Oh, I didn't ever tell you about that, did I?' And she proceeded to tell him about what had happened after he had left the Castledene, how Mr Thwaites had returned, how he had virtually bullied her into leaving, and how the Castledene Hotel and bar was now closed for business. Leander sat opposite her, listening intently and sipping his tea, saying nothing.

'Why didn't you talk to me about this before?' he asked when she had finished.

She shrugged. 'I think I just wanted to forget about the odious man. I mean, he and Charlotte were married in all but name, after all, weren't they? Although, I was disappointed to hear that Mr Matthews had gone back to Sydney without coming down to Dunedin to see me. I can only assume he didn't have enough money.' She saw his thoughtful expression and put down her cup slowly. 'You think there's something wrong, don't you?'

'I don't know. Maybe not.' He leaned back from the

table, his frown deepening. 'And the Castledene is still closed?'

'So it appears. Although sometimes when I've knocked on the door I've been almost sure that I can hear someone moving around inside.'

He did not like to tell her that he had observed a curtain moving on the one occasion he had seen her knock at the hotel door. Something was definitely not right about this. 'I think I'll pay a visit to the Castledene. Today.'

'You won't be able to get in,' she warned. 'And I don't have a key.'

'I do.' He grinned broadly at her expression. 'Well, I'm assuming it's still there. Mr Matthews kept a spare key behind a loose board at the side of the veranda. It was in case you ever took it into your head to lock me out at night. Although I'm sure the thought never entered your head.'

'No more than half a dozen times,' she returned. 'Very well, then, but I think it's best if I come with you.' As he began to shake his head, she went on quickly, 'After all, it is—or was—my aunt's hotel. As her niece, no one can say that I would be entering illegally, would they?'

He considered that, and then agreed that there was sense in what she said.

It was afternoon by the time they washed and dressed, and Caro called in at her hotel to change her clothes. By then Dunedin's streets were all but deserted, being too late for the morning shoppers, and too early for the evening revellers. At first they knocked and tried the Castledene doors, but there was no response. The curtains remained drawn and there was nothing but silence and the echo of their knocks. Leander disappeared around the corner and returned, brandishing a front-door key.

'Now, assuming that no one has changed the locks…'

No one had. The entry hall was cool and gloomy, and Leander immediately went to pull back one of the heavy curtains covering the front windows. Caro sniffed. The air still smelled of timber and, more faintly, of the beeswax she had applied with such vigour to the staircase and furnishings just a few months before. Plainly, the hotel had not been closed for long.

'It all looks fine,' she said wonderingly. 'Look, the ledgers are still here, where I used to keep them behind the desk. Surely, if the hotel was being sold, these would have been taken?'

'Yes, the place looks completely untouched,' Leander said. Then he opened the doors to the dining room and added, 'I spoke too soon, it would appear.'

She peered over his shoulder at the shambles that had once been the Castledene's finest room. Bricks lay in piles on the costly rugs, and fine mortar dust covered every surface. She stepped over the wreckage, heedless of Leander's cautionings, and peered through the dust and gloom at what lay on the tables.

'Leander, what are these?'

He gave a short laugh. 'Gold bars is what those are. Fresh from the rear of the Gold Office vaults, if I'm not mistaken.'

There were dozens of them, glistening like small bricks against the white dust. She tried to pick one up, but it was almost too heavy to manage. Leander made his way to the kitchen and gave a low whistle.

'What a mess.'

The Castledene's back wall was completely demolished, and the brick wall of the Gold Office, now fully exposed, looked decidedly insecure. Leander leaned forward and pulled at the masonry, and then jumped back as a pile of bricks landed at his feet. He swore.

'Clever beggars. God knows how much they've taken out already. All they need to do is repair the masonry and the Gold Office will be left scratching their heads and wondering where all the gold in the vault has got to.'

'Who would have done this?'

'Three guesses.' He took her hand and gave it a comforting squeeze as he began to lead her out of the kitchen. 'But Thwaites has to be one of them. We'd better go and raise the constabulary...'

He never got to finish his sentence, because two huge hands wielding a gold bar swung into his face, and he dropped like a stone. Caro stared in disbelief at the huge man filling the doorway.

'Don't you even think about it!' he snarled as she opened her mouth to scream. 'Or you'll get the same and I'll finish him off while I'm at it!'

'Who the...who the hell are you?' she demanded breathlessly, even as she searched around for a weapon, any weapon. The knife drawer under the kitchen table... He was there before her, squeezing her hand so hard that she heard it crack. The carving knife fell to the floor and he flung her back against the wall, leaving her winded.

'Don't you bleeding listen, you stupid bitch? I told you not to move!' He reached to cover her mouth and she bit it as hard as she could even as she brought her knee up very hard. She had the momentary satisfaction of making contact and hearing him grunt in pain, before he snarled, 'Oh, I've just about had enough of you.' Then everything went black.

Leander drifted in and out of consciousness for what seemed like hours but which was, in reality, only minutes. Someone kicked him in the ribs at one stage but he managed to stifle his grunt of pain before it left his lips, helped by the rag that had been stuffed in his mouth. His hands were tied behind his back, and what he suspected was blood was dripping into his left eye. Heroic actions were out for the time being, he decided.

Between his lashes he could make out the burly form of a man standing in the far side of the kitchen, looking down at something. When he moved away, Leander saw that it was his wife. Like him, she was bound and gagged. Her eyes were closed, and she was so pale that for one heart-stopping moment he thought she was dead. Then he told himself that the bastard who had tied her up would hardly have bothered if he had killed her. That was the one thought that kept him sane.

There was considerable activity in the dining room, and he could easily guess what was happening. Unsure of what repercussions there might be to the disappearance of two young people, the thieves were preparing to take the gold that they had and leave. That would account for the grumbling complaints about weight and the sound of heavy boxes being dragged along the floor. There would be a dray waiting outside, and any passers-by would simply assume that the closed Castledene was being emptied out for sale.

To his huge relief Caro's eyes fluttered and opened. She saw him at once and began to rise, but he shook his head and she understood. When the man responsible for knocking them both out came back into the kitchen came back in, they were both still apparently deeply unconscious.

There was another set of footsteps and the first man was joined by another.

'All finished. Here you are.'

There was the sound of a tin cap being unscrewed and then the unmistakable reek of paraffin oil. Leander watched as the oil was poured over the table, the floor, Caro's skirt and himself. As the man backed out through the door and into the dining room, Caro's eyes met his in horror. She knew as well as he did what was intended for them.

From the other room, they heard a match being struck.

'Oy, blow that out, will you?' a voice said angrily. 'You haven't finished.'

'Yes, I have. Them two are trussed up nice and tight like plucked chooks ready for roastin'…'

'Exactly. So when they go looking through the hotel afterwards, what are they going to find?'

'Two bodies—'

'Trussed up like chooks. Stupid!' There was the sound of someone's hand meeting the back of someone's neck. 'Now, go and untie their hands and their feet and make them look like they got trapped in there by accident. You got that?'

Muttering angrily, the first man came back into the kitchen and roughly sawed through the ropes tying Leander's hands and legs. He bent over Caro for somewhat longer, and Leander was very tempted to spring on him while he was groping his wife. Patience, he thought, tensing his hands and feet. There was still the other man waiting outside. Whatever was being done to Caro, she had the self-control to continue feigning unconsciousness, and he had to do the same.

A low shout from the dining room had the man straighten up and stamp out into the dining room. Now Leander got unsteadily to his feet. Caro was only seconds behind him, holding on to the wall for support.

'Now! We have to run for it!' he whispered.

'Take a knife, first!' she hissed back. 'Just in case they try to stop us!'

'Knife be damned!' Leander could hear a match being struck in the next room. 'Caroline…'

But she already had a knife in each hand and was heading for the door. He snatched up the first thing to hand from the kitchen drawer—a carving fork—and followed closely on her heels.

In the dining room, the two men were swearing at each other and fighting for possession of the box of matches.

'Here, give it to me! You're incapable, you are!'

'Stop it! They're mine. Give 'em back!'

They looked up in amazement as two filthy, oil-soaked, furious people bearing carving implements bore down on them.

'My Gawd!'

'Stop 'em!'

But nothing was going to stop Caro and Leander. Caro dived under the outstretched arm of one man, Leander brutally shouldered aside the other. They staggered through the entry hall and burst out on to the street.

As their two pursuers reached the front door of the hotel, Caro turned and raised both knives in warning. 'One step closer and I'll slit your goddamned throats!' she screamed. 'Just try it, you bastards!'

She grinned triumphantly at Leander, her teeth white against the grime and dust on her face, and took a step backwards into a solid wall of chest. She spun around, knives high, to face the tall, solidly built man who was staring at her in amazement.

'What the *hell*,' said Ben Morgan, 'are you doing?'

Much later that evening, Caro and Leander sat, scrubbed and in clean clothing, around a dining table at the Royal Hotel and listened to Caro's father tersely describe their collective lack of intelligence. He had listened patiently enough while they told their story to the constables and held his peace while their cuts and bruises were tended to. Leander had filled him in on recent events while Caro was dressing. But Ben still seemed to hold the view that what they had done was extremely foolhardy.

'And don't you roll your eyes like that at me, young woman!' he thundered.

'Then stop being such a bully!' she retorted. 'You're treating me like a child again. No wonder I left Sydney—'

'To run around like a screaming harridan in the streets of Dunedin, brandishing forks! Oh, very grown-up!'

'Leander had the fork. I had the knives,' she corrected him. 'But we did nothing wrong! How could we have known that those men were inside the Castledene? I was worried about Aunt Charlotte…'

He snorted rudely. 'Charlotte? She's fine. She should be here next week.'

Caro frowned. 'But she married Mr Thwaites, and now that the police know he was behind the gold theft, he's going to be arrested, and she will lose absolutely everything!'

Ben suddenly looked quite diverted. 'I don't think so, Caro. She isn't married to Thwaites.'

'But he told me—'

'And he doubtless thought he was. But your aunt has…how can I put this?…a rather poor memory when it comes to husbands. She was never married to the late Jonas Wilks, for a start.'

'But…'

'And I'm sure he thought he was legally married to her, too. But she had neglected to mention the minor detail that the husband before that—that's the man she married after she married my father, if you're following all of this—was still very much alive, but had fled to America to get away from her. Thank heavens she's felt compelled to keep your mother abreast of all her convoluted affairs over the years.'

'Two bigamous marriages? Oh, no. Poor, poor Aunt Charlotte. So I suppose she can't keep the Castledene. What a mess,' she said sadly and then scowled across the table at her husband. 'It's not funny, Leander! Stop it!'

Ben's lips twitched.

'So now she's all alone.'

'Not quite. Your aunt now has company.' Ben poured himself another large whisky and sat back in his seat, his previous foul mood descending upon him again. 'I suppose the saying is true that there's no fool like an old fool.'

'Who? Aunt Charlotte?'

'No! Mr Matthews. They've become quite… attached to each other.'

'But he told me once that he was married!'

Ben shrugged. 'If he was ever married, it was never official. When he came as convict labour to my father, twenty-six years ago, he was listed as a single man. It suited him to invent a wife back in England, I suspect, to keep any interested female at bay. Why he should suddenly decide in his dotage that your aunt, of all women...' Ben took a deep swig of whisky to steady himself. 'That's why I came over here, to try and extricate him from her clutches when Thwaites had got what he wanted from her and left her in Auckland. She wrote some stupid flight of fancy about her latest great love to your mother. When I realised who the poor bastard was, I took the first ship to Auckland. But damned if I can talk any sense into him.' He shook his head helplessly.

Caro looked pained. 'I thought you'd come to see how *I* was.'

'Oh, I knew you were all right. Mr Matthews told me you'd hatched up some damn-fool scheme to raise money so you'd married a complete stranger. Well, you're your husband's problem now, God help him.' Ben raised his glass to Leander. 'Good luck, mate. You're going to need it.'

'Thank you,' Leander said politely. Caro's heart sank. The two men were not getting on. Ben was too bombastic and Leander was playing it far too cool. And when her father found out she had married an artist, that most effete of occupations... She thought frantically of the best light to put on the situation.

'Why aren't you drinking?' Ben demanded of his new son-in-law, waving his own glass at Leander's untouched one.

'Because I'm an alcoholic, sir,' came the calm reply.

Caro wanted to slide quietly under the table.

'You're being sensible, then,' her father said after a short silence. 'Any other vices?'

'Just your daughter, sir.'

'Hmph.' The sound might have been one of amusement—Caro was staring too hard at her untouched dessert plate to check. 'So what work do you do?'

'I play poker and I paint.'

Caro was biting the inside of her cheek so hard that she tasted blood.

'Any good at either?'

'Very good at both.'

'Hmph.'

Caro couldn't stand it any more. 'I'm going upstairs to bed,' she announced. Her father and her husband politely stood when she did. 'Are you coming, Leander? Or are you going to stay here and be insulted by my father all night?'

Ben raised his eyebrows at Leander. 'Are you being insulted?'

'Not by you, sir.'

'Good. I'll bid you goodnight then, Caro. No doubt I'll see you in the morning if you haven't done a runner and embroiled yourself in another harebrained scheme before dawn.'

Leander slid into bed with her hours later, only to find her rigid with worry and full of apologies. She flung her arms around him and held him closely.

'He's such a beast, darling! He always has been. Now you understand why I had to leave Sydney, don't you? Was he too dreadful? What did you talk about?'

She felt him shrug in the darkness. 'Everything, really. Sydney, Dunedin, your family, business, money, politics, you…'

'Oh, I'm sure he had lots to tell you about me,' she said bitterly.

He cupped her worried face in his hands and kissed her gently. 'Caroline, I know he's hard on you, but it's because he loves you so very dearly. You don't need me to tell you that, do you?'

Some of the tension left her shoulders. 'No, I suppose not. But he shouldn't pick on you…'

'He didn't pick on me, Caroline. In fact, we got on very well. I really like him. He's as tough as old boots, and he won't tolerate fools, but he made me feel as welcome to your family as he could.'

She drew back in amazement. 'What did he say to you?'

'He shook me by the hand, clapped me on the shoulder and said you couldn't have done better for yourself. I think it was a compliment.'

Caro thought about that for a long time.

'I'm not so sure,' she said at last.

Epilogue

The opening of Willoughby's new art gallery a month later was regarded by Dunedin society as one of the more interesting cultural events of the year. Invitations were keenly sought after by anyone with artistic pretensions, and not just because of the lavish, newly refurbished premises on The Octagon.

For a start, there was the young couple hosting the opening along with old Mr Willoughby. Both tall, fair and extraordinarily good-looking, the pair had managed to charm Dunedinites quite effortlessly. Mrs Gray was already held to be solely responsible for the remarkable emergence of the Willoughby Gallery as the leading art gallery in the city. She combined a sharp business intelligence with an eye for design, and the rumours of vast family wealth behind the venture certainly did her no harm.

And then there was her husband, who was rumoured to be of an aristocratic background, possessed looks good enough to make women go giddy, and whose paintings and sketches were snapped up by eager buyers almost before the paint was dry.

Some people are most unfairly blessed, was the most common verdict.

Caro picked up two glasses of champagne and handed one to Charlotte, frail in pale blue organza and perched elegantly on a chair in the corner.

'Are you quite all right there, Aunt Charlotte?'

'I'm perfectly fine, thank you, darling.' She reached up and patted the gloved and protective hand of Mr Matthews, who was looking most uncomfortable in his evening suit. 'Aren't I?'

He beamed adoringly down at her. 'Yer perfect all right, my love.'

Oh, dear, thought Caro, and moved away out of their intimacy. She caught her father's eye.

'I give it a month,' he muttered.

'You said that a month ago,' she teased him. 'Father, they're in love. And Mr Matthews might be besotted, but I think he can handle Charlotte. Leave them alone and let them enjoy themselves. We none of us know how long we have together.'

He sighed heavily. 'You'd best take care, young woman—you're beginning to sound almost sensible.'

'You can blame it on Leander.' She tucked her hand under his arm. 'I'm so pleased that the two of you get on.'

'He's yet to meet your mother. There's no guarantee that she'll take to him.'

She shook his arm reprovingly. 'She will love him, and you know it! Do you really have to leave tomorrow? I'm going to miss you so much.'

'I've been away too long as it is. Besides, you'll be over to see us soon enough, or so you promised. Maybe to stay, eh?'

'Maybe,' she said uncertainly.

He moved to stand between her and the crowd, forcing her to meet his eyes squarely. 'Listen, girl,' he said quietly. 'I know I've asked you before and you've given me the same answer. But think seriously on it. I like your husband. He's not got the land that young Benton would have brought with him, but he's got something else. The ability to stand up to you.'

Despite her best resolutions, Caro's lips twitched. 'True. But he's no farmer, and never will be.'

'But you are. You always told me you could run the property with one hand tied behind your back. I think you're wrong—it will take both hands and a good man beside you. And that's what you've got. Please, just think about it.'

Caro rested her head for an instant on his shoulder, determined not to let him see the sudden, hot tears of joy blurring her vision.

'I'll think about it,' she promised.

Ben looked around the room, at the richly panelled walls on which hung Leander's brilliant, exuberant paintings. At the milling throng fêting his daughter and son-in-law's success. At the tall, handsome young man who had so profoundly and deservedly captured his daughter's heart. And he looked at his daughter, glowing in an elegant evening dress of oyster silk, positively radiating happiness.

'I'm proud of you,' he said simply.

'Thank you. That means a lot to me, Father.'

Leander was deep in conversation with a buyer across the room, but—with the telepathic communication they often shared—he felt her eyes on him and he looked up with a smile. The look they exchanged was intensely private, a sharing of hope and love and a belief in the future. He began to make his way through the crowd towards her.

I'm proud of me, too, thought Caro. I think I've done rather well for myself.

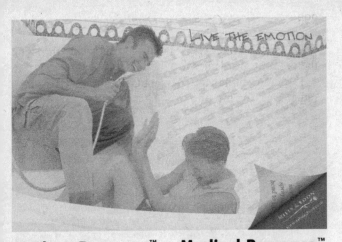

Modern Romance™
...international affairs
– seduction and
passion guaranteed

Medical Romance™
...pulse-raising
romance – heart-
racing medical drama

Tender Romance™
...sparkling, emotional,
feel-good romance

Sensual Romance™
...teasing, tempting,
provocatively playful

Historical Romance™
...rich, vivid and
passionate

Blaze Romance™
...scorching hot
sexy reads

27 new titles every month.

Live the emotion

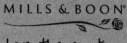

MILLS & BOON®

Live the emotion

Historical Romance™

THE RUNAWAY HEIRESS
by Anne O'Brien

Miss Frances Hanwell effects a daring night-time escape – in the
Earl of Aldeborough's carriage! With scandal imminent,
marriage seems the only course of action. But reluctance turns to
respect when Hugh uncovers the brutal marks of her unhappy
life, and suddenly he will do all in his power to protect her…

Regency

THE WIDOW'S BARGAIN
by Juliet Landon

1319 Scottish Borders

When her Scottish home is invaded by a dangerous band of
reivers, Lady Ebony Moffat's first thought is to keep her young
son safe. She is prepared to strike a bargain with the men's
leader – her body for her child's life. Sir Alex Somers is
intrigued. He means no harm to the boy, but he can't help but
be drawn by her offer…

MY LADY'S TRUST by Julia Justiss

Laura Martin assures herself that she will be safe among
strangers – but will anonymity protect her from the discerning
gaze of the Earl of Beaulieu? Or will he discover her secrets as
easily as he has the key to her heart? Desire fills the Earl when
he looks at Laura – but can he earn her trust…and her affection?

Regency

On sale 4th June 2004

*Available at most branches of WHSmith, Tesco, Martins, Borders,
Eason, Sainsbury's and all good paperback bookshops.*

0504/04

2 Books
and a surprise gift!

We would like to take this opportunity to thank you for reading this Mills & Boon® book by offering you the chance to take TWO more specially selected titles from the Historical Romance™ series absolutely FREE! We're also making this offer to introduce you to the benefits of the Reader Service™—

- ★ FREE home delivery
- ★ FREE gifts and competitions
- ★ FREE monthly Newsletter
- ★ Books available before they're in the shops
- ★ Exclusive Reader Service discount

Accepting these FREE books and gift places you under no obligation to buy; you may cancel at any time, even after receiving your free shipment. Simply complete your details below and return the entire page to the address below. *You don't even need a stamp!*

YES! Please send me 2 free Historical Romance books and a surprise gift. I understand that unless you hear from me, I will receive 4 superb new titles every month for just £3.59 each, postage and packing free. I am under no obligation to purchase any books and may cancel my subscription at any time. The free books and gift will be mine to keep in any case.

H4ZEE

Ms/Mrs/Miss/Mr ....Initials....................................
BLOCK CAPITALS PLEASE

Surname..

Address..

....

....Postcode ....

Send this whole page to:
UK: The Reader Service, FREEPOST CN81, Croydon, CR9 3WZ
EIRE: The Reader Service, PO Box 4546, Kilcock, County Kildare (stamp required)

Offer not valid to current Reader Service subscribers to this series. We reserve the right to refuse an application and applicants must be aged 18 years or over. Only one application per household. Terms and prices subject to change without notice. Offer expires 29th August 2004. As a result of this application, you may receive offers from Harlequin Mills & Boon and other carefully selected companies. If you would prefer not to share in this opportunity please write to The Data Manager at PO Box 676, Richmond TW9 1WU.

Mills & Boon® is a registered trademark owned by Harlequin Mills & Boon Limited.
Historical Romance™ is being used as a trademark.
The Reader Service™ is being used as a trademark.